speed
shrinking

speed shrinking

∾

Susan Shapiro

Thomas Dunne Books
St. Martin's Press
New York

THOMAS DUNNE BOOKS.
An imprint of St. Martin's Press.

SPEED SHRINKING. Copyright © 2009 by Susan Shapiro. All rights reserved. Printed in the United States of America. For information, address St. Martin's Press, 175 Fifth Avenue, New York, N.Y. 10010.

www.thomasdunnebooks.com
www.stmartins.com

Book design by Rich Arnold

ISBN 978-0-312-58156-5

First Edition: August 2009

10 9 8 7 6 5 4 3 2 1

for stacey & fred,
         with eternal love

part
one

chapter one
the art of losing

July 14

I'm stacking the basket of bride-and-groom candles on the counter at Party City on Fourteenth Street in a last-minute stop to fill Sarah's goody bags when she says, "There's been a change of plans. Andrew took the museum job."

"Which job is that again?" I ask, adding the final miniature wax couple, balancing the bonbons we just bought at the chic chocolatier around the corner on my other arm. I'm worried they'll melt before her rehearsal dinner tonight and that the overpriced confections look too tiny. If I could eat candy, I'd devour twenty of the truffles and pralines in one gulp.

"He'll be renovating Cleveland's Natural History Museum," she says.

The cashier rings up eighty-nine dollars. Expensive little tchotchkes. I reach for my wallet to treat, but she whips out her American Express, mumbles "Don't be silly," and swipes.

"So you two will be long-distance for a few months?" I ask. "We did that when Jake was shooting the cop show in L.A."

"No." She signs the receipt. "We're subletting my apartment."

"Buying a bigger place? In the meantime, you can crash with us." The last time we roomed together a decade ago, we were both single. It was right after my live-in lying ex, a.k.a. the Sociopath, dumped me. Sarah and I would stay up all night drinking cheap wine, chain-smoking, and making crank calls to all our exes. Why do breakups suddenly seem more fun than weddings?

"Julie, the museum's undergoing a fifty-million-dollar renovation."

"That means they really like Andrew, right?"

"It means he has to make a three-year commitment," she says. "And I'm going with him."

"What?" My mouth drops. "You're moving? For three years? Quitting your job? What will you do?"

"I'll be his wife. Dr. Zane says you don't land a great husband, then ruin it with long-distance right after you close the deal." She laughs as I follow her out of the store. I'm carrying her bags in both hands, surprised they're so heavy.

My therapist, Dr. Ness, says "Love doesn't make you happy, you make yourself happy." But the beginning of Sarah's weekend wedding extravaganza is probably not the best time to play dueling shrinks.

"You're really leaving?" I try to keep up as she zigzags through the ragtag crowd to reach the corner of Sixth Avenue. "When?"

"After the brunch on Sunday. You and Jake are coming, aren't you?"

"Wouldn't miss it." I nod, totally stunned, pretending not to be devastated.

I know Andrew's from the Midwest, but so are we. Sarah and I grew up next door to each other in the Chicago suburbs. Our mothers, best friends and fellow domestic goddesses, remained so thin and stylish during four simultaneous pregnancies that Sarah and I, the only girls, eternally bonded over feelings of inadequacy. In between being Mommy's Little Helpers at multiple brothers' brises and bar mitzvahs ("Blessed with a boy, mazel tov!") we plotted escape. No wonder we became career-obsessed urbanites—it's the only arena where our maternal figures can't compete. We like to joke that we're mutant left-wing aliens who were mistakenly dropped into the wrong plaid-wearing, conservative, sexist clans.

Which is why I'm flabbergasted that she's throwing away the city and work she adores for a guy. Since Sarah and Andrew sparked at their SoHo architecture firm a year ago, he's never once mentioned moving back to his hometown—or kidnapping her. If he had, I wonder if I still could have been his biggest advocate, reassuring her that his grad-school wardrobe and eyeglass frames are easily upgradable, that his habit of quoting Homer Simpson isn't juvenile, and that the square soul patch on his chin looks hip. Not to mention constantly disputing her long-held dogma that marriage only leads to divorce, domestic abuse, or brain death. Now I feel duped. Along with my gift of crystal wine goblets from ABC Carpet, I have an urge to slip Andrew a plastic razor with a note saying we're all over ironic facial hair. Luckily Dr. Ness never lets me act impulsively.

"You'll get there early tonight with the camera and sign-in book, right?" Sarah asks. "There's a cab. Love you madly." As the yellow taxi comes to a halt in front of her, she grabs the bags of meltable newlyweds and chocolates from me and climbs into the backseat, leaving me standing alone on the curb, arms empty.

"You won't believe what happened," I shout, running into our Greenwich Village apartment, where I find my husband in the bedroom. "Sarah's moving! Andrew took a job renovating the Cleveland history museum."

"I hear they have a cool planetarium," says Jake.

"What's the point of a planetarium if it's in Ohio? She's deserting me!" I wonder how he can possibly not grasp the impact of this catastrophe. Why is Jake taking his favorite gray button-down shirt from the closet and putting it in his suitcase? "What are you doing?"

"Great news. They picked up the *Doctors on Mars* pilot. Shooting starts Monday in Studio City." He folds two pairs of jeans into the black Italian leather suitcase I bought him at Barneys to celebrate his last pilot deal.

"That's in California," I say rhetorically, recognizing the excited "I just got free dugout tickets to the World Series" gleam in his eye.

"They wanted me to fly to L.A. tonight," he says.

"You can't! My whole family's flying in for the wedding!" I panic at the thought of being bombarded by the Illinois branch without my Jake shield. I hate this feeling; it's like trying to put my hand in a subway door that's closing too fast to catch.

"Don't worry. I told them I can't miss my wife's best

friend's wedding. So they switched the meeting. I'm leaving Sunday morning."

He looks proud of himself, as if it proves he's Husband of the Year. But he's packing two days early. This isn't up for discussion. He's already there.

"What about the HBO show in Jersey?" I sputter.

"That's half-hour cable. You said push for the big time—network, prime time, one-hour dramas. NBC's green-lighted thirteen episodes. I'm doing what you told me."

I recall my exact words: You have to promote yourself in this cutthroat biz 'cause nobody else will. Since when does he listen to me?

"I have to run to my agent's to hammer out the contract." His lopsided curly brown hair falls in his eyes as he ties the laces of his new white and blue Nikes, making him look like a little boy about to sprint away. "I'll meet you at Sarah's dinner at eight."

He rushes out, forgetting to kiss me good-bye.

"What a double sucker punch. First Sarah, then Jake. Both leaving on Sunday," I tell Dr. Ness, thanking God I decided to keep my 6 P.M. Friday shrink appointment. "Maybe I should just relax and eat whatever I want this weekend."

"Why don't you snort some heroin too while you're at it?" He smiles.

"Heroin was never my style." I smile back.

"With your personality, you could get addicted to carrot sticks."

He scrutinizes a note in his leather date book, shuts it, then takes off his glasses and rubs his eyes. Hasn't he been sleeping well? I tighten the buckles of my new Prada sandals, thinking they're worth the three hundred bucks for making my size-ten clown feet look sleek.

"It's not like they're going off to war," I venture. "Sarah's found her soul mate and this could be Jake's big break. I should be happy for them." I cross my bare legs from the chill. Did he turn up the air-conditioning? Damn the fashionista who says you can't wear pantyhose with open-toed shoes. Obviously a thoughtless, thighless size two. (Even at my skinniest in control-top Spanx, I'm a six.) "I'm just not good at surprises, that's all."

He gives me his "you're being an idiot" eye roll.

"What? I'm denying my darkness and pain again?"

"Yes. You're in shock and denial."

If anyone would know, it's Dr. Ness. He's the dashing substance-abuse specialist whose claim to fame is unhooking me. I call him the Superman of Psychotherapy since he's a peculiar mix of moralistic and reckless, with a savior complex on the side. His dark wavy hair, chiseled features, and thick gold-framed lenses give him a nerdy Clark Kent aura, as if he's concealing his real identity.

"Well, I'm not going to drink or smoke, if that's your worry," I say, craving a Virginia Slims menthol and a vodka martini. "Sarah hired the best caterer in the city. Why can't I loosen up my diet for two days?"

He moves his cell phone from the shelf to the table next to him and stares at it, as though he's expecting an important call. Then he looks up, as if just remembering I'm here, puts his glasses back on, and says, "Don't use food to quell distress. You have to make friends with your hunger."

"I have enough friends," I snap. "I'm sick of starving on twelve hundred calories a day. Last night I dreamed of vanilla cupcakes with candy hearts on top. What would Freud say?"

"It's not physical hunger. You're *emotionally* ravenous," he reminds me. "Pinpoint what's missing inside."

"Aren't you listening? It's pinpointed! Sarah and Jake are leaving while my whole crazy Midwest *mishpocheh*'s flying in to shove food and alcohol in my face." My brain understands why Sarah's moving, but my selfish heart is not letting her go. "What if I just wing it for dinner at the reception tomorrow?"

"Huge mistake."

He's pissing me off, but that's what I pay him for. Over the last two years, Michael Ness has been my critical sounding board, career counselor, diet doctor, and father figure, despite being only thirteen years my senior. A nutrition and exercise fanatic, he's six feet tall and a slender 165 pounds. (I ask and keep track.) His willingness to answer my personal questions and expose his own addiction history made him the most potent expert in my bestselling self-help book *Up in Smoke*, which chronicles how he helped me quit toking and smoking after two decades of two packs a day and other debauchery. If it weren't for him, I'd never have banished my bad habits or nailed the book deal.

"When you're careless with food, everything feels chaotic and you spiral out of control," he's still hectoring.

"Give me a break! I'm 128 pounds. For a big-boned, five-foot-seven thirty-seven-year-old, that's perfect." I tug on the loose waist of my black skirt to show him. "I've got your Nazi diet laws down. I can chill for one weekend."

"Julia, do not ask for trouble."

Right after I nixed nicotine, he made me give up alcohol, the diet pills I became dependent on, and the Juicy Fruit gum I was shoving into my mouth two packs at a time to replace the cigarettes. He then banned all bread products and food freedom, insisting that if I'm not careful my orally fixated internal wiring will only perpetuate "the substance shuffle."

"I'm not. I'm skinny, smoke-free, happily married, with a skyrocketing career." How defensive and superficial I sound. Yet since finally getting my own byline, after toiling as a low-paid women's magazine copyeditor since college, I'm not letting a bit of bad news set me back. I'm no sore loser who resents others' good fortune. Just the opposite. I teach my readers how to get clean by finding their bliss. I'm a bliss pusher! "With *Up in Smoke* royalties and signing my second book deal last month, I've tripled my income."

"You've tripled your megalomania," he says. "Don't exaggerate or deviate from the truth."

"I'm not deviating!" Is it my imagination or is he being more extreme than usual? "You know, the *Today* show producers want me back. I could be their on-air addiction expert." I brush my hair behind my ears. I had it cut in the editrix Anna Wintour's Cleopatra style and blown dry, treating myself and Sarah to a French manicure and pedicure this afternoon, so he'd see me dolled up before her dinner. Does he notice? "I can handle a few special meals. I'll stick to protein."

"Five thousand calories of cheese, nuts, and meat will make you sick—and fat. Figure out your menu beforehand. Have fish, vegetables, and salad," he instructs in his stern principal's voice, then adds, "Julia, there's something we have to talk about."

"Why you're being such a prick today?"

"Look, I told you, addicts can't handle spontaneity. Shocking changes are about to take place. You're not the type who can roll with it. Make sure you get enough sleep. Don't give yourself choices or allow last-minute substitutions based on your mood."

"Please. I haven't touched a cigarette, joint, pill, or piece of bread in twenty-four fucking months. *Entertainment Weekly* calls me the Diva of Deprivation. You're the only addiction I have left."

In my "save the world" fantasy, I'm the white Oprah and he's my more handsome Dr. Phil, with hair. Okay, so being a feminist fervently dependent on a male is oxymoronic, but he's my magic elixir. Aside from his two-hundred-dollars-an-hour fee, there's no downside. For the last two years I've tasted joy for the first time in my life.

"Listen, Julia…"

"I know. Food's the hardest dependency to conquer because you can't quit. You have to be moderate and eat three times a day. I get it. For Christ's sake, I just sold a whole book about it." Following his strict low-carb regimen and "learning to suffer well" system, I dropped twenty-two pounds while remaining substance-free—the miraculous feat I'm recounting in *Food Crazy*, my new self-help sequel.

"So how will you handle the emptiness?" he asks.

"My rewrite's due in six months. I'll throw myself into finishing," I say, but something's wrong with the leather strap of my sandal; it's hurting my ankle.

"You won't miss Jake?"

Dr. Ness calls my workaholic husband's demanding TV jobs his mistresses, christening the latest two Laverne and Shirley. But since my spouse's agent is married to my agent, and he makes three times my salary, I can't kvetch about a few months apart. "Too much vork should be the vorst problem ve ever have. *Nu?*" Jake often says in his grandfather Alfie's Yiddish accent.

"I'll miss the hell out of him. But his last L.A. show about those buff cops screwing each other was canceled in three weeks. I warned him no female police captain in the history of the force is built like Gisele." I scan Dr. Ness's spiky cactus plants and ebony shelves. The quirky antique clocks telling different times look mysterious, like him. This is my safe place, two blocks from home, a confessional where I go religiously every Monday and Friday, like bookends framing my week. "Right now I have to focus on getting Sarah wed. It'll be such a trip to have both families in town."

"Trip, as in nuclear explosion?" he asks.

How well he reads me.

"Last night, when I e-mailed my dad that I can't wait to show him the new Italian and French editions of *Up in Smoke*, he wrote back: 'Stop wasting your talent on psychobabble. Repression is the greatest gift of the human intellect.' He always makes me feel inadequate." I bend down to loosen the shoe's strap and rub my sore skin.

"Feelings are misleading," Dr. Ness reiterates.

That's his main mantra, along with "Don't trust your instincts" and "Live your least secretive life"; he writes them down for me on the back of his business cards. I keep them all in my bedroom drawer, checking them frequently, the way some women reread letters from old lovers.

"Your book is smart, honest, and has helped many people," he says. "I'm proud of you."

Finally, a rare compliment! But the digital clock says five to seven; we've gone over. I have to hurry uptown to make sure Sarah won't screw up marrying Mr. Mistake-on-the-Lake.

"Listen, I have something for you." Standing up, I hand him a silver shopping bag. "For your birthday. A little early." He was born in August, the day before my father. It's a black suede laptop tote from the Flight 001 store in the West Village. "Figured you could use it on your annual summer trek to Arizona."

"Thank you." He takes my present hesitantly, staring at me with a strange expression. "Julia, there's something I need to tell you."

Is he not accepting presents anymore? Jake and Sarah find it bizarre that I bring my therapist gifts. But I couldn't have published my book without him since he reviewed and edited every single page as I cranked them out. "Don't tell me. You're firing me as a patient because I'm too taxing?"

"I wish I had longer to prepare you. I know the timing is terrible, but I don't really have a choice." He pauses awkwardly. "I need to move to Arizona year-round."

"But you're keeping your place here, right? You'll be bicoastal, like Jake?"

"Unfortunately, I can't." He looks anguished.

"Is everything okay?"

"I'm fine—it's my wife's family. But I'll be keeping this office and I can see you in New York every few months. My protégé will be taking over the day-to-day operations of the institute, and when you're ready, I'd like you to meet him."

I fall back on the couch, clutching the armrest. Dr. Ness is taking off too? Pawning me off on a guy I've never met? I'm confused. Dizzy. His words don't compute. He promised me twice-weekly feedback on my new manuscript, like last time. I can't stay clean or make my deadline without him.

"When do you leave?" I ask, my breath knotting in my chest.

"In three weeks," he says. "But I'll be back to visit in the fall."

"Can we do phone sessions? Can I e-mail you my chapters?"

"Yes, of course. And we'll talk about this more on Monday."

"Isn't there some shrink rule that you have to give neu-rotics more than three weeks' notice?" I try to make light as I run out, not waiting for his reply.

Outside his building I switch to my comfortable, ugly rubber-bottomed flats, but my stride is off, as if my soles are too stunned to trust the ground. Dr. Ness is the one who insists I stop depending on substances and depend on people. But what if they all become undependable at once?

What a disaster—I'm an acclaimed self-help guru who suddenly can't help herself.

chapter two

i don't

July 15

"Now my best friend will come up to share *her* expertise on what makes a good marriage," says Sarah.

She's standing at the microphone in front of two hundred wedding guests at Capitale, the magnificent 1893 Stanford White Beaux Arts landmark building on the Bowery. She looks gorgeous—but nervous—in her long pearl silk gown. In the middle of her elegant Saturday-evening reception, she's ambushing me with this request to share my recommendations for marital happiness.

"Julie's been like a sister to me since our days in Evanston, when we played together in the sandbox."

The real story is that I bashed her in the back with my brother's Tonka truck and had to give her my Malibu Barbie in a hostage negotiation so she wouldn't tattle. And I switched my name to the more mature "Julia" in sixth grade. Yet to Sarah and the rest of this crowd, I'm stuck with the cutesy "Julie." Still, I'm awash in nostalgia as I join the bride at the podium, trying not to trip on my long black lacy Anna Sui dress. I hug Sarah carefully, so as not to ruin her flawlessness for the flashbulbs. Taking my turn at the mike, I run through my repertoire of relationship aphorisms in my head, wishing we could all just make inebriated, passive-aggressive toasts like normal wedding guests.

Sarah's parents have already advised the couple to practice saying "I was in the wrong, dear, I'm sorry," because if you don't, "you could be very right and very alone." Sarah's mother-in-law, a recent widow, warned against separate beds and complaining if he snores, "because now I can't sleep without the noise." Sarah's sisters-in-law lightheartedly chimed in with the importance of weekly date nights, full-time help, and ugly nannies. Her brothers did a comedy routine, telling the groom that when he screws up there are easy remedies. Then they held up sign cards that read FLOWERS, CHOCOLATE, and EXPENSIVE JEWELRY.

Their shtick is a tough act to follow since I feel compelled to share actual, meaningful words of wisdom. After all, I'm someone who takes—and gives—advice very seriously.

"Well, my therapist, who's a man, insists that women underestimate how much criticism can hurt your spouse. So he made a rule that I'm never allowed to criticize my husband," I ad lib. "The first words I utter every morning and the last words I speak every night have to be kind—even if I just say, 'I like that shirt, honey,' or 'Thanks for picking up toilet paper.' Instead of shouting 'Listen, lazy ass, take out the damn trash,' I say, 'Hey, handsome, think you can help me with the garbage?' This way he hears the 'Hey, handsome' part, then does what I want while feeling good about himself and thinking it's his idea."

Everyone laughs and applauds while the waiters bring out elaborate bread baskets and Caesar salads with croutons.

"You can read more about Julie's husband and shrink when you buy her book *Up in Smoke*," Sarah says, throwing in a generous plug right before the ten-piece swing band behind her launches into Louis Armstrong's "Dream a Little Dream of Me."

As I walk off the stage and pass by him, Sarah's oldest brother, Gary, yells, "You can say that again, sweetheart," and winks at me, to the obvious chagrin of his pretty wife seated next to him. She hasn't been my fan since Sarah let slip that Gary and I used to get stoned and make out during summers home from college.

"Your rule should also apply to male siblings," shouts my oldest brother, Scott, from his seat at the Goodman table, right next to the Suttons.

"I second that motion," adds brother number two, Bradley, as they click beer glasses.

"Why don't you tell that rule to your mother?" my father asks.

"She needs therapy after being married four years—wait till she's married four decades," my mom answers, pinching his arm.

"You New Yorkers pay shrinks for navel-gazing," my dad bellows.

What? He's just landed in the city where I launched my

bestseller and he's publicly trashing me and Dr. Ness in one swipe.

"Wait till I publish *my* self-help book, *How to Tame the Shrew Beside You*," Jake chimes in.

"Now that one I'll buy," says Bradley. "I thought everyone was getting free copies of *Up in Smoke*."

"Sarah offered to put one in the goody bags for all the out-of-towners, but it's her night, not mine," I say, knowing my book is more apt for an AA convention than a celebration filled with closed-off therapy-phobes like my father.

Taking my seat, I marvel at the forty-thousand-square-foot space's Venetian glass skylights, sixty-five-foot ceilings, and Roman classic mosaic floors. It's the perfect place for two New York architects to wed, though the external splendor seems to be mocking my internal nervousness. Dr. Ness's warning really spooked me. Scanning the guests giddily chatting, getting drunk, and devouring every edible in sight, I feel as if the rest of the room is in the comedy *The Wedding Crashers* while I'm stumbling into the second act of *Titanic*.

I focus on avoiding danger, which is everywhere. I remain on addiction alert all night—avoiding smokers and boozers; nixing the buttered rolls, fried appetizers, creamy sauces, starchy side dishes, and alcoholic drinks being served; opting for plain vegetables, broiled salmon, and ice water. Since my quitting spree began two years earlier, attending social events is like navigating a minefield. My book's "Get out of Dodge" rule insists you're allowed to flee any occasion where you're tempted to abuse your substance. But I'm not the fleeing type. I'm the rock who stays.

Ness probably thinks his relocation will instigate an emotional avalanche. And he calls *me* myopic. What an egomaniac he is. I'll be fine without him. He's just another bad habit I have to kick.

To spite my fleeing shrink, I get along famously with my entire family. This requires avoiding subjects that might arouse their disapproval: my politics, my career, my penchant for self-confession and psychotherapy, my substance issues (which, I've surmised, hold a mirror to *their* substance issues), or any inference of the superiority of Manhattan. For the next five hours, I suck in all big-city sarcasm and suck up, expertly doing small talk. I quiet my cravings and "everyone leaving me" anxiety by getting up from the table to take five rolls of pictures with my prehistoric, predigital film camera, ignoring that Jake rudely keeps taking calls and texts from his damn producer.

Alan, my youngest brother, notices my annoyance at the CrackBerry glued to Jake's ear and asks, "Do I get a dance with my favorite sister?"

As the band plays Frank Sinatra's "Fly Me to the Moon," we make our way to the dance floor.

"Good marriage speech," he says. "I thought you killed it."

I lean my head on his rugged shoulder. The three Goodman boys stand six feet, like my father. The Sutton men are all tall too, but slimmer. They used to complain that Mrs. Sutton was a lousy cook and would all show up at our house right before dinner. "If it wasn't for your mom, we would have starved," Sarah often says.

"Freaking out that Sarah's moving?" Alan asks as Sarah's parents, elegantly mimicking a tango dip for the videographer, wave at us.

"Just a little." Out of all my relatives, Alan's the only one who can tell when I'm on edge. Appropriate for an internist specializing in diseases of the gut. "She just told me yesterday. Timing sucks. My shrink's moving too, and as it turns out, Jake's taking off for L.A. tomorrow."

"I know about Jake," Alan says. "I agreed to be his medical consultant for *Doctors on Mars*."

"Really? That's great." When the hell did Jake have time to talk business with my brother? He couldn't even show up early tonight to take a few pictures. "Cindy couldn't come?"

"They didn't invite kids under ten and we didn't want to leave Aliyah with a hotel babysitter we've never met," he explains.

Their adorable little girl is three, but the only babysitter Alan and Cindy ever trust is my mother. Knowing my mom, I'm surprised she didn't offer to miss the wedding to take care of her granddaughter.

"Can you believe what Dad's been shoving in his face all night?" I ask. "He ate ten of those little hot dog appetizers, three rolls, and the steak main course with extra potatoes."

"I love those pigs in a blanket. Haven't seen them since my bar mitzvah," Alan says, and I wish I could eat ten of them too, dipped in mustard.

"Did you hear Dad's sarcasm about my shrink? I don't mind my role as black sheep when we're home, but he doesn't need to trash me on my turf, at my best friend's wedding."

As Sarah and Andrew glide by, we step aside, out of the photographer's path.

"In your book you said you grew up in 'a family of oral-fixation fanatics,' with Dad as 'the right-wing Vesuvius' and Mom 'the overfeeding orphan,'" Alan reminds me. "And they loved the part where you did cocaine on the Greyhound with the bus driver."

"Sounds like you really read it." I'm touched.

"It was pretty good. About time you and Dad gave up those cancer sticks," he says. "Listen, since you moved away I'm the black sheep because I'm a doctor, not a lawyer like him, and we decided to only have one kid."

"I know, thanks. Now Dad's hounding me to give him more grandkids."

"You're smart that you don't let him get to you," he says.

He thinks my father doesn't get to me? Does that mean Dad gets to Alan too?

As the song ends we walk back to the table, now adorned with four-tiered silver plates of chocolates. The waiters bring the luscious-looking, vanilla-frosted wedding cake and serve more wine and champagne. I ask for a water refill and chew on the ice.

Alan joins the Goodman-Sutton brother sextet taking turns making silly speeches on stage. They chide Sarah's choice to wed in a building that by day serves as a bank on the Bowery, a strip legendary for its bums, and relay her childhood foibles: how she once stuck a raisin up her nose that a doctor had to remove; how she almost got thrown out of our private high school for supergluing the locker-room keyhole, imprisoning the gym teacher inside for two hours. In between dumb anecdotes, the six boys do shots of whiskey. When they leave the stage, I walk over.

"Six shots is excessive," I tell Scott.

"Nobody's driving tonight," he slurs.

"You already had three beers," I admonish.

"You're such a self-righteous killjoy since you stopped partying," he accuses.

"It's true. You've become this straight-ass narc," Gary pipes in, then looks pale. "Please excuse me while I go puke."

"They're right," I tell Jake, finally off the phone. "After I quit everything, I became this boring, born-again prude."

"You're better straight," Jake reassures, before bowing out at midnight to finish packing. His glee at getting away from me for thirteen weeks doesn't exactly prove his point.

When I get home at 3 A.M., he's out cold but I'm too wound up to sleep.

Early Sunday, Jake kisses me good-bye, saying, "I love you. I'll call you late tonight, after my meeting." I want to get more shut-eye but Sarah's postwedding brunch at the Palace hotel starts at 10. It's for out-of-town guests, but she specifically requested my presence. I force myself into the shower, don my DKNY black sundress and new sandals, switch to a small purse, and bustle out at the ungodly hour of 8:50. Since I'm proud my camera's predigital, my first stop is the Forty-five-Minute Photo Shop on Sixth Avenue.

"I've never seen you in daylight," says the owner, Raj. He rushes three sets of prints while I do the *New York Times* Sunday crossword puzzle in red pen. I superstitiously tell myself that if I finish the entire puzzle, Sarah will change her mind and stay in Manhattan. But I get stuck on the big clue—a pun involving the letters "Q" and "A."

"Here, Julia. I threw in the last set for free," Raj offers.

I thank him and hop a cab to the Palace hotel, making it to the dining room by ten.

"Hey, long time no see," I say, hugging my mom. "Where's the boys?"

"They just left for La Guardia. They're taking the early flight back."

I'm disappointed I missed hugging my brothers good-bye

and hope they're not mad at me for trashing their inane drinking games. "Look, I already got three sets of the pictures from last night developed at Forty-five-Minute Photo." I hand her the envelope.

"That's funny, an hour isn't fast enough. Like everything in New York," she says.

"That's why Julie loves it here," says my dad. "Everyone's as manic as she is."

"You're not exactly famous for your patience and restraint," I shoot back, poking the big belly of my father, whose addictive genes I've inherited. Probably why he's so threatened by my book.

"In Manhattan being manic is an asset, not a vice," my mother adds. "Isn't it, Julie?"

"Mom, I've been going by 'Julia' for twenty-five years," I remind her.

"To me you're always my little Julie," she says. "Jake left for L.A.?" When I nod yes, she puts her arm around me.

"I get more work done when he's out of town," I say.

My folks look at the wedding pictures while eating bagels and lox. I look at the buffet, dismayed there are no eggs, omelets, vegetables, or cheese. Not a drop of protein. It's only bagels, Danish, muffins, and rolls. I decide to eat later and just drink a Diet Coke. Dr. Ness says be careful with caffeine, but I'm not a monk.

"You look beautiful in the pictures," Mom flatters. "So does Sarah. But I look fat."

"You do not." With her bright auburn beauty-shop hair and sequined green and gold dress, I think she looks lovely. Have I inherited her weight obsession, or is it an inescapable female trait? My mother, an orphan, grew up on the South Side of Chicago. While she overfed us all for decades she stayed a size-six fashion plate—until she turned sixty. When Dad quit smoking around the same time I did, they both put on weight. Neither of them exercises. None of my relatives do. The Goodmans are avid readers and eaters.

"Aliyah and Teddy left me a message saying, 'Grandpa, make sure you bring us presents from New York,'" my father says. "They're so cute. Can I put in an order for more grand-kids?"

"Hey, did I tell you the *Today* show might want me back for my new book?" I ask.

"So Jake's doing well," my father says. "In the paper today, the *New York Times* TV critic says *Doctors on Mars* is supposed to be the smartest fall show on television."

"Jake calls that the kiss of death," I say.

Back at the buffet table, I can't help but spy an extremely attractive glazed donut. Dr. Ness does not allow dough. But it's not public knowledge that I've officially sworn off sugar until my new book comes out this summer. So I take it, lick-ing the white frosting off. It's so good I eat the topping off an-other one, stashing the rest under a napkin. Tacky, but I've been a good girl all weekend and deserve a treat. Ever since my first book came out, I fear a Page Six paparazzo will catch me with a contraband cigarette, joint, or drink—the way they nabbed diet spokeswoman Kirstie Alley shoving French fries in her mouth, and Suzanne Somers, Ms. Thighmaster, flash-ing flabby legs at the beach in Cabo. But icing is not techni-cally a violation of any addiction I've already renounced. So I'm slipping through a loophole.

The newly knotted couple sweep in right before my par-ents' airport limo arrives. I walk my folks to the lobby to see them off, then return to the dining room. I'm dying to show Sarah the pictures, but she's too busy. I drink a second Diet

Coke, then a third. As the room thins out, it hits me again that Jake's on his way to the West Coast, and Dr. Ness and Sarah are also taking off. The backs of my feet are throbbing from dancing in heels. Last call for food is announced. Brunch is over? My caffeine buzz makes the time move too quickly, which means watching Sarah go sooner. I grab another donut, plopping on cream cheese and jam, which I lick off while sitting alone at a cocktail table outside the dining room. Sarah sits down next to me—at last.

"Oh my God, Julie. Can you believe we actually pulled it off?" she asks.

I'm not sure whether "we" means her and Andrew, her and her family, or her and me.

"The wedding was out of this world," I fawn. "You have never looked so stunning."

"You're thinner than I am," she says.

"You're an inch taller with tighter abs," I counter. Fellow addicts, we've struggled with the same diet—of cigarettes, joints, alcohol, junk food, and jerky boyfriends—since junior high.

She eyes my plate and says, "Thought your new book says you're off bread."

"I am. I'm just eating the cream cheese and jam."

"You were the one who convinced me to get off cigarettes, alcohol, and starch," she says, but then grabs my donut and takes a bite. When the waiter walks by, she orders a decaf coffee. He eyeballs me suspiciously. Has he traced the stash of donut carcasses to me? I slip him a ten, just in case he has any tabloid cohorts on speed dial.

"They never get paid enough," I tell Sarah, shrugging at her confusion.

"I haven't eaten carbs in months. Now that I'm a Mrs. can

I order in pizza and stop exercising? Did you see Carolyn last night? Didn't she look like hell?"

Her ex-friend Carolyn stole the last guy Sarah dated before Andrew. "She's single, jobless, fat, gone to seed," I agree. "While you're in your glory. Great idea to invite her."

"I know. Amazing what a difference a year can make. Thanks for getting me photos so quickly. Let me see." I'm so glad she's noticed the effort I went through to get her early hard copies to take on her honeymoon. "Look how happy my parents look. They're all but dancing on the tables shouting hallelujah." She sips my Diet Coke.

"When I told my father Jake and I eloped, his exact words were 'Thank the Lord. I'm so relieved,' like he could rest easier knowing I was off the streets," I admit.

"After the advice you gave last night, every guy in the place wants to marry you," she says, laughing her full-bodied, warm laugh. "Or they want to send their wives to your shrink."

"Hey, the marriage sermons were your idea. Not mine."

"You were supposed to share romantic lunacy, not sexist adages, with the Chicago contingent. I mean, come on, you can't *ever* criticize your husband? What did you say when Jake sprung his new L.A. show on you? 'That's nice, honey, go hang with gorgeous actresses in la-la land and I'll see you in four months'?" she says with a chuckle. "Isn't being in love with your shrink the real trick to your ideal marriage?"

"Oh, I never got the chance to tell you. You're not going to believe this, but Dr. Ness is moving!"

"What? No way! Where's he going? If he's in Cleveland, can I have him?" She finishes my donut. I want more cream cheese and jam but they're shutting the dining room doors.

"Arizona, where his wife is from. They already own a summer place there," I say. "What am I going to do without you or Ness?" It occurs to me that I usually see Sarah twice weekly, the same amount I see him.

Andrew joins us and pats my head sweetly as he sits down. "Great advice you gave."

"See? He wants to marry you too," Sarah says.

That's an odd joke. I sense she's distancing herself from me before she goes as a preemptive strike. Or I could just be too tired and paranoid.

"Did you see the pictures I took?" I ask Andrew, trying not to resent him for whisking her so far away.

He shuffles through the stack. "These are terrific," he says. "Can I give a few to my mom?"

"Sure. I made you guys two sets." How can I dislike a guy who is so kind to his widowed mother?

"It's almost noon, honey," he tells Sarah.

She looks at her watch, stands up, and points toward the elevator, where a bellman is bringing out their bags on a luggage trolley.

I feel a stab in my gut. "Are you guys coming back Labor Day? That's only six weeks. You can stay with us."

"We won't have time. I gave Sarah a one-way plane ticket," he says, smirking. "If I never saw Manhattan again it would be too soon."

Is this a joke? He's got to be teasing. "I thought you loved the city."

"Nope. Never liked it here. I'm a Midwest boy at heart." His mother calls him away. What about Sarah? She's a city mouse! What about where *she* prefers to live?

"He's kidding." She hugs me. "I'm ten days late," she whispers. "Two rabbit tests were positive."

What? Rabbit tests means pregnancy? When did this happen? Why didn't she tell me before? I'm losing her to a

husband, the state of Ohio—*and* a baby. What happened to
our solemn vow to be the only members of our clans with
big-city careers and no kids? She was the one who christened
our group of childless pals the Empty Womb Club.

"Congratulations!" I croak. "Why didn't you tell me?"

"I promised Andrew I wouldn't tell anybody until the
gyno confirms it, but you're not anybody."

She means this as a compliment.

Andrew calls her over. "We should go, honey."

"I can't believe you're taking off, Sutty." I can feel myself
starting to panic.

"Love you madly, Goods. Call if you get weird," she adds,
our sign-off code since second grade.

Before I can say "Over and out, weirdo," she's gone.

I stay at the table, standing up to bid farewell to each of
Sarah's relatives as they depart, until I'm the last one there.
The clock says noon. I'm so out of it, it seems like midnight.
On my way out, I catch a bellboy sneaking a cigarette in the
hall and consider bumming one. But I don't want to relapse.
I can't risk ruining the spotlight I finally stole by becoming
known as a hypocrite—or another inane poster girl for partying. Dr. Ness has deemed me a good role model for young
readers. I can't disappoint him.

Walking down Madison Avenue and Fiftieth Street, I'm
boiling hot, too dressed up with nowhere to go and nobody
to get home to. Loud Latin music and the smell of burned
meat startles me; I've stumbled onto a street fair.

"Back rub? You need massage, twelve dollar." A Chinese
man puts his hand on my neck.

"Thanks, not today," I say.

Heading for the curb, I slip and tumble, breaking my shoe's
heel. I reach into my bag for my flats but I left them in my big-

ger bag when I switched purses. Rushing into a drug store for black duct tape to perform surgery on my expensive sandal, I pass the candy aisle. Staring out at me are bags of Necco Wafers and candy corn, which Sarah and I used to eat on Halloween. There are no bread products in candy, so I won't be breaking any oath. Dr. Ness has strict regulations against sugar pig-outs, but my sugarless vows aren't published yet. They're in *Food Crazy,* which I haven't even finished or handed in to my agent or editor yet. Thus I have some leeway, I convince myself, impulsively snatching the pastel wafers and candy corn. Then I can't help but grab Hershey's chocolate, Reese's Peanut Butter Cups, Twizzlers, and Almond Joys. I spot the chocolate Hostess Cup Cakes with their white swirls. I haven't had a cupcake in two years. I pick up a package, thinking I'll eat only the frosting on top.

I put on my Dior sunglasses and slink to the register. Nervous someone I know will see me, I tell the cashier, "For the kids," as if he cares, feeling like a crack addict about to score.

Taping my heel back on, I hobble outside. The second I'm out the revolving door, I eat the thin sandpaper-tasting Necco Wafers two at a time, chewing instead of sucking like you're supposed to. Sweaty and sugar-rushing on this strange street, I'm completely disoriented. I've spent so long piecing the tiny parts of my life into place, like a jigsaw that finally fits together. Now it feels as if someone's unexpectedly stolen essential pieces, leaving gaping holes in the middle that I don't know how to replace.

I hail a cab to my high-rise, longing to fall into Jake's arms. But the only trace of him is the garbage overstuffing his wicker basket. I throw it out in a huff. He's a slob, and it's not my job to take out the trash he left behind. I sink into the blue couch. Everybody's leaving but me! Have I done

something to cause all this desertion? Has my recent success made me too strong and independent? Starting to cry, I
spark Sarah's bride-and-groom candle with my Bic lighter
and watch it burn as I finish the goody bag I've filled with
cheap drugstore candy and cupcakes, throwing myself a
party in my mouth.

I haven't wept this much since the Sociopath jilted me. I
recall I survived that breakup by figuring out I liked living
with Sarah better than with him. She had to find me a studio
apartment in her building to get rid of me. But she's not a cad,
and I'm not a poor single girl left in the lurch. I'm a married,
published guru, for God's sake, and she's been a great sport.
Sarah has finally found her other half and I have no right
to feel deserted. I can't summon Jake for a reality check—he
hasn't even called with his Los Angeles number yet. I try to
reach Dr. Ness, e-mailing his work and private addresses and
leaving messages on his office machine. Next I call his emergency cell, though I'm not suicidal, relapsing on drugs or cigarettes, or about to cut myself. Does crying while devouring
retro candy and icing constitute a crisis?

If I confess my simmering sugar issues to my mother, she'll
say, "So you ate too much? Big deal. You're too skinny anyway."
Only Sarah would get it. Dr. Ness has deemed her one of my
three "core pillars," an essential support beam I lean on, along
with him and Jake. I try her iPhone, but this is a pathetic new
low, interrupting her while she's honeymooning with a food
freak-out. She's the vulnerable person here, going through
metamorphosis. I'm not allowed to piggyback on her life pas-
sage. I hang up before spilling my guts in a way I'll regret, hoping she doesn't see my number on her caller ID.

For the rest of the afternoon, I can't stop consuming
different-flavored cornstarch confections, as if the continu-

ous dose of sugar can heal where it hurts, like medicine administered intravenously. When my phone does ring I don't get it, all of a sudden glad everyone's gone so I can be alone with my fix. If Sarah's returning my call, what would I say, anyway? "Trash your husband so you'll split up and come back here because I can't handle living without you"?

Dr. Ness and I never had a chance to discuss what happens when all your pillars disappear. Does everything fall down?

chapter three
the shrink shuffle

August 28

Eating pink Hostess Sno Balls that make my computer keys sticky, I'm distraught that Ness and Sarah keep ignoring my e-mails while Jake's unavailable on set for twelve-hour stretches. I decide to call Sarah's therapist, Dr. Zane, though most therapists are on vacation until after Labor Day. I leave a message, then fear she'll think I'm a shrink stalker. Luckily, she returns my call ten minutes later, saying "What's up?" in her bemused, sturdy voice. I give her the update.

"Sarah's move feels like a divorce. I miss her more than my wayward husband and analyst combined," I wail. "She's like the love of my life. I'm trying to give her space, but I can't stop eating and crying."

"Screw giving her space. Let her know you miss her. She

needs her friends more than ever," instructs Dr. Zane, a seventy-year-old no-nonsense Holocaust survivor.

"She's been home from her honeymoon ten days, but hasn't gotten back to me," I say with a sniffle.

"She will," Dr. Zane assures. "Call her again."

I'm concerned this connection with Sarah's confidante is inappropriate. Yet I rationalize that I turned Sarah on to the talking cure a dozen years earlier, when she was afraid to apply to architecture school. My first psychologist, Dr. Pamela Gold, said Sarah and I were too close to share a couch, so she recommended her supervisor, Dr. Gayle Zane, who turned out to be Sarah's godsend. I've contacted Zane several times over the years, soliciting sharp quotes for psychminded service pieces for *Femme*. Now I need her help for the femme moi.

"After their wedding brunch, Andrew said he got her a one-way ticket," I tattle. "He wants her to stay in the Midwest and not even visit here."

"That won't last long." Dr. Zane sounds sure. "Julie, grooms test out a lot of different roars to see if any of them work. This one probably won't."

I introduced myself to her as Julia, but Dr. Zane calls me Julie. I blow my nose and thank her, guessing I'm the recurring "Julie" character in Sarah's psychodramas. At least, I used to be.

Sure enough, two days later Sarah calls to say, "I'm here. When can we meet?" She's in the Big Apple for three days to see her baby doc and finalize her apartment sublet. Her quick reappearance fuels my fantasy she'll move back. I ask if she's spoken to Dr. Zane but she says no. We make plans for lunch at noon. I try on my black skinny jeans with the twenty-seven-inch waist, which won't get past my knees. My twenty-eight-inch relaxed-fit stonewashed middleweight pair stop at my thighs. I manage to zip up the twenty-nine-inch good-for-bloat baggies, which are tight. I throw on one of Jake's over-sized sweaters and rush to the diner around the block, our old hangout.

Forty-five minutes later Sarah runs in, waving. "Julie, how are you?"

We hug. We've only been apart six weeks but it feels like six months. She's wearing a lavender sundress and a flowered shawl. A month and a half away from New York and she's already pastel.

"I'm great. Really busy." I try not to cry.

"I'm showing. Can you tell?" She points to her belly, then slides into the booth. "I've been eating nonstop. I'm already a fat cow."

"You look fabulous." I reach out to touch her hand, noting her new diamond wedding band. "Nice bling."

"My fingers got so thick, I have to have it resized. It's not just baby weight. Don't they say you gain ten pounds on the newlywed diet?" She laughs.

She doesn't mention my weight gain. What's my excuse? I can't stop eating since *she's* gotten married and pregnant? If she has twins, I'll really be in trouble. "How are you?"

"Love Andrew, miss New York. I can't believe you called Dr. Zane." She laughs again.

"She told you?" I suppose there isn't doctor-patient privilege when you're mooching free advice from your best friend's therapist.

"No, you told me in your last e-mail." She takes off her shawl, showing off tan shoulders.

Oh, right, I'd forgotten that missive—one of the many she hasn't answered. She already doesn't need me. "I'm sorry, I was freaking out after Andrew mentioned your one-way ticket."

"It's adorable that you called Zane. Anything mine is yours, you know that." She takes a sip from my diet soda and looks at the menu.

"Julia's Salad?" asks George, my favorite waiter, in his Greek accent.

"I'll have Julia's Salad too," Sarah says.

George looks at her. "Where you been?"

"Cleveland, of all places."

"You look good. You gained a little weight?"

"I sure did." She beams. "I'm pregnant."

"Congratulations. Julia too?" he asks in a jolly voice.

"What, everything she gets, I get?" I ask, trying to hide that I'm mortified.

Figuring out he's committed a major faux pas, he adds, "You were too skinny before. Now you beautiful, like real woman. In Athens, where I born, women have meat on bones, like Sophia Loren."

"Isn't she Italian?" Sarah giggles.

"Quit while you're ahead if you want a tip," I tell George.

"Julia's the best." He walks to the kitchen and barks our order to the cook.

"Do I get to retaliate by calling Dr. Ness in Arizona?" Sarah asks.

"Maybe he'll return your calls. He's not returning mine. Though I got an e-mail promise for a webcam session in September. You and I should try it. I miss your face."

Her iPhone rings and she checks the caller ID but doesn't pick up. I picture her not answering all the times she sees my number.

"Here's Julia's Salad for two: turkey, cheese, egg, no roast beef or ham, chopped up good just for you," George sings, putting our food down, trying to make nice.

Her phone rings again. This time she checks the number and picks up. "Hi, sweetie. Wow, that's fantastic. I'm having lunch with Goods. Can I call you back?" She puts the phone away, smiles, and says, "Andrew sends his love."

"Me too," I mumble.

"You wouldn't believe the scope of Andrew's project. He's overseeing ten contractors and five hundred workers at the museum. He's like the Frank Gehry of Cleveland," she gushes.

"Why don't you pick up when I call?" I pour dressing over my salad. "You've been back from your honeymoon for two weeks." I sound pathetic, like a spurned lover.

"I know, I'm sorry. It's been a whirlwind. We bought that two-story house I told you about and I'm overseeing the renovation while puking ten times a day. We got two new puppies. Here's pictures." She shows me one on her phone. "Aren't they adorable?"

I take a quick look and nod, then dig in, eating fast, thinking she shouldn't get dogs before having a baby, she has enough to take care of. Bad enough to be jealous of her husband and kid, now I'm making rivals of her pets. And her fancy phone. I feel like a cave woman without a state-of-the-art, Web-connecting, picture-taking, music-and-TV-playing gizmo, though its best use seems to be catching flashers on the subway.

"We need a new code, like 'Crazy, more later.' So if you e-mail 'CML,' I'll know you still love me but you're busy," I say, picking the bell pepper out of my salad, wanting to believe her lame alibi. "Oh, I made that weight-bearing wall into wraparound bookshelves like you suggested. You have to see how regal it came out," I tell her. "What do I owe you for all the plans you drew up?"

"It's my gift—for all your help with my wedding," she says, now checking her e-mail. "So the wraparound shelves make your place look bigger?"

"You were exactly right. Dr. Ness thought so too."

"He saw them? When?"

"A few weeks ago, the day before he left town."

Dr. Ness convinced me that Jake and I could afford to buy the apartment next door to ours and that combining them would double their value. So it seemed essential that I show him my newly expanded, though still dusty, space.

"Spectacular," he fawned when he walked in that Thursday, at noon.

"Construction's fun for an impatient addict. How would it look without that wall? Bang. Bang. All gone," I said, trying not to mention his departure the next morning. But when he turned toward the door, "How can I ever thank you?" spilled from my lips. I was really asking, "How can I live without you?"

"You're good," he said before he dashed out. No hug, no pat on the shoulder. Just that two-word benediction.

Ness and Sarah have the best visual taste of anybody I've ever known. Whose eyes can I rely on now?

"So he's become your therapist, business advisor, real estate agent, and project manager?" Sarah asks with a sarcastic lilt.

"Mostly he's the good father," I answer. "Younger than the real one. And this dad actually likes me and my career."

"Or he gets paid to pretend he does," she throws out there.

"Why do you still need him when you have a great husband, gigantic apartment, and second book coming out? You're like on top of the world."

"I'm actually having a rough time." Without you holding me up, I don't say, not wanting to pressure or guilt her.

"Explain again why you think he fixes you so much." She pours dressing on her salad and digs in. I'm almost done with mine.

"His intense paternal attention and approval make me stronger and more successful."

"But you never slept with him or anything?" she asks for the twentieth time. I speak about him so passionately, she's not the only one concerned.

"Out of the million inappropriate things about my relationship with Dr. Ness, that's not one of them." I grab an olive off her lettuce mound.

"Having him inspect your construction beats me having Zane on speed dial while we registered at Bergdorf's. You win. I never met anyone so crazy for their shrink."

We have an ongoing, very Manhattan competition about who's more obsessively linked to their analyst. When Zane recommended her dentist and ob-gyn, both of whom Sarah is still seeing because she prefers female and not my male doctors, she was winning. But Sarah says I trumped her when Ness came to my book party and pitched my agent the idea of cowriting a book with me, in his voice. (Lilly— an antiacademic—didn't bite.)

"You know addiction therapy is behavioral and unorthodox. Sometimes he's getting somebody off crack before they kill themselves or their child, whatever the cost."

"So is he charging two hundred dollars for a video chat?" Her tone is sarcastic.

"Well, taking his advice, we went from being in debt to having six figures in the bank, and doubling our real estate holdings. Then my insurance reimburses sixty percent of his fees and my accountant claims the rest of therapy as a deduction, since it's research for my books."

"Didn't the *Femme* staffers hate his quotes in the article they excerpted?"

Okay, my boss did ask how a self-proclaimed feminist could let a man control her, while our staff critic decided I was paying Ness to be my higher power. Even the reviewers couldn't agree if he was heroic, eccentric, or too dictatorial. The *Daily News* called him "the head doctor of depravity" while *People* said *Up in Smoke* offered "the most funny, psychologically astute kick-the-habit strategies of the century."

For my career alone, keeping Ness around is a no-brainer.

Just as I'm ready to confess the extent of my sugar binges, Sarah's phone rings again. "Doctor's office," she says, looking at the number and taking the call. "I have to go. My gyno's fitting me in at three thirty."

"Don't you want to see the bookshelves?"

"Not now, I'll be late."

"Let's go out tonight. We never had a girls' last night out or bachelorette party."

"We'd been partying since we were thirteen. Our life was a bachelorette party." She laughs. "Now my idea of a thrill is being a stay-at-home wife and mommy."

I smile, haplessly watching my hip comrade-in-arms morph into a wannabe version of the mothers we've spent our lives swearing we'll never become.

"How about we order in sushi?"

"Can't eat raw fish while I'm pregnant."

I'm about to remind her we're in the Village, where a

United Nations of cuisines can be delivered to your doorstep within twenty minutes (except Indian, which takes forty-five), when she lowers the boom.

"I made plans to stay with Katy in New Jersey. She's a vegan who cooks organic," she adds.

I had assumed Sarah was staying at her old apartment before the sublet officially starts. Otherwise, why isn't she crashing in the city with me? She's only known Katy, a work colleague with two kids, for a year. So this recent interloper gets more time with Sarah than I do. I surmise it's because Katy's in the Secret Mommy Society and I'm not.

"Why aren't you staying with me?" I can tell I'm regressing back to fifth grade, when Sarah and I had Goth-looking ripped black "Sutty & Goods Club" T-shirts made at the mall and took a solemn oath not to let anybody else join. Dr. Ness tells me, "Sometimes you get so overly sensitive that you're like a burn victim who has no skin, so when you go outside, even the air hurts." But that's when I'm withdrawing from substances. I can't blame recovery symptoms for my immaturity while I'm using food to block the pain of pillar withdrawal, can I?

"Look." She grabs her shawl, sitting on the edge of the booth. "This is hard for me too. I'm the one leading the double life, half East, half Midwest. If we stay like we were, I'll never connect with my husband or make any new friends. Nobody can compete."

I feel myself soften. How can I argue with that?

She reaches for her wallet but I say, "I got it."

"You sure? I'll get it next time." She blows me a kiss. "You know I love you, Goods."

"Love you, Sutty," I mumble, throwing cash on the table.

But I don't get up. I sit there, reading the *Post*'s cover scandal "Punch Drunk Prison Party" about a local starlet's latest drama—a DWI arrest after the fistfight she and her lesbian lover had with a guard while visiting her father in jail—which puts my pig-out problems into perspective as I down the remains of Sarah's salad and ask for more melba toast.

On the way home, I stop at Crumbs and buy Fluffernutter, Heathbar, Red Velvet, Caramel Chew, Strawberry Butterscotch, Fudge Chocolate Chip, Strawberry Banana Split, and Devil Dog cupcakes. At home I slurp the thick candy-filled icing off each one, then polish off the cake part too.

Checking my e-mail that night, I open this seven-word message from Jake: "Hate asshole producers. Too tired. Talk tomorrow." Just what I need, a demented cliché L.A. haiku. Next, finally, is Dr. Ness's response to my previous missives: "Sugar's a dead-end drug you must abstain from to suffer well." I print a hard copy and wind up crashing with the page next to me in bed, where Jake is supposed to be.

chapter four
speed dating for dr. right

September 8

Triple-pillar desertion keeps sending shock waves through my system. Dr. Ness sends an e-mail promising we'll dissect how my candy-cupcake usage exacerbates my abandonment complex over the phone, on webcam, and in person when he comes to town this month, so I agree to continue therapy with him long-distance. But he's not yet ready to resume weekly sessions and it takes him five days to return my next voice mail. Then he responds to my daily e-mails a week later in reverse order, which disorients me, and postpones his supposed fall trip back east until Halloween.

"Listen, buddy. I already have an emotionally distant dad. I don't need to pay my pseudo–father figure to reneglect me," I e-mail. "I've decided to look for your replacement."

Six days later my AWOL shrink responds, "Good idea," not sounding the least bit anguished about my threat to move on without him.

"Can I call your guy, Bryan Cox?" I ask. Ness has described Dr. Cox, his guru, as "his sage, seer, and savior."

"Cox is out of the country," he says, but jauntily offers the number of his protégé, who has taken over Ness's office and his blunt behavioral approach. Ready to play musical couches, I set up a session, revisiting Dr. Ness's classy Tenth Street work space without him.

Protégé—a blond, stocky guy who looks my age—leads me inside. I notice a cheesy painting of daisies on the wall where an old-fashioned bronze ship clock with a barometer used to hang.

"Since Ness left, my husband's been working out west, my best friend moved to Cleveland, and I've been eating more," I confess, trying not to stare at the hideous white flowers.

"Why is that a problem?" he asks.

"I'm gaining weight at the same time I'm finishing a book on conquering my food addiction. It's due in three months. They could cancel the project," I explain. "I need to slim down by the pub date so I can promote it and it does as well as my last book."

"None of that will make you happy," Protégé declares, crossing his beefy arms.

"What are you, a Buddhist?" I guess.

He nods yes.

"Did your kid paint the daisies?" I can't help but ask.

"They're lilies," he snaps. "From an antique fair."

When I get home, I e-mail Dr. Ness, "Your protégé's a pudgy Zen hypocrite with bad taste in art. Meanwhile, Mr.

Antimaterialist is charging two hundred dollars for forty-five unenlightened minutes."

"E-mail him your negative reaction directly," Dr. Ness promptly suggests, suddenly more interested. "And then forward me his response."

Just where I don't want to be—in the middle of a subconscious pissing contest between Freud and Jung.

Instead I Google "psychologist" and "Greenwich Village." Thousands of names pop up, along with an article saying the highest concentration of American Psychiatric Association members is in my neighborhood, and six psychoanalytic training centers are within twelve blocks. The perk of living in New York City. The Web site of my medical insurance provider shows listings of Ph.D.s in its network who charge only a twenty-five-dollar copayment a session. What a deal!

Determined to land Dr. Ness's lower-priced clone, I sit in the dark with my black Apple laptop and click "male," "addiction," and "food disorders," locating eighty local masculine mind tenders in my health plan. Since Ness charges two hundred dollars for forty-five minutes, for the same price as seeing him once I can play the field by going on eight blind dates with eight professionals in eight days. Still viewing the world in terms of the punchy women's magazine headlines I used to write, instead of Speed Dating for a Husband, I'm going Speed Dating for Dr. Right!

Some of the doctors have pictures online, so I scan for a handsome healer who'll make me forget Ness fast. I leave messages on ten machines and most of the eligibles return my call within six hours, passing my impatience test. They all give good phone. I make my first date with the photo-gallery face who resembles a younger version of Gabriel Byrne's psychoanalyst on HBO's *In Treatment*. Byrne Jr. also works on West Tenth Street, a block I associate with good shrink vibes.

Yet walking there Monday afternoon, I feel guilty passing my ex's office, as if I'm cheating on Ness. Even though he left me first! In person Byrne Jr. is tall and slim, an aqua shirt and matching tie accentuating nice blue eyes. As I share my recent left-in-the-lurch lament, he nods silently, taking notes. His office is beige and neat. Too neat. Why is he so quiet and reserved? Ballbuster father who squelched his power? Too many siblings too close in age? Can I be projecting my own pathology this quickly?

"It sounds like you depended on Ness and Sarah like surrogate parents," he finally says, enunciating carefully. "Their absence shakes your foundation, making you feel orphaned and unfed."

"Yes, but the mind fuck is they're fine. So the minute I start sitting shiva, they call back in a great mood, like I'm crazy to be hurt. My mom grew up poor and an orphan, by the way, that's why she's an overfeeder."

"Do you always speak so quickly?" he inquires.

"I have three smart, loud brothers, so as a kid I had to rush to get a word in edgewise. Have you always spoken so slowly?" I fire back. "Do you have siblings?"

"Do you have family issues?"

"Who doesn't?" I snap. "How old are you?"

"Why do you want to know?"

I hate the restrictive "blank slate" approach. All this mystery makes me hungry for Dr. Ness, a surprisingly open WASP who—when it comes to his personal life—can't shut up.

"Do you ever consider leaving Manhattan for someplace quieter, like the suburbs?" he asks.

Next.

On Tuesday at a nearby prewar building, I visit contender number two. He's my height, slim, with a navy jacket and know-it-all foreign air, regal, like Napoleon. His inner office has a burgundy couch, brown leather chair, a bold South American rug, oversized plants, and Asian prints on the wall, as if to say "I am worldly."

"I like residing in the neighborhood with the most shrinks in the world," I throw out.

"Actually, there are more per square foot in Buenos Aires," he corrects.

"I wonder why."

"German Jewish immigration to Argentina after World War II. Who doesn't know that?" he asks. "So why are you here?"

I share my addiction history, "separation and shoving my face with sugar" saga.

"Instead of dealing honestly with changes you've found devastating, you're too concerned with looking like a winner on TV," deduces Napoleon. "It's like you're on trial and need externals like press clippings to prove you're worthy on a daily basis."

He's right, I do. He seems confident, erudite, sophisticated, like someone who can teach me something.

"I've seen this syndrome in American media professionals," he continues. "I recommend a relaxing vacation and a Mediterranean diet with a glass of red wine every night."

What kind of doctor tells a self-described recovering addict to go get a drink?

My third tryst, on Thursday, is with another doc in Byrne Jr.'s building. I recall that the article on downtown-as-psychmall says a hundred therapists share this very address.

Indian music plays in the waiting room, where I'm summoned by a slightly built, gray-haired guy with glasses, wearing a white shirt and khakis. I learn he teaches at Adelphi and is "eclectic in an analytic frame." He sits on a couch with his legs crossed like a Swami pretzel as I present my backstory.

"You're the type who makes the right choices for the wrong reasons," he deduces.

Am I?

"Where did your loss originate?"

Good question. Encouraged, I tell him, "I grew up the old-est of four with a workaholic lawyer dad and an overfeeding mom who encouraged me to recite 'I Have a Little Shadow' when I was three."

"You're still performing to get attention," Swami declares.

"By auditioning my one-woman monologue to an audi-ence of male psychologists?" I ask.

"Yes." Swami nods. "Still trying to win Daddy's love."

"Of course I am."

"You should be meditating daily," he says, adding, "my wife runs the Vipassana Meditation Center in New Hampshire, where my patients get a discount for weekend retreats."

Another karma pusher looking for cash? I'm starting to rethink my decision to dump Ness.

On the way home I call Jake in California and leave a mes-sage on his machine, asking, "If I commit to seeing someone weekly, do I tell the new guy I might also see Dr. Ness when he's in town?"

"That's like warning someone on a first date you're still sleeping with your ex," he later e-mails back.

I forward this to Ness, who responds, "It's more like get-ting married but telling your mate that you won't give up your family of origin."

Typical male. Now that I'm leaving him, he's answering immediately, as if we're instant messaging.

That night, channel-surfing with Jake's remote, I analyze why I'm really speed dating head doctors like a madwoman. Rather than getting a second opinion, I want eight? I'm obviously just feeling lonely and need company. I fear my frenetic hunt for Dr. Replacement is designed to hide discomfort. But there's a surprising side effect: Over the last few days I'm eating less. What an unusual diet plan—a shrink workout a day keeps the pounds away. While my spouse is out west, all the messages from male shrinks make me feel popular. I relish the attention, my neighborhood absurdly hopping with the possibility of a nurturing man just around the corner. Optimistically, I hope the process of searching for a fresh Freudian can cure me. On the bad side, I could probably blow my annual mental health budget in one week, gorging myself on shrinks.

On Friday afternoon, at another prewar building with elaborate moldings and high ceilings, number four is wearing brown cords and a sweater. He's fast talking, bald, in robust shape, Yul Brynner in *The King and I*. I relay my pathetic "I miss Ness, Sarah, and Jake and can't stop shoving frosting in my fat face" song and dance.

"Are you sugar-rushing?" he asks. "You present with manic energy, like you're on overdrive."

"You talk fast too," I comment.

"I talk faster around you to compete," he counters. "And I know exactly who you are. I read *Up in Smoke*."

"You did?" It would be a dumb reason to pick him—since he doesn't add that he liked it.

"Having trouble coping with loneliness, you had a garden-variety relapse. So you're reverting to self-destructive eating behavior," Yul diagnoses. "Here's the million-dollar question: Why are you so consumed with rage?"

Wow! *Am* I enraged? At being hooked on another substance despite all my addiction therapy? At everybody who's deserting me? Because my fickle publisher won't love me as a chubette?

"Are you taking my steady two P.M. Friday slot?" He demands an answer.

He seems a little pushy. "I still have a few therapists I'm checking out," I respond honestly.

"What? You didn't tell me you're shrinking around!" he yells, pounding his fist on his desk.

No wonder he has rage radar. "You didn't tell me you expect exclusivity when we've barely met!" I yell on my way out.

On Saturday, my session is at a homey brownstone. But brain bender number five is late. Bad sign; Dr. Ness is never on time. I'm determined to find a more punctual practitioner. (To paraphrase Erica Jong: Every therapist is a reaction against your last.) Twelve minutes later, I meet a burly type who looks like the antihero of *The Shield*. Is marriage to a TV/film director making all my visual references actors?

This one's profile said he's sixty-two, an Episcopalian of Scottish descent, "psychodynamically" trained at Columbia.

After sharing my spiel, I inquire, "Why do you think I'm eating less during my shrink search?"

"Instead of feeling rejected that Ness, your husband, and Sarah left, you're taking control and giving yourself choices, which is liberating."

It really is, I think excitedly.

"I should let you know my only opening is nine on Saturday mornings."

Next.

At noon on Monday, my sixth specialist is clean-cut, a bit heavy, wearing a striped shirt and bow tie. He has red hair and glasses, an intellectual David Caruso's Detective Horatio on *CSI: Miami.* (I really have to turn off the TV and read a book.) Horatio divulges that he's married with two kids, Catholic, from California, in his midfifties, and had an alcohol problem he conquered. Enjoying his openness, I quickly recite my whole "marooned alone on this island with sugar mania" megillah.

"Dr. Ness is a daddy substitute," Horatio opines. "You want to please him, to be his favorite patient just as you wanted to be your father's favorite child."

Exactly. I never got over that desire. This one's perceptive.

"Some men don't like scrawny bodies. I personally prefer a woman with meat on her bones. I think you look very voluptuous and sexy," he continues, ogling.

Yick! I reconsider the upside of the blank slate.

Despite failing so far to find a new object of transference, during my first week of speed shrinking I finish three chapters of *Food Crazy* and shrink myself two pounds. If I keep it up and stick to network guys at twenty-five dollars a pop, it's cheaper than Slim-Fast. Is it anxiety? The breakup diet? Does running to all these sessions burn up calories? I bet therapy feeds me, and getting back out there for this marathon meeting of so many new males is more fun than eating.

On Tuesday morning, I walk into number seven's waiting room, find a ferret in a cage, and walk right back out.

. . .

My Tuesday-afternoon session turns out to be not only in the building of my literary agency, but on the same floor, right across the hall. What if contender number eight is a nut-job like Horny Horatio or Raging Yul and I end up bumping into him whenever I visit my agent? At least he's on time—and attractive. He wears casual black jeans and a button-down flannel shirt, a big, tall bohemian bear with a mustache, dark hair to his shoulders, and soulful brown eyes. Just my type. He's a "cognitive behavioral therapist" experienced in impulse disorders but admits he smokes cigars. A problem, since I've become an antismoking zealot.

"Have you analyzed that terrible habit?" I ask.

"No, but I will," Dr. Cigar says with a laugh. After I disclose my neuroses, he has no issue spilling his stats: He's fifty, a Brooklynite Virgo, married, Jewish, and childless, like me. His graduate psychology degree is from NYU, like Ness's, where he knew and admired him!

"You seem exceptionally bright. I'm not sure I can keep up with the ghost of Dr. Ness intellectually," Dr. Cigar admits.

Complimentary, humble, and self-critical? It catches me off guard. He's the only one calling me smart. He's respectful of my connection with Ness. He isn't auditioning for the role of my next mentor, playing hard-to-get. I'm intrigued.

"Why? Are you insecure about your brains?"

"No. But I don't lead with my brain," he explains. "I lead with my intuition."

"So intuit," says I.

"Okay. You come off hypomanic, blurring work and life, an urban extremity we could work to temper."

I don't want to toil less, I want to hurt and eat less while selling more books. But he seems sane and sharp enough. No pets in sight. I'll forfeit some of Dr. Ness's edgy genius for empathy and proximity.

"Are you planning on moving anytime soon?" I must ask.

"No, I'm staying put," he swears.

"One more essential question. What do you read?"

"Lately, books by Amy Bloom, Irvin Yalom, Deborah Tannen," he answers with authors I admire. Plus, he has a prime time slot at 6 P.M. on Fridays open three times a month.

"My agent is right across the hall," I say.

"You could join the gym on this floor for one-stop shopping," he quips.

A sense of humor too, though he had me at "exceptionally bright." On my eighth try, has my maniacal mind met its match?

On my way out, I stop at my agent's office to see if she's received my latest *Food Crazy* advance check, mentioning my quick quest for another analyst.

"So instead of speed dating, you're speed shrinking?" Lilly asks. "Sounds like a *Femme* feature."

She would know. She plucked me from the *Femme* masthead the day my "How to Quit Anything" article—about how Dr. Ness was helping me quit all my addictions—hit the newsstands, saying, "Lilly Rem here. I'm buying you lunch. There's an editor at a top house who wants this expanded into a book pronto. Are you up for it?" After Ness's pep talk about how I couldn't say no and had to quit my job to become a self-help author, I was.

"'How to Find Your New Guru'?" I now suggest.

"Too *Eat, Pray, Love*. I'm so over it." She takes off her glasses to scrutinize me. "You're not pregnant, are you?"

This again! What a punch in the gut—which I just reduced a few pounds by speed shrinking. Can't a woman my age eat a cupcake or two without everyone jumping on the baby-bump bandwagon?

"No, I'm not."

"Avoid everyone at your publisher until you drop a few," she says.

"That bad?" I ask, and she nods her head yes. I picked Lilly because she never lies, though I'm currently wishing she'd make a polite attempt.

That night I e-mail Dr. Ness the update that I'm officially choosing Dr. Cigar—whose real name is Dr. Gregory Holder—as his successor.

"I know Holder, he's good," Dr. Ness replies. "But when I come to town, let's talk this over in person."

I make a mental note to ask Dr. Cigar his opinion, afraid I've just started therapy to psychoanalyze my relationship with my ex-shrink.

chapter five

reprogramming

November 11

When I get on the scale I'm depressed to see that I'm up to 153. I hate being fat and feel determined to find a way to get my slim body back.

"The only way to change is to change" is my new book's top slogan. After I finish fine-tuning the last chapter's "Are You Ready to Transform Yourself?" test I take it myself, add up the score, and the answer is yes. Along with quitting cupcakes and candy, I better listen to my own advice: "Don't attempt to morph into your maximum self on your own. First, embark on an all-out assault to get the right mavens, mentors, or gurus to guide you."

Okay, since Dr. Cigar has only a twenty-five-dollar copay per session, I can afford to add an exercise expert to my day-to-day existence. I'll work out three hours a day, like Madonna. I leave a message for Junior, my former personal trainer, a chiseled African-American nightclub DJ who lives in my building. We met a few years before, when I was a chubby chain-smoker. He checked me out and said, "You're not really fat, you're average. But this is Manhattan, where nobody can bear being average anything." How could I not hire him?

He turned me on to an elaborate, sweat-inducing weights routine set to Missy Elliott's "Get Ur Freak On" and Kanye West's "Jesus Walks," which we did for an hour three times a week for sixty dollars a session. He even threw in a short back massage afterward. So three hours of funky aerobics with a rub was cheaper and more fun than forty-five minutes of Dr. Ness kicking my brain into shape.

But this time Junior calls back to say he's relocating to Tokyo, where his spouse is being transferred. A geographically desirable male trainer who can teach hip-hop moves to a cerebral Jewess will be as hard as Ness to replace. It isn't fair—all the important men in my life are leaving me for their wives!

I send notes to both Dr. Ness and Sarah, asking why the hell they haven't returned my calls in the last ten days, feeling like a hungry little kid who can't get the attention of her parents. This reminds me of my speed-shrinking session with Dr. Byrne Jr., who surmised that I'm experiencing their loss as orphanhood. My mother lost her mom and dad when she was just a toddler. Am I transferring her childhood angst? Internalizing her lack of attaching? Object relating? No, that's too psychoanalytic. Since I'm a believer in blunt behavioral approaches, I breeze through *Food Crazy*'s chapter headings, debating whether to try to dispute my misconceptions, stop catastrophizing, overcome victimization, create positive illusions, or quit feeling hurt by who's not there and focus on who is.

Just then my laptop pings with an update from my friend Victoria, who has attached her piece on being the first supersized Asian in her family that I recommended she submit to *Femme*. In it she documents losing thirty pounds with the Janey Peg diet and includes a picture of herself looking svelte. How I long to be svelter. There's a link to the Janey Peg Web site. Unlike Weight Winners, they don't do meetings or weigh you in public. It's good for a busy freelancer on deadline—I can do this plan on my own, without leaving my apartment, and it's nobody's business what the scale says. Janey Peg it is.

Calling 1-800-FAT-AWAY, I talk to a representative named Tim who says that if I enroll today, he'll waive their joining fee and send me a week's worth of food for $125. Seems reasonable since I spent that much last week on Crumbs' cupcakes. Tim asks my name, birth date, height, weight, exercise and eating habits. Liking his attention, I admit that I've gained twenty-five pounds. In a bout of paranoia, I give Tim a false last name so he won't rat me out to the media, and pretend I need to drop weight fast "for an important high school reunion." He calculates that to get back to 128 and lose the amount I gained in the same time frame, I need 1,200 daily calories of their prepackaged food—the same amount of calories as the diet Dr. Ness had me on.

"Listen, I'm a fussy eater who doesn't want any red meat, ham, peppers, or onions."

"No problem, Julia," Tim says. "Go to our Web site for special orders."

I like the multimedia consultation and the looks of their pasta, cheesecake, muffins, pizza, French fries, and fish and chips. Surely Dr. Ness would tell me not to gobble up that starchy garbage.

"There's too much bread and potatoes here," I tell Tim. "I get thinner on high protein, low carbs. I gain weight on diets filled with starch."

"Our clients have luck with small two-hundred-and-fifty-calorie portions. We think low carbs make you feel deprived. We believe in a variety of foods you'll enjoy. Try it for one week. I think you'll find that it could work for you, Julia," he amiably insists.

"Can I just get one meal delivered?" I ask.

"We deliver once a week. You want delivery more often than that, Julia?"

"I can't do moderation. Isn't there any way I can buy one meal at a time?"

"I bet you could at a local Janey Peg outlet. But I can't do it from here."

"Why not?"

"I'm in Texas."

"I thought you were in New York." He sounds very young. "How old are you?"

"Why do you want to know?"

The blank-slate therapists are bad enough. Now my Janey Peg guy has a privacy policy?

"Have you ever been on Janey Peg yourself?" I ask.

"Yeah, they made us try it when we started. I was surprised how good the food is, Julia."

"How much do you weigh?"

"I'm five-eleven, used to weigh 200. Now I'm 187," he says. "They taught us about portion control. And I work out five times a week at the gym."

Yeah, I could drop twenty pounds in two weeks if I

stopped drinking beer when I was in college too, I don't say. "But Tim, I have an extremely addictive personality." I give him the crash course on Goodman addiction history, concluding with cupcake compulsion, turning him into yet another shrink.

"Hey, Julia, I hear you, it can be hard." He turns into Dr. Phil Jr. "But how about this? When you receive the food, put it in the freezer right away, except for one day's worth. That way it won't be in front of your face, so you might not be tempted."

"If two hundred and fifty calories won't fill me up, can I eat two or three meals for lunch?" I ask, since on Ness's plan I used to eat my thousand-calorie chef salad early in the day, and then just have yogurt or veggies for dinner.

"You know, Julia, you might be allowed to do that. Hold on, I'll check." He comes back and says, "You can eat two at once if you want. Your food will be delivered on Wednesday, so I'll have a food consultant call you at five P.M. Does that work for you, Julia?"

Repeating my first name so often is an effective way to create false intimacy; I have to steal that technique for my next seminar. "Okay, Tim, I'll try."

On Wednesday morning I rush to my volunteering gig, running an antiaddiction workshop at the local soup kitchen. I don't have time to grab a bite beforehand and it's too tacky to waste a state-subsidized free church lunch on a rich Jewish girl. I figure I'll eat later.

"Boy, you packed on some pounds since last year," says Petey, my schizophrenic homeless friend. He gives me a huge smile, clearly meaning it as a compliment.

"Thanks, Petey," I gulp.

"You got a kid in there?" Petey points to my stomach as I hold my tongue and tears back.

"How long have you been clean now?" I change the subject.

"Three years and three days sober as an ugly nun," Petey says. "One day a time."

As I return late that afternoon, my doorman hands me a big box from Janey Direct. Starving, I tear it open in the elevator, skimming the explanatory booklet. In my apartment I put the fourteen mini TV-dinner-looking boxes in my freezer. They're packaged with pictures of the meals on the front and calories, carbs, and fat breakdown on the back. Ripping off the plastic, I start microwaving and soon devour Janey's Breakfast Scramble (pretty good), Chicken Salad kit (yuck), Chicken Fettuccine (yum), and a tiny bag of microwave popcorn, one-tenth the amount I normally eat. I assume polishing off four packages means I've blown the diet sky-high. When my Janey Peg consultant Carla calls, I confess my sins.

"No problem, Julia. That's only eight hundred and fifty calories so far. It doesn't matter what combo you eat as long as it's twelve hundred calories. You can even eat more today, Julia."

Carla, like Tim, is a twenty-three-year-old Texan whose upbeat attitude is kind of contagious. I should stop wasting money on Manhattan psychoanalysts in favor of free phone sessions with young cheerful Southern salespeople who say my name twenty times in a row.

"Hey, Carla, are you on Janey Peg too?"

"I've tried some of the food that they gave us for free. I haven't gone on the diet yet."

"Why?" I ask. "Are you already thin?"

"No. I'm five foot five and weigh 180 pounds. Honestly, Julia, they don't pay us enough."

Her admission makes me like her. "That doesn't seem fair."

"You don't know the half of it, Julia," she sighs.

"Tell me."

"My boyfriend dumped me, then they transferred me to this office where I have to answer phones seven days a week, for hardly any money. Any wonder I'm eating too much?"

"Drinking and smoking too?" I ask her.

"How did you know?" she asks me.

"'Cause I was there too, Carla. But you have to believe your pain instead of suppressing it. Underlying every substance problem is a deep depression that feels unbearable," I quote from my book. "But it's not unbearable, Carla, it just feels that way."

"Wow, that's so heavy, Julia," she says.

Completely blowing my cover, I wind up sending Carla the free e-version of *Up in Smoke* and the pamphlet from my "How to Quit Anything" seminar, while she sends me a list of "free foods" I can eat anytime.

After we hang up, I go grocery shopping for lettuce, tomatoes, carrots, broccoli, and fat-free salad dressing. I bouncily breeze past the cupcakes and candy aisle in favor of fruits and vegetables, realizing I'm the type who needs a new mission every few weeks. Usually it's to convert others, but now I'm hoping to reconvert myself.

On Thursday I have Chicken Pasta Parmigiana (not terrible), Pesto Pizza (nothing to write home about), Pasta Fagioli (zesty), and Chocolate Cheesecake (too minuscule), downing the food in one sitting, adding up the calories, all sated and not even hungry later. This isn't so hard. I'm enjoying myself. After all my overintellectualizations on addictions, how corny that the answer's been one infomercial away.

On Friday, I order in organic artichokes and green beans, eating the "free foods" at night, feeling full and fine. Hey, this regimen is doable. I envision being a slender author with a kitchen filled with cute Janey Peg cuisine. For the first time in years I'm not afraid to keep food within reach. My thirty-one-inch-waist baggy Levi's feel a little looser. The skin under my chin looks tighter. But after three days on the diet, I get on the scale—to find I've gained four pounds!

I leave an emergency message for Carla, who calls back. By following my mandates she hasn't had a drink in forty-eight hours. She thinks three days isn't enough time to tell if my diet is working, and says give it a week. It's the same thing I'd say to a client. But "Let yourself know what you know" is another of my pet mantras. I know I never lose an ounce eating bread products. If I keep going, I'll keep gaining. The company assumes there's a one-for-all diet when every person's different. After I praise Carla's sobriety, I tell her to call if she gets weird. Then I march into my kitchen and see the Janey Peg chocolate nutrition snacks for what they are: candy bars in disguise, about to trick me so they can glom onto my gullible thighs.

Before I inhale the rest of the bars and make myself sick, I toss them down my building's incinerator. I feel bad throwing away perfectly fine nourishment. Yet if it's in my freezer, I'll finish it off in a food fit at three A.M. On Friday at 5:30 I go online to find out if the Janey Peg outlet nearby is open weekends—so I can return the leftovers—but it's already closed. At six Jake texts me from LAX, surprising me by flying home for the weekend to see me!

"Can't wait to hold you, baby," I respond to the one person who never notices my weight fluctuations.

Because I rarely cook, when he walks in the door a few hours later, he's pleasantly shocked that I offer a tasting platter of the leftovers I have to get rid of pronto. I expertly microwave the hell out of the Southwestern-Style Chicken Burrito, Luscious Lasagna in Marinara Sauce, Chicken Strips with Rice Medley, Vegetable and Shrimp Pot Pie, and a final Breakfast Scramble. My hubby loves being served by my Manhattan version of Suzy Homemaker, and we feed each other the tastier items with our fingers. Then we have sizzling sex on the living room floor, my favorite way to burn up calories. Just as I'm about to climax, the telephone rings and my old phone machine—which I forgot to turn off—picks up.

"Julia, it's Dr. Ness. Call me right away on my emergency cell."

chapter six
e-therapy

November 16

"Can you hear me now?" asks mini-Ness, staring at me from my computer screen.

"Yes, finally." I turn up my microphone.

I've wasted two hours this morning setting up the video iChat program on my Apple MacBook, adding Dr. Ness, a.k.a. MNPHD, to my buddy list so we can see each other's faces for this technotherapy experiment he was so eager to schedule last night. The fact that he has a mac.com e-mail address somehow makes it harder to connect with my AOL address. Although we've exchanged e-mails and quick calls, I haven't had a real forty-five-minute appointment with him in months. A regular phone session would have sufficed. All this hassle, just to see my larger-than-life shrink shrunk to the size of one of the goofballs on the YouTube clips my young fans send me.

"Can you see me now?" he inquires.

I nod. They promise a good picture through the high-quality CCD camera sensor, but he looks pale and grainy, a moving mug shot. It's noon and I'm sitting at my desk barefoot, in extra-large sweats and a T-shirt. Testing the equipment earlier, I caught my own mug shot, and vanity motivated me to take a shower, put on makeup, and blow-dry my hair. One benefit of cybersessions—he can only see my head, not my bloated body. I look down when I speak to hide my double chin. I could be naked below the shoulders and he'd have no clue.

"This doesn't feel like you're closer," I say. "More like Big Brother is watching." It's hard to see his huge personality and stature in my life being reduced to a dwarfed cyberhead. I feel as if his body is disappearing while mine is magnifying, as if I've eaten him.

"Why are you so upset with me?" mini-Ness wants to know.

"You haven't been able to resume our therapy, you haven't read the manuscript I sent you. You said you'd be back to New York soon but it's been fourteen and a half weeks!" I flash to the sex movie *9½ Weeks*, fearing my need for him is sadomasochistic. Nothing's worse than making an impatient addict like me wait. It's like a hundred-day prison sentence, though now he's the one encaged through the eye of the hidden camera I didn't even know was lurking on my laptop's edge.

"I'm sorry. It's taken me much longer than expected to get settled in Arizona. There have been some problems here. And last week I had a trauma conference in Texas I had to attend."

"I don't give a fuck where you went," I say. I don't have to be rational; that's his job.

"I did read the entire first draft of *Food Crazy*, like I promised. It's excellent. Sharp, sincere. I'll e-mail you back a few word changes. But it looks like you'll be making your December deadline."

"You really like it? Thanks! But if I look like Porky Pig, my agent says they'll cancel my contract. Can you tell I gained weight?"

"I can't see your body but your face does look a bit fuller," he admits.

"I feel like it's partially your fault."

"Tell me what I did wrong again."

"It's bad enough being without Jake and Sarah. But you can't help me deal with the loss if you're gone too. Your absence is the final straw. It's making me go sugar crazy."

"Because you're feeling abandoned," he says in a sincere tone that pisses me off.

"Because you abandoned me." I twist around in my swivel chair.

"Being sad and missing me isn't a bad thing," says my Lilliputian shrink.

"It's more than being sad. I feel bereft, like I'm in mourning. It's setting me back. Reopening old daddy-ignoring-me wounds. I can't stop stuffing myself—which could wreck everything I've worked so hard for." I feel like touching his face on the computer, but it would blur the screen. This is the technology families use as a link to soldiers at war. How painful an actual separation must be, versus my allegorical attachment to my fake father.

"I'm here now," he announces. "Doesn't this help?"

"No. It's worse." If I depended on him instead of substances, it shouldn't be surprising that his departure is causing a relapse. I think of the Joni Mitchell song about the guy she can "drink a case of" and still be on her feet. "It's like I'm getting too weak a dose of you."

"Our chemistry changed when I moved," he confirms.

"It's better for me to connect with someone here. I've seen Dr. Cigar three times so far. He's really warm and empathetic."

"Sounds like you're hitting it off with the new guy," he says. Or is that a question?

"He thought *Up in Smoke* was intelligent, brave, and did a great turn for therapy," I read from the journal I keep by my desk. It's quite a compliment for Ness since he's my book's rock star.

"He certainly knows how to connect with you" is his response.

Is he implying that Dr. Cigar doesn't really love my book? "Why so hostile?"

"That's not hostile." He sounds defensive. "That's being protective of you."

Protective? I'm beginning to think I need someone to shield me from Dr. Ness.

"For a self-help guru who teaches people how to change, change is quite difficult for you," he says. "My protégé's flower painting made you cry."

"It was a very ugly painting," I laugh. "Listen, I quit every bad habit for you. That's all I can handle. Now I have to quit feeling rejected."

He nods his diminutive head. "Listen, Julia, this transition was hard for me too. I did not want to move. But my wife spent twenty-five years in Manhattan for my work. Her mother isn't well. As the only child, she needs to be closer to her."

He often pushes his patients to take responsibility for the welfare of their mates and children. So at least he's walking the walk. I just wish it wasn't so far away from me.

"Have you spoken to Dr. Cox about your move?" I find it reassuring that he has his own shrink. Or is Cox his supervisor? On the board of Ness's institute? Whenever I ask, all he reveals is that he talks to Cox monthly, if not in person, then by phone. Do *they* do e-therapy?

"Yes. Bryan says it's time to put my family's needs before my own," Ness admits.

"I didn't know you didn't want to leave New York," I say. "What a horrible position to be put in."

"Oh, it's not such a big hardship for me. We own several acres of land we're building a house on. It's twenty times cheaper here."

"Your wife likes it better in Alabama?" It's been a running gag that in my e-mails I refuse to write the name of his new state. I switch off among Arkansas, Alaska, Antarctica, and Anaheim.

"Well, I wouldn't say she likes it better. Her mother had a stroke and needs around-the-clock care. The change has been pretty traumatizing for her and her folks."

"I'm so sorry. I had no idea."

I suddenly feel stupid and selfish for babbling on about my problems, now that I picture his wife selflessly caring for her elderly parent. It's so guilt-inducing, I almost wish he'd stop divulging the truth. Dr. Ness never wants to be a blank slate. But when he shares his own story, it feeds my fantasy that our feelings of closeness are mutual. In reality, I fear it's all one-sided. He's simply a man I pay to listen to me. What a bizarre concept—like hiring a gigolo, but without the sex. For all that money, I don't even get to be in the same room with a real body anymore. I just get this scintilla of my former psychoanalyst, a McShrink on my MacBook screen. I go away to blow my nose but he doesn't appear to notice.

"I'll be back east soon," he says. "In the meantime, with my wife so busy, I have to take care of my daughter. She's seven and having trouble with the transition, so we can't leave her in day care or with a stranger. I'm not cut out to be a full-time babysitter, but there's no choice right now."

"Why are you telling me all of this?"

"I'm explaining why I had to leave you," he says.

See, he has left me. He's admitting it.

"It's tragic." His small shoulders shrug on the screen.

What's tragic? His wife's mother's illness? Giving up Manhattan? Having to prematurely sever our intense link? When he confides in me, it only makes me more curious about his private world.

"Is your older daughter upset that you moved so far away?"

"She's in school at Yale," he says. "So it doesn't affect her so much."

"What about your mother? Doesn't she live in Texas? Are you going to visit her?"

"No plan so far. But she wrote a letter thanking me for the flowers I sent on her birthday."

Dr. Ness hasn't seen his eighty-five-year-old mother in thirty years but still hopes for a reconciliation. Sarah finds it off-putting that he shares his alcoholic mom's antics with me. But I'm hooked on the story, like a fan following the next installment of a favorite soap opera.

"Now that I'm set up here, do you want to do video sessions every Friday?"

I've wanted to resume our treatment so badly. But by the time he's ready, it seems too late. "I'm seeing Dr. Holder three

Fridays a month now. I'm starting to bond with him. Maybe it's better this way."

"Why don't we make an appointment for next Friday and you can cancel last-minute if you want?"

"The long distance is too hard. It hurts. It just reminds me you're not really here."

"I'm trying to be here."

"I think I need to break up with you," I blurt out. "You have to let me."

"I most certainly will let you." He raises his voice, which sounds scratchy.

"Then let me NOT make an appointment," I tell mini-Ness. "This isn't helping me."

"I'm helping you by endorsing your therapy with Dr. Holder, thank you very much."

"Isn't it weird that an addiction specialist famous for getting people to end long-term drug dependencies is incapable of terminating a relationship with a patient?"

"I'm not incapable. I just don't want to shut doors," he says. "Listen, it's okay to be upset with me for being erratic and unpredictable. That doesn't mean I'm not good for you."

I used to like his arrogance, but it's starting to feel maddening. I'm anxious to see the available Dr. Cigar while literally turning off the distant Ness. After all, he's the one who says I have to put as many blockades between myself and my addiction as possible.

"I bet you and Dr. Ness can negotiate a posttherapeutic relationship," Dr. Cigar suggests. "But it won't be easy. You two swam in such deep waters."

"I know. We clicked on so many levels. I fear too many."

His office is less organized than Ness's, crammed with coffee tables, chairs, ottomans, overlapping rugs, piles of books, and primitive Indian art on the windowsill. His waiting room is on one side of the hall, his bathroom on the other side. You need a key, which is inconvenient. But I'm glad to have a real man in the flesh to help me digest the video version of Ness.

"Why can't we unclick?" I ask, crossing my legs. I'm wearing my thirty-two-inch-waist relaxed-fit jeans, along with the same two-inch high-heeled black boots I often wore to see Ness. Are they my shrink boots? Or my date boots?

"This guy's been line editing your whole life," Dr. Cigar surmises.

"He literally edited every chapter of *Up in Smoke.* Each session he'd hand me back corrections and say, 'This is excellent. I love it.' My father hates my work. Having Ness's praise made the book write itself. One time he wouldn't read the chapter I'd given him and said, 'I'll wait to read it all when you're done.' I got blocked and couldn't work till he resumed reading, saying he loved it again." I tear up at the thought.

"You are your work, so that means Ness loves you?" Dr. Cigar pushes a box of Kleenex close.

I take one, sniffling. "By the end we were switching roles. I was psychoanalyzing him and his mom, and he was starting his own self-help book called *Unhooked* that he wanted me to ghostwrite."

"Cool title," Dr. Cigar says.

"During our e-therapy session, he admitted he didn't really want to leave the city. He only moved because his wife's mother had a stroke and needs around-the-clock care. He's stuck taking care of their little daughter. It really upset me. I couldn't sleep all night."

"That reminds me of when Freud invited a patient to go hiking with him," says Dr. Cigar. "The patient spied his daughter Anna and then had weird dreams that Freud was adopting him."

"Yes, like overdosing on too much information." I nod vigorously. "It's hard to handle seeing Ness as human or hurt. I want to be the weak, needy one."

"He hijacked your session and freaked you out with his vulnerability. That's a low blow."

"He thought my understanding why he left would get me out of pain," I defend Ness.

"His intentions were noble. But you're paying to be the emoting patient. He turned the tables, emotional jujitsu. Cathartic for him but devastating for you, and now you can't catch up with it." Dr. Cigar's on a roll, spewing mixed metaphors like a performance poet.

He's right. I can't handle it. "So is it better if I just see you in person?"

"What if you don't need a therapist anymore?" he asks. "You're a smart, acclaimed author with a good husband. I bet you'll do fine without therapy."

Is he going to desert me too? "The years I wasn't in treatment, I was broke, chain-smoking, hooked on diet pills, hated my job. I came out far ahead with Ness."

"But you got better. Why continue now?" He looks sincerely confused.

"I know that gaining weight and being afraid they'll cancel my book doesn't seem like a dangerous emergency to you. But it's a huge crisis to me."

"You look absolutely fine. You're a real person, not a stick-thin model," Dr. Cigar says. "Lots of people eat for emotional reasons."

"My whole family does. They think I'm crazy to be in therapy. My brother Scott says, 'You're neurotic, not psychotic.' His idea of a compliment. He's a lawyer at my dad's firm, married with four kids. When I was growing up my father only talked business with the boys, ignoring me."

"It didn't get better as an adult?"

"No. He hated when I dragged our whole family's addiction history into my book. At my launch party, he said, 'Now write something important—like history, or politics.' Interesting that a guy who quit smoking at age sixty hates a chronicle of an addict's recovery."

"I liked the anecdote about how he replaced cigarettes with cigars and oatmeal raisin cookies and gained fifty pounds, becoming the walking textbook of what not to do," Dr. Cigar jumps in.

Has he memorized *Up in Smoke*? How endearing. But if I'm going to transfer my transference from Ness to him, it seems imperative to learn more of his secrets. "How much do you weigh? How tall are you?"

"Six-one, 220."

I'm surprised it's so much. No wonder he thinks I look fine; he's tipping the scales himself. He's more than fifty pounds heavier than Ness. "How many kids in your family?"

"There are four of us."

"Really? Just like me. Ness's clan too." Growing up in a quartet, I gravitate to shrinks who are also one of four, who get that particular brand of agony. "We have a lot in common."

"Like we both wear black jeans?" he asks, making fun of my desire for superficial ties. "Lucky you only see me on Fridays when I wear them in anticipation of the weekend."

"What do you do weekends? Work out? Running? Tennis?" I want to picture him behind the scenes.

"I eat too much ethnic food and explore different neighborhoods, smoking cigars."

"My new shrink's hobbies are overeating and smoking? You're the Antichrist." I laugh. "Are you the oldest kid? What do your siblings do? Is your wife a shrink too?"

"Wife's a sculptor. Sister's a mom. Brother's a dentist, like my dad. Other brother is a psychiatrist."

"You and your brother do shrink talk?"

"No," he says. "We smoke cigars together."

Too great—the Freud twins chomping on their extended penises. "Your brothers went to dental and medical school. Why not you?"

"Are you asking why I don't have a more substantial career?" He smiles.

"Yes. You should be more ambitious. Doesn't your wife want you to make more money?"

"Look, I admire your capacity to ride the Jet Sled of life. But I'll be your contrast. Your spiritual anchor who won't pick up speed to meet you."

"How old were you when you got married?"

"In my early thirties, like you."

I envision Dr. Cigar tying the knot wearing shorts, sandals, and love beads on a foreign beach. "When did you lose your virginity?" When I asked Dr. Ness, he asked why I cared. I said I wanted to know who he used to be and he coughed up "nineteen."

"Fifteen," Dr. Cigar says. "Same age as you were in *Up in Smoke*. That was a good scene, where you were in the backseat of the silver Camaro with the guy who smoked Marlboros."

Boy, he really read my book carefully. The guy gets an A in literary retention. "Losing it at fifteen means you were hip and randy?"

"Nope. I was self-conscious, depressed, and filled with inner turmoil," he admits.

Now I picture him as an angst-ridden teenage stoner with long stringy hair and a Led Zeppelin T-shirt who I want to save. "Because your brothers got all your father's love and approval like mine did?"

"Man, you're intense. Have you ever heard of object transference?" he asks. "When physical traits impact on therapy, like a limp or a cleft lip."

"You're comparing my intensity to a physical deformity?" I ask, amused.

"Your hyper speed-of-lightning instant deluge of questions presents an unusual onslaught."

I'm known to impatiently gobble up the relevant facts to chew on and swallow to figure out what someone's deal is. Ness once said, "Everything about you is insatiable." But it's the quality that makes my "How to Quit Anything" seminars soar because I pinpoint underlying problems and solutions quickly, the way Suze Orman gets to the emotions behind a financial crisis. "You think it's about the mortgage but you secretly don't trust your husband," Orman says, and a second later the caller's crying while confessing her suspicion that her husband's screwing the neighbor.

"One reason I chose you is because you answer my personal questions, like Ness. The other shrinks did the boring blank-slate dance. Who wants to spill their guts into a void?" I ask. "It's like being naked with a lover who keeps their clothes on."

"I see why you're a good self-help guru. You're an assertive, nimble speaker," Dr. Cigar says. "You invoke richness and uncover weakness. So perceptive and quick rhetorically, you win on speed alone. Dr. Ness could match your urgency. I'm not prepared for the scrimmage."

Scrimmage is a football term? "What's with all the tangled allegories?"

"You're focusing on my issues to avoid your own."

"You don't want to treat me?"

"You want me to play the role of the good father who understands you?" He hits the ball back to my court.

"Probably. My dad will never get me. He still tells me it's not too late to go to law school. When we bought the apartment next door and combined them, I bragged that the investment value increased by seven figures. I thought he'd be proud. I told Jake, 'I had the best talk with my dad about business.' Jake said that afterward, my dad called him and said, 'You've done wonders with her.' Can you believe that?"

"He thinks if you're doing well, the only reason is because of your husband?"

"Right. Which is dumb 'cause Jake didn't want to buy the place. We fought about it for months." I shrug. "This gap in paternal attention was limiting me and Ness fixed it. He was my secret weapon. The trick is to keep getting what I want without him."

"There's a transference cure where you get fixed by sheer devotion, responding to the shrink's magical power."

"Really? I bet that was me and Ness."

"But Julia, I'm different. I don't want to be your deity."

"I don't need another god," I reassure him. "I don't care if it's a shrink, personal trainer, work mentor, tarot card reader. My motto is, you can do anything as long as it works."

"You'd pay the village idiot if he helps with your diet?" he asks.

"Probably." I want to be honest. "Am I allowed to e-mail you?"

He nods yes. After a full hour (Dr. Cigar never seems in a rush), I put on my coat and bid him good-bye. On the way out he gives me his business card, which has his electronic address. Though he doesn't write an adage on the back, the way Dr. Ness would, Dr. Cigar is one of the few people I know still on AOL, like me. When I get to the street, I switch my high-heeled boots for the sneakers stashed in my bag and then put my hand in my pocket, fingers touching Dr. Cigar's card, as if we're walking home holding hands.

Later that night, running over our session in my head, I'm afraid he's not really interested in seeing me. I e-mail him, "Thanks for trying." He responds right away, in all small letters, like e. e. cummings: "okay i'm in. glad we're wired and on the same system."

This makes me feel safer. But then I get an e-mail from Dr. Ness, asking "When's our next iChat?" Before I can answer, I get six more in a row from him. He's accidentally sent the same message over and over. Like repetition compulsion, even his technology's projecting our malfunction.

chapter seven
uncovered
December 7

Uh-oh. Though I postponed the next iChat with Ness, the echo of Dr. Cigar's assessment that I look "absolutely fine, like a real woman, not a stick figure" is perplexing my subconscious by providing permission to perpetuate my pighood. I know it's pathetic to polish off a dozen cupcakes and slurp up six caffeine-filled Diet Cokes while completing a manuscript on how to stem eating addiction. But at least—with the help of Ness's careful edits of *Food Crazy* via computer— I'm making my final book deadline before the holidays.

I just need to deal with the bills that have piled up since Jake left. While he's in L.A., I've taken over our finances. I'm sure my newfound business acumen will make my husband— and dad—proud. But when I get today's mail I find a statement from our insurance company claiming I already reached my threshold for mental-health sessions for the year with Dr. Ness. Thus, they're denying payment for all of the supposedly in-network therapists I saw over the fall. I can't believe how badly I've screwed up my shrink shopping quest.

I go over the process I played out. I researched our medical coverage on the insurance company's Web site, attained the authorized number I needed, dutifully made each of the therapists from my speed-shrinking week sign an authorization form, sent each one in, and wrote checks for their twenty-five-dollar copays. I then left polite rejection messages, explaining that I'd chosen Dr. Cigar, before I moved on. But now, carefully reading the explanation-of-benefits form, I see to my horror that Swami, Yul, Horatio, Napoleon, Byrne Jr., the Shield, and Ferret Man (whom I never even met but didn't give twenty-four-hour cancellation notice) are back—to bill me!

Like when bad boyfriends from the past pop up to claim you owe them money, it turns out it isn't over, after all. My insurance firm insists I pay the Ph.D.s out of pocket between one hundred and two hundred dollars each, their regular fees for those brief, unsatisfying sessions. I can't get back to my skinny weight, can't get over my ex-shrink and my best friend moving away, and I've failed the one task I thought I aced—nailing a replacement for Ness. Now I have to call back all my quickies to explain my mistake. What a psychodramatic nightmare. My imagination conjures seven dwarfs circling around, like seven mean father figures, all making fun of me.

I e-mail the manager of appeals in Schaumburg, Illinois, explaining this misguided billing botch. "What the hell's wrong with you corporate bozos?" I want to dash off. But I use Dr. Ness's techniques to harness my emotions by slowly crafting a response that's rational and effective. I start by thanking them for their coverage and fine medical care, mentioning I'm an Illinois native. But it feels helpless, as if no real person will receive my correspondence and I'll be stuck with the headache of renegotiating with head doctors I already rejected.

Then Dr. Cigar e-mails that my insurance has denied payment for our last four sessions, so I owe *him* $500. I chose Dr. Cigar at $25 a session. Would I have signed on for $125? I begin doubting him, questioning if he's worth the financial risk. I question why a good-looking, intelligent guy—the best of the bunch I met on my shrinking spree—has an office inferior to the others, and irrationally become disturbed that his waiting room, bathroom, and inner sanctum are spread across the eleventh floor of the building. It's as if he's fractured himself, his head, heart, and body not yet aligned. At our last session, I asked, "Why don't you have a better office? Don't you think you deserve one?" When he just shrugged, I was afraid I'd hurt his feelings.

Now that I've completed my rewrite of *Food Crazy*, I have to go back to his building to drop off a hard copy with my agent. She works in a beautiful 2,500-square-foot suite with two bathrooms inside right across the hall. To avoid bumping into Dr. Cigar or Lilly (who might notice I put on a few more pounds), I sneak in during lunch hour when I hope they'll both be out. Lilly's assistant says I can leave my pages on Lilly's desk. On the cabinet where Lilly shows off recent books she's sold, I'm pleased to see an advance copy of the paperback edition of *Up in Smoke*, which will be released in January. Hey, when do I get my soft covers? A more dire issue is that displayed on the top is my competition—a hardcover *Further Reasons Why French Women Are Never Flabby*. I thumb through it and check the info on the back. Damn, it's coming out next week—a pre-Christmas release they're undoubtedly playing up for the holidays. That means they're making a much bigger deal about it than about *Food Crazy, my* buried-in-the-summer sequel.

The author of this annoying sure-to-be megaseller is the skinny French woman Frederica Follet. She's still championing her "eat, smoke, and drink everything you want in moderation" paradigm that soared to number one the same month my addiction debut was only number nineteen on the charts. I find Frederica's axiom to be downright dangerous for me and millions of addicts, a state defined by the inability to be moderate. Since her sophomore attempt will be in stores so much sooner, it'll surely beat mine again. My cell phone rings and it's Jake.

"Hey, honey. Good, you're the only voice I want to hear now," I say.

"Me too. What's up?"

"I'm at Lilly's office," I tell him. "She's not here. I'm dropping off my finished pages."

"Congratulations. I knew you'd have no trouble making your deadline."

"But Lilly's displaying Frederica's sequel more prominently than *Up in Smoke*. Why is it coming out two seasons before my new one? She doesn't admit that French women have more smoking and drinking addictions, so she's a liar who's getting a second book that's going to be bigger than mine!"

"Oh, the French diet-book thing again?"

Okay, I've ranted about this a few times before.

"Yours is so much more soulful and important," he says.

"If women follow her suggestions, they'll turn into obese alcoholics dying of lung cancer. I hear she has a thyroid condition that keeps her from gaining weight. She's never even worked in publishing—she works for a wine company. Why did a book so biased and off base sell more copies than mine?"

"She says to smoke, drink wine, go to fancy restaurants, and order chocolate desserts every night and you'll get thin," Jake says. "You say to quit smoking, drinking, overeating, go to therapy, and deal with pain that never totally goes away. Which message do most Americans prefer?"

"Oh, yeah," I say, sitting down on Lilly's brown leather swivel chair. I look out her window's wide view, the Empire State Building in the distance. Jake was the one who'd argued against calling my book *Up in Smoke: How to Stop Your Bad Habits in Ten Hard Steps*, insisting my subtitle wouldn't entice your average self-help book buyer, who'd prefer to pay for the illusion that change will be easy.

"Listen," he says, "my agent at CAA negotiated a bigger deal for this *C.S.I.* guy ten years younger than I am, someone I recommended. He makes more than I do at a dumber show and I'm their best director." He sounds incredulous.

"That's so unfair. I'm sorry," I tell him.

"What makes my life fair is that I get to come home to you."

I'm lucky to have such a great husband. "I'm so glad they're giving you five days off. Can't wait to see you next week. I've been having a rough time without you, Sarah, or Dr. Ness around."

"Why don't you call your new shrink for a few extra sessions?" he asks.

"You think I should?" Usually Jake teases me about being overtherapied.

"Yeah, I like the sound of Cigar," Jake says. "He seems like a mensch."

Cigar also says nice things about Jake. Walking home, I

decide I'll reimburse Dr. Cigar the five hundred dollars and send checks to the rest of the therapists I speed shrunk through. After spending most of my career broke and stuck in the sale and layaway bins for everything, I can finally afford to pay full price. I need to fight my food demons, not my ex-doctors. That's one of *Up in Smoke*'s dictums: Always err on the side of generosity.

Opening my apartment door, I hear the phone ringing and run to answer. It's the lady from the insurance firm, letting me know she's read my e-mail and that I'm absolutely right! They found a record of okaying all my network sessions, understand the importance of addiction therapy, and will cover the bills—including the sessions with Dr. Cigar. I can continue seeing him three Fridays a month at the bargain-basement rate.

"I read *Up in Smoke* and loved it," she adds. "I haven't had a cigarette in four months."

"Congratulations," I say, feeling supported and exonerated. I promise to send her a signed copy pronto. What a nice way to end a difficult year. The world is fair, after all.

When the phone rings at nine P.M., I'm surprised to hear Sarah's voice. "Hey, Goods. How are you?"

"Sutty. So glad you're finally calling back." I've only left seven messages for her in the last seven days. "How are you?"

"I'm fine. Everything's fine."

"What's wrong?"

"Oh, man, Julie, I'm the worst fish out of water in cow country. I don't get Cleveland. I miss you. I miss New York." She starts to cry. "I want to get on a plane and visit. Can I stay at your place?"

"Of course, you can always stay with me. When are you thinking?"

"Tonight. I called the airline and there's a ten P.M. flight."

There's no other holiday present I'd prefer than seeing Sarah's face at my door, but this seems crazy and she sounds boozy. "Are you sitting down, sweetie? Tell me what's going on."

"Nothing. I'm losing it. Andrew's always working and I don't have any friends here. And the dogs were limping and didn't want to go out. So I thought great, leave it to me to find bipolar pets who need Prozac. But it turns out they got Lyme disease from a tick and almost died and have to stay overnight at the vet's. I feel like it's my fault. I'm so lonely. My neighbor, Jenny Lynn, this college kid, was going to the local hangout for happy hour and invited me. So just for company I went but wound up drinking and smoking and now I'm freaking out."

Oh, God, she's freaking me out. Over the years we've both had our dark, addictive, and morose moments. Yet in Illinois I would run over to her house in minutes and in Manhattan we could quickly hop a subway or cab to save each other. There's not much I can do from five hundred miles away. "You know, you can't smoke and drink while you're pregnant."

"I know." She's sobbing. "Look what I've done. I've ruined everything."

"How many drinks did you have?"

"Three glasses of cabernet. I haven't touched alcohol in six months. I don't know what came over me."

"Did you eat today?"

"I tried, but I'm still puking up food. Everyone else gets morning sickness for three months. I'm getting it my whole pregnancy."

No wonder she sounds so out of it.

"Did I hurt my baby?"

"No. No. You're okay. You're fine. My sister-in-law Melissa drank that much wine all the time during her pregnancies and her kids are perfect."

"Do you swear?"

"I swear." Actually, Melissa only had a few glasses a week—not all at once—and I have no idea what I'm talking about, but panic won't help Sarah, that's for sure. "Is Andrew at the museum?"

"Where else would he be? Why did I marry a geek?"

"I know, they work too much. It's maddening. But you need to call him."

"I did. Before I could tell him what happened, he said, 'You sound hormonal.' Can you believe what a sexist fuckhead he is? I hung up on him."

"No, I can't believe he said that," I say, thinking she sounds hormonal. Pregnant, drunk, no food in her system, alone in Ohio with sick dogs and hormones going batty—not a good combo platter.

"What if I've killed my baby?"

She's making me feel guilty since my sugar mania topped with missing her can't compete with her thinking she's Medea.

"I swear to God you haven't. Courtney Love shot up while pregnant and her kid is healthier than she is. Look, here's what you need to do." I switch into my antiaddiction self-help guru mode. "First, call Dr. Zane and make a phone appointment right away."

"After I get off with you. You're probably busy working," she says. "I should let you go."

"Don't be crazy. I have nothing else to do in the world

except shove candy in my mouth like a piglet. My tummy's bigger than yours but instead of a human fetus, it's a Hershey baby."

This makes her laugh, which makes me feel less disturbed.

"Call Zane from your landline and tell her you need an emergency phone session. Okay? I'll stay on the phone. Remember when I lost it and called her too?"

"Yeah, you lost it and called her too," she says, and I wait until I hear Sarah leave the message.

"What time is Andrew supposed to get home?"

"He said midnight. But if I call him now I'm going to tell him I hate his guts."

I think of a technique Dr. Ness once suggested when Jake and I were fighting and I was about to get on a plane home to my parents.

"Does Andrew check his e-mail at work?"

"Constantly," she says. "That's more important than me and his baby."

"Okay. Turn on your computer and send him this sentence: 'I need you to come home immediately and hold me for an hour without talking.'"

"But he's an idiot I don't want to touch."

"I know. Men can be jerks, but I need you to trust me," I tell her.

"I can't come see you?"

"You can come see me, but first e-mail Andrew."

When I asked Dr. Ness why sending this sentence through cyberspace helped Jake and me make up so quickly, he explained that it's often easier to e-mail than to speak, that men understand directives better than emotions, that being held for an hour is a primal way to soothe anxiety, and that if a couple is hugging but not talking, they're connecting but can't argue.

"Okay," she agrees. "I'm a little dizzy. How do you spell 'immediately'?"

I spell it for her, then wait a few minutes. When she's done, I ask, "Do you have any more wine or cigarettes in the house?"

"No wine. I took the rest of Jenny's Marlboros before I left."

"Let's get rid of them right now. I'm going to stay on the line and listen while you flush them down the toilet."

"Can I break them first?" She laughs, then hiccups.

"Yeah. Smash them to smithereens."

"Okay. I'm smashing and throwing them down the toilet."

"Good." Waiting to hear the flush, I remember the night I heard a rat rattling around my kitchenette at four A.M. and I was too petrified to get out of bed. Sarah was in Chicago at the time, but she stayed on the phone with me for five hours, until the exterminator came at nine o'clock.

"Do you have Paul Newman in your house?" I ask. That's our college code for microwave popcorn, our crunchy way to drown our sorrows. We'd usually get stoned first, but luckily we're past that stage.

"The organic no-trans-fat kind," she says.

"Does popcorn stay down?" I recall reading that starch was good for morning sickness.

"I never know."

"Okay, well put the bag in the micro and get a Diet Coke." I'm hoping a little food and caffeine will sober her up before Andrew gets home. "Now turn on Natalie Merchant's *Tigerlily*."

I wait until I can hear the popcorn popping and the song "Jealousy," her favorite.

"Okay. I have to pee. I pee fifty times a day," she says, sounding sad but more serene. "I'm going to go."

"I'll call you back in half an hour. If you're not feeling better, I'm getting on a plane to see you."

"Have I made a big mistake?" she asks.

I'm not sure if she means the wine and cigarettes, her marriage and pregnancy, leaving New York, or (how narcissistic I am) leaving me.

"No, not at all. Changing so much at our age is really hard," I say. "But let's lose this Jenny Lynn. Don't hang out with her anymore."

"What the hell's wrong with me, Julie? It takes me till thirty-seven years old to marry a good guy and I'm already sabotaging it."

"You're allowed to have a bad day. You're pregnant in Podunk with sick dogs and a workaholic. You moved there for him, so he needs to be home more."

"I'm allowed to have a bad day," she repeats, loudly chomping.

"Love you madly, Sutty," I say.

"Love you madly, Goods," she says. "Want some popcorn?"

When I call back in twenty minutes to check up on her, Andrew picks up the phone.

"It's Julia. I'm glad you're there. Is she okay?" I ask.

"She's fine. She'll catch you later," he says in a curt tone, then abruptly hangs up.

I wait by the phone, but she doesn't call back. How rude. But maybe she's a mess and he's just got his hands full.

Haunted by our talk, I can't sleep the rest of night. I order in microwave popcorn from the deli and eat three bagfuls myself. My brother Alan says I'd make a decent doctor because I'm good in emergencies. I only sweat the small, neurotic stuff. I use one of *Food Crazy*'s techniques and try journaling, marking down changes I'm determined to make for New Year's resolutions. With bullets in red pen, I swear to myself that I'll quit depending on sugar, my best friend, and my ex–head doctor cold turkey.

part
two

chapter eight
the secret cure-all
January 7

While Jake is crushed to learn they gave him time off because the low-rated *Doctors on Mars* is canceled, I'm hoping that having my husband back in my bed every night will nix my jonesing for junk food. He's busy unpacking Monday morning, so I run out to xerox flyers for my next seminars, which I'm adding more of to plug the paperback *Up in Smoke*. I'm in my elastic-waist sweatpants (the only garment still comfortable), along with sneakers and my large Gap parka. My neighbor Karen is pushing her six-month-old twin daughters in a high-tech stroller in the lobby. Noticing how slim she is in her jeans and tailored peacoat, I say, "Hey, you look terrific. What's your secret?"

"I've been doing Strollersize classes six days a week." She

lifts her shirt to show me her tight ab muscles. "Never felt better."

Great, so a woman five years older who gave birth to two babies half a year ago is in better shape than I am.

"Sounds like fun," I say.

"You should join too! When are you due?" she asks.

Maybe she assumes I'm pregnant because I'm dressed in sloppy, loose clothing? Yet this is the third time it's happened. Have I put on that much weight? I feel dejected, ugly, and obese.

"Congratulations on the cover story," she adds.

"What cover story?" I ask.

"*New York* magazine."

I've done tons of interviews over the past year and last spoke to the *New York* reporter two months ago. But my publicist, Bonnie, thought the article on me had been killed. I didn't know they were considering making me their cover girl. I wonder what turned it around. "It's in this week's issue?" I ask.

"My subscription just came in the mail." She points to the stack of mail but doesn't hold it out to me. "Do you want my copy?"

No, I want to wait two whole days to see huge press on myself, I don't respond. Does having babies dull your brain? "That would be fantastic," I say, as she reaches under the mammoth stroller to grab the issue and hand it to me. "I'll give it right back to you."

"Keep it," she says. "I never have time to read anymore."

As she strolls her kids out, I stare at the magazine, shocked to see that I am not alone on the cover. The reporter interviewed me extensively for my own profile, but they've lumped me with a crowd of four faces with the bold headline THE NEW GIRL GURUS. I've been demoted from soloist to part of a quartet, including Ronit, a protégé of mine, using the name I gave her—the Israeli House Whisperer—along with my nemesis, Nurse Nancy the British Cure-all Bimbo, and Frederica, the *French Women Are Never Flabby* lush. Worse—they've included an inset of a sucky solo recent candid picture of me that shows my double chin. Drats! When was this photo taken?

Inside, the description reads, "Move over Deepak and Docs Phil, Oz and Gray. This junior league has breasts, brains and hot self-help books selling better than yours." Not bad. I turn to the article, happy that it mentions the success of *Up in Smoke*. But then I read: "Right before the debut of her new food addiction book, a fellow author revealed that Goodman and her happening TV director husband have a bun in the oven." Very bad. Not only the pun but the implication that I'm carrying so much extra belly blubber, I must be with child. What author friend would lie like this?

Dr. Ness insists that addicts with impulse disorders should not impulsively respond when upset, and that I should try to postpone all negative reactions. So I take a breath, tell myself that no press is bad press, throw the magazine in my purse, and run to Kinko's to xerox a thousand copies of the seminar flyer. Waiting in line, I check my messages, pleased to hear Sarah's voice saying she's okay, and she hasn't touched a cigarette or drink or seen that college dolt who took her to happy hour since our phone call. And she and Andrew are doing much better. Phew!

A blond girl ahead of me in line keeps turning around and staring.

"You're Julia Goodman, aren't you?" she asks. When I nod, she says, "I loved *Up in Smoke*! I quit smoking and drinking because of your book. I believed my pain, honored my own needs first. It worked!"

"That's great," I say, lamenting that I've gone out of my apartment looking like such a schlub. Still, it's gratifying to know that I've been able to help this cute young person I've never even met, along with my best friend in the world. Why am I always so brilliant with other people's lives?

"You were right—quitting addictions really enhanced my work," the blond goes on. "I landed the lead in a new play at a downtown theater. I'm Tina, by the way."

"Nice to meet you, Tina." I shake her hand. "Cool about the role."

"Come check it out." She hands me a promotional post-card and says, "Congrats on *New York* magazine—and your pregnancy."

"I'm not having a baby." I cross my arms over my chest.

"Oh, sorry. I just read about it in the article. You know, just between us girls, it's not your best pic. They should use the author photo from your book—much better. Talk to your publicist about it," she throws out before the person behind the counter calls out "Next," and she skips away, leaving me mortified.

Since I'm so colloquial and honest in my book and seminars, strangers often speak to me as if they know me. Ms. Actress is wearing a miniskirt, heels, and crisscross hose, just to go to the copy shop in freezing weather. I'm not into acting or modeling and unlike her don't have to depend on my figure for my livelihood. Luckily, the shape of my body is less important than my body of work, I tell myself. Isn't it?

Now I'm paranoid that I'm making a mistake calling too much attention to my diet and shape in the upcoming *Food Crazy*. I don't need any more negative scrutiny. I call my publicist, Bonnie.

"How much do you love me?" she asks.

"You knew about this?"

"Knew about it? I've been hocking the editor in chief to include you for a month!"

"Why didn't you tell me?"

"Because I didn't want you to get your hopes up. I was still haggling with them last week. Do you have any idea how hard it is for a self-help author who isn't Suze Orman to land the cover for a paperback? You are so lucky she turned them down."

Probably because she wanted her own cover. "I didn't know I was going to be one of a team." I want to be singled out but I'm stuck being one of four—the story of my life.

"Well, you were only included because of me! I lied and told them the *Times* Style section was running something on you next week. So they wanted to scoop them."

"But I hate Nancy and Frederica."

"Yeah, so how would you feel if they were on the cover and you weren't?"

Excellent point. "But don't you think my picture sucks?"

"You've looked better." She pauses. "Is there any news you want to share?"

"I'm not pregnant!"

"Really?"

"It's just an unflattering angle," I insist.

"'Cause we're going to be pitching the four of you to *The View*."

"The four of us? But I'm a solo attraction. I'm not a team player."

"Now you are. Everybody loves a girl group. So stop acting like Diana Ross."

If I don't drop weight fast, I fear I'll wind up with the role of Effie.

"These are now your best girlfriends in the world. Did you read Ronit's book?"

"I practically wrote Ronit's book. My agent sent me Frederica's. But not *The Cure-all.*"

"Go get it. This minute," she says. "Got it?"

"I got it." My vanity over my looks is overlapping with my vanity over my work. Thankfully, work is winning. If the choice is being on *The View* fat or no *View* at all I'll waddle to the freaking studio. "Listen, Bonnie, thank you for fighting for me."

After I get my flyers copied on different-color paper, I rush to Barnes & Noble to purchase *The Cure-all,* which I've bemoaned as monopolizing my market. So nobody will recognize me from *New York*'s cover—which I see on sale at the register—I put my black pashmina scarf over my head a bit, pretending I'm Muslim.

"How are you today?" chirps the girl at the register.

"Fine." I take out my money to get this over with quickly, worried that the magazine will be splattered all over newsstands everywhere I go this week. How does one lose thirty-five pounds in twenty-four hours? Too bad *Up in Smoke* trashes lipo, along with all other cosmetic surgery. My exact chapter heading is: "Forget Liposuction, Try Happiness." What a self-righteous prig I am—not to mention poor predictor of the future. Hey, why is my hardcover $21.95 when Nurse Nancy's is $24.95?

"Do you have one of our discount cards?" asks the saleswoman, smiling.

"No, I'm in a hurry. Just put it in a bag." I pray I won't bump into anybody else who knows me today, slinking out with the package under my arm.

It's no wonder *The Cure-all* bugs me, since my mother keeps

mentioning that she and Sarah's mother, Marsha, are fasci-
nated by this megahit claiming you can think yourself slender. They haven't, and I don't believe for a minute that *The
Cure-all* will help me downsize myself without going back on
the plan I'm promoting in *Food Crazy*: strict low-carb diet, exercise, and intense psychological self-scrutiny that demands
daily emotional honesty. I'm already incensed that Nurse
Nancy's sales numbers are four million, much fatter than
those for *Up in Smoke*—though I've tried to entice the same
wide audience using my similarly empowering but much
more realistic mantra. I'm itching to figure out why the hell
the country is falling for a thick hardcover by a skinny British
nurse with the basic premise that "wishing will make it so,"
rather than my realistic book by an American author promoting candor, hard work, and therapy.

I start reading the book on the street. Nurse Nancy says
to stop focusing on "fat thoughts" because if you obsess over
dieting, negative energy will attract back the continual need
to diet. *You have the power to attain your goals if only you want them
badly enough.* I do! Before I'm even home she's hooked me into
hoping that with the right attitude, I'll lose weight without
exercising, eating less, or dealing with my denial. Damn—
how does she do that? I turn to the middle chapter, where
Nurse Nancy chronicles how she's gone from "a hefty 150" to
her current weight of 116. Shit, I'm heftier than her at her
worst. How tall is she? I'm sure I'm taller. And bigger boned.

Back at my place, I follow her instructions to find pictures of myself at my ideal size and put them up everywhere.
I pull out the skinny publicity stills taken for *Up in Smoke*.
Bonnie and my editor, Priscilla, nixed the sultry photograph
of me in a tight black dress and high heels and told me to
pose outside wearing a bright-colored top and blue jeans

instead. They insisted I should smile widely to look more "girl next door"—healthy and trustworthy, like a best friend you'd confide in. "Ask yourself the *Gilligan's Island* question: Would women buy a book from Ginger or Mary Ann?" Bonnie asked, while Priscilla showed me bestseller Rachel Day's adorable poses with her puppy, and more recently Nurse Nancy in her white nurse's uniform (which I think looks more *Penthouse* than hospital).

Still, I find myself taping the minier-Mary-Ann-like me to my refrigerator, trying to broadcast "thin thoughts," thus "placing an order with the catalogue of the world" to regain my former lithe form.

"Hey, you're back," Jake says, coming into the kitchen, putting his arm around me, and looking at the pic I've taped to the fridge. "Pretty picture of you. I had this one up at my office in L.A. Everybody walked by and asked, 'Who's the babe?'"

"Thanks." I kiss him, but loathe the fact that he's still drooling over my former self. He wants to have a fun domestic day together, but I'm in a mood and on a solitary mission. I write down the number 128 on a Post-it note and, instead of weighing myself, place it over the readout of my new digital scale in the bathroom, pretending it can make me lose all my extra pounds by Monday.

"What are you doing?" Jake inquires, coming into the bathroom to take clothes from my hamper to do laundry—the one household chore he can handle to commemorate being back home.

"It's this new strategy that says writing down your ideal weight and putting it over the scale will help you get back to your thin weight," I admit, waiting for him to make fun of me.

"You're not going to try to make me do it, I hope" is his response.

He's less a skeptic than a narcissist; he only worries about how everything in the universe affects him personally. Whenever I mention that the husband of someone I know is having an affair, gets addicted to gambling, asks for a divorce, or is diagnosed with a serious illness, Jake listens quietly, then comments, "This makes me look pretty good, doesn't it?

"I spend months in L.A. but you're the one becoming a New Age loony tune?" he asks.

He picks up the black towel hanging over my shower door, puts it into the laundry bag, then heads to his bathroom to collect his own dirty clothing.

He's been teasing me since he came home Thursday night to find me with Ronit the Israeli feng shui guru, whose article on being the House Whisperer I recommended to *Femme*. To pay me back for helping her turn her article into a hot self-help design concept, she came over to our apartment to reveal what it was saying telepathically.

"The empty vases on the mantle show that your career energy is drained and vacant," she declared, so I followed her advice to fill them with foreign coins. The next day my agent sold *Up in Smoke* to an Israeli publisher, and Jake was called in for an interview to direct a *Law & Order* spin-off shooting at Chelsea Piers, less than a mile away.

Since Ronit also found our "romantic flow" lacking, I put a picture of us in a big red heart frame in the bedroom and that same morning my mate initiated a rare passionate morning session. (We're usually night lovers.) When I point to the cute picture postcoitus, he cracks up and asks, "Now you're using voodoo to control me sexually?"

"Do we have any more Cling Frees?" he's now yelling from the hallway.

"Under the sink." For the hundredth time I show him where we keep our cleaning supplies.

"You're not still obsessing about that other self-help author selling more copies than you?"

I hand him *New York* magazine.

"Hey, you're on the cover! Wow! That's fantastic!"

"Now I'm obsessing over three other authors. Bad picture of me and the story sucks."

"Sorry," he says. "You don't want me to read it?"

"No," I say, not wanting him to see that I'm so fat someone's saying I'm pregnant.

"I think you look good," he adds.

This is the one benefit of my old rule never to sleep with men who have smaller thighs than I do. Jake, who is six foot four and a hefty 240-pound big eater himself, only sees my body in terms of how often it's offered to him.

Staring down at our high-tech Weight Winners precision electronic scale, the digital display listing both pounds and ounces, I debate whether to remove the Post-it note and weigh myself for real. Nurse Nancy recommends getting clear on your ideal weight. I look most beautiful at 128, which I'm determined to get back down to.

Jake walks in the bathroom, sees me, and says, "It's cute you're so preoccupied with your weight. It's so fifteen-year-old girl of you."

As a hot fifteen-year-old teenager, I was 128. Who knew that chain-smoking, drinking, popping diet pills, and chewing gum constantly make such fabulous appetite suppressants? I'm feeling determined to be that svelte again—without the addictions or Dr. Ness.

After loading the laundry into the washer, Jake goes to his den to watch some DVDs the producers sent of the *Law & Order* spin-off. I step on the scale. When I see the number is 160, I scream. I'm ten pounds heavier than I guessed. When did I gain even more weight?

He rushes into the bathroom. "What's wrong? Are you okay? What happened?"

"I have to lose THIRTY-TWO POUNDS before my pub date! That's what happened!" I slide to the floor, devastated. It's worse than I expected.

He looks at me quietly, trying to assess just how insane I am while also trying to mask his irritation that this is what has dragged him away from a show about an OCD serial killer. "You're still beautiful."

"Fuck off!" I scream. "Don't lie to me! I'm a disgusting pig!"

"Okay, fine, you're a disgusting pig. Is that better?"

"Yes," I say as he helps me up from the tile.

"I have to run to my office to pick up some stuff," he says. "Want to go out to dinner later? I wouldn't mind trying that new Indian restaurant in the East Village."

"No! I don't want to go out to an Indian restaurant—where breads and sauces are a million calories. How selfish are you? I just said I gained thirty-two pounds. Are you even listening to me? Why is the only social activity you ever suggest going out to eat?" I scream, realizing I've broken my rule about never criticizing my husband and I don't even care.

He looks enraged and yells, "Fine! I'll eat alone. Don't wait up." He grabs his coat and briefcase. "You can finish the fucking laundry yourself." He marches out and slams the door.

I take out a box of twenty-four low-cal frozen chocolate Popsicles from the freezer. Unable to summon happy, thin, perfect thoughts, I finish off the entire box, which makes me feel ill. Nurse Nancy is offering no insight whatsoever in solving the enigma of my never-ending emptiness. Aside from the temporary loss—and resurfacing and reloss—of a few core pillars, I have to take my own advice and dig deeper to get to the bottom of what could possibly be eating me.

chapter nine

speed stepping

January 10

Instead of getting better, I'm becoming more needy by the minute, and both Dr. Cigar (in person) and Dr. Ness (by e-mail) suggest I try free daily Overeating Anonymous meetings. I Google, finding local gatherings for every flavor of food fanaticism. There's a klatch for compulsive eaters/alcoholics, a band for bulimic/anorexics, a group for gay and transgender addicts, a twelve-step assortment for agnostics, a sect for victims of incest/sexual abuse, and a "big winners qualification" for members who've lost a hundred pounds. I don't know which cluster of fellow feeding fanatics I'll click with. Still semi in denial about my weight gain, I pretend I'm researching *Food Crazy* (though it's already handed in). I decide to hurl myself headfirst into this self-help subculture.

I'll dine on eight different OA meetings in eight days, speed stepping.

Usually I toil at my laptop every day till sundown. But on Saturday at noon I try my first OA meeting at a downtown hospital. Unlike my seminars, where my goal is to look successful and slender, here I hope to blend in and not be recognized. Wearing baggy jeans, a loose sweater, flat boots, sunglasses, no makeup, and my hair in a ponytail is liberating. I aim for anonymity, lest I be taken for a skeptic, spy, or faker.

At meeting number one, "for females only," a dozen older, very heavy women slowly gather around a boardroom table in a conference room. I appear to be the youngest, thinnest, least depressed one here. Five foot seven and 160 is apparently on the slender side for such serious intervention. While waiting to start, I scan a pamphlet about how OA is an offshoot of AA, founded in 1960, that lists the 12 Steps, replacing "alcoholic" with "compulsive overeater." I take the "Are You a Compulsive Overeater" test: Do you eat when you're not hungry? Do you give too much time and thought to food? Do you eat normally in company but find yourself overeating when you're alone? I answer yes to these and the rest of the thirteen questions. I do belong here.

A nutritionist or doctor should recommend an eating plan with three daily meals and two snacks, the pamphlet says. That's more than I ate on Ness's diet. I stayed 128 pounds for two years on 1,200 calories in two early meals, no snacks. Maybe that's just not enough food? As a reform Jew who's into fix-yourself-fast behavioral psychotherapy, I'm intrigued with OA's offer of "spiritual mentors." With Ness out west, and Dr. Cigar admitting that his main outlets are shrimp fried rice and stogies, I could use some spiritual mentoring.

As we're called to order, everyone holds hands, recites

the AA Serenity Prayer, and takes turns reading aloud from an OA book. I read as fast as I talk, so during my turn someone yells out, "Slow the hell down." Next a "spiritual timer" clocks three minutes for each "share."

"Hi, I'm Dana, an overeater who uses food to sedate, fulfill, soothe, and excite."

"I'm Mary and I'm a diabetic yo-yo dieter."

"I'm Debbie and I have major sugar issues."

Hey, so do I.

A college-age girl comes late (stealing the youngest crown) and says, "I'm Natasha, I don't know how to define myself." When she says she's hypoglycemic, the matronly members nod with a nurturing aura.

A Jewish grandmother doesn't like to hear about higher powers. I'm also a Yid, I feel like telling her. But there's no "cross talk, questions or feedback allowed," so I nod. She says she's the biggest overeater on the planet, the way I used to brag I was the worst nicotine fiend. When she mentions her son has died, I want to show her the Yehuda Amichai poem where Mr. Barringer loses his oldest child: "He has grown very thin, has lost / the weight of his son." I wonder if she's gained the weight of her baby, wanting to give birth to him again.

A gray-haired secretary used to be 380 pounds, feels she has no right to exist, and can't keep toxic people out of her personal space. A redhead with a hat, off sugar, wheat, and flour, is upset that her sponsor is not off the same stuff and is fatter than she is. A fast-talking lawyer "grabby" with food worries there's never enough for her. At the opera she found brown gloves on an empty seat. "But I wouldn't steal brown gloves—only black." I wouldn't take brown either.

I overidentify with every story, each member of the chorus of sadness illustrating a familiar mood. I mentally diagnose the storytellers, matching them with solutions from the up-coming *Food Crazy*: Find what really feeds you; try one-on-one therapy with a great shrink, a career counselor, a healthier love relationship, a better haircut and dye. The hypoglycemic can send a piece about her medical restrictions to my *Femme* editor friend. The no-self-esteemer would benefit from my "Dispute Yourself" exercise. The Jewish grandma should fill out my "Why Instant Gratification Takes Too Long" question-naire.

When attendees at my seminars confide pain, I give guid-ance. I make them journal, focus on past problems they've conquered to recall their strengths. I offer job ideas and re-ferrals for therapists, matchmakers, coaches, classes, and personal trainers. Here I have to shut up and listen to the suffering. It's agonizing. I don't tell anyone who I am; nobody recognizes me. I'm not in charge. I can't play the wise, best-selling guru who gets special treatment. I don't look pretty or sound smart. Without my usual identity I feel blank and invisible.

The leader asks if I'll share. Self-conscious, I use Sarah's moniker for me and say, "My nickname is Goods, I'm an over-eater," choosing not to go further. I wish Sarah were here. If she were, would I not be?

Next is a call for donations. A homeless-looking lady shuf-fles around with a cart. When the attendees hand her money, she puts it in a plastic bag and adds it to her cart's pile. Fasci-nating! "She's stealing the money," I whisper to the woman next to me, but she informs me, "That's our treasurer." I hand Cart Lady three dollars in guilt money, feeling like a snitch.

Unnerved by the confessions, I have steamed chicken and vegetables for lunch. But then Jake shows up with good news—he got the *Law & Order* spin-off job—along with chicken cacciatore for two. He wants to break bread to celebrate. Not wanting to disappoint, I dig in. Is OA's "preferring to eat alone" taboo worse than their rule about not eating when you're not hungry? I guess switching a cupcake compulsion for being overpoultried is progress.

For the second beginners group, on Sunday I hop a cab to a Murray Hill complex, rationalizing that an addiction guru can claim transportation expenses for twelve-step meetings. In a stuffy room there are ten gals and two guys, all middle-aged, average weight, dressed schleppy like me. The leader, who has braids and looks like a plump Pippi Longstocking, "qualifies" about her four-year sugar abstinence. Another sucrose maniac! Maybe I'm just a cliché.

"Do you ever go to the special sugar-addicts-only meeting?" I ask.

"There's no questions allowed," Pippi cuts me off.

"Oh, I'm sorry." In my seminars I answer all inquiries and no question is ever unwelcome.

"And there's no cross talk either," she snarls.

I take off, tossing a quarter in the donation cup on my way out.

Walking downtown, I buy a sixteen-ounce bag of nuts and raisins at a bodega. At home Jake wants to fool around, but I'm sick from too much health mix. That night I dream I'm doing therapy with Dr. Ness while we're naked in bed. I have chapters of my book to show him, but he's not interested. I find Jake in his TV trailer and we have sex but I don't climax. Waking up, I guess it's about feeling insatiable, unfilled, and still emotionally naked with Ness.

At my third meeting, for anorexics and bulimics, in Chelsea on Monday at 6 P.M., thirty cute skinny girls and four buff guys sit in a circle. When the leader asks for "burning desires," they all fight to speak, mentioning acting and dancing credits, as if auditioning for *America's Next Top Model*. They share vignettes of hating themselves, feeling belittled by families, being judged by their looks, and bingeing, starving, or purging to squelch hurt. I put five dollars in the box going around, grateful I'm older, boring, and too secure with my insecurities to starve or stick my finger down my throat.

At my fourth meeting, for victims of sexual abuse, ten members tell of being molested by doctors, parents, cousins. One guy abused by his father says food is his only shield and weapon. An obese girl who was raped by her foster brother shows pictures of herself at every weight, from 120 to 350. I slip four worn singles in the envelope that's passed around, feeling like I'm unscathed and a lightweight in every way. Then the woman with sponsor issues from the other meeting again shares her fat-phobic codependency saga, which I sense she shows up every day at different meetings to repeat. So get a thin sponsor! I want to yell, annoyed she's perpetuating her own problem. Until I picture the 220-pound Dr. Cigar, overeating and puffing away, and realize I'm caught in the same conundrum.

That night I eat only vanilla yogurt for dinner and have sex with my husband, not hungry for food, as if the smorgasbord of sorrow I can't heal is killing my appetite.

On Thursday I get an e-mail from Haley, a charming client from my last seminar, asking me to have coffee. When I mention I'm going to OA, she wants to come since, while getting sober in AA, she's had eating issues. Haley's a five-foot-seven, twenty-three-year-old, slim, red-headed, doe-eyed Southern yoga teacher. Did I miss signs of anorexia or bulimia? My new book says, "Bringing a buddy with you makes everything easier," so I invite her to my fifth conclave.

I meet Haley, who calls herself "a recovering Baptist from Kansas," at the agnostic overeaters meeting at 8:45 P.M., at a Union Square outpatient addiction center. Only problem—there're multiple meetings on the same floor. We follow ten good-looking people into a room, but they turn out to be sex and love addicts. Switching to another space across the hall, I'm surprised it's all thin straight men. But we're in Debtors Anonymous. After sidestepping Crystal Meth Dependents, we find five big bespectacled elders in a dark hovel with pea green walls.

"Are you the agnostic/atheist/humanist sect?" I ask, reading from the listing.

"Yes, we're the heretics," says a white guy with glasses. "I'm Stan."

"Are you two beginners?" asks a heavier black man who introduces himself as Henry.

"I'm an alcoholic but it's crossing over," Haley answers.

They shake our hands gregariously, happy for new blood. Unlike the other groups, the agnostics have no regular leaders, no religion references, and few regulations, and they chat casually. Their motto reads: "No matter who you are, where you come from, what you've done, or who you've slept with, loved, or hated, we extend acceptance."

"Isn't that beautiful?" Henry asks.

"The other groups omit who you've slept with," adds Annabel, a bespectacled Brit.

Henry used to weigh 600 pounds, having since lost 300, and has kept his food rules for seventeen years. At his first meeting, he explains, a huge woman shared her rule to never eat more than one whole chicken at a time. He adopted that limit too. "I used to stash candy bars under the bed so nobody would see me, hiding out in chocolate. So I banned hiding, but I don't ban any specific foods. My personality is that if it's banned, I binge."

"Me too," adds a bedraggled, pale woman named Irene. "My mom committed suicide when I was two. Doctors diagnosed bipolar panic disorder, but I call it self-hatred. Feeling abandoned, I used junk food to soothe and mother me."

"Look, it's a program of clichés," says Stan. "But a cliché starts because it's so common. Nobody can quit food. You have to confront your illness three times a day. Go to multiple meetings. Take what helps and leave the rest."

I want Stan for my sponsor. How does one propose the idea? Is it like asking someone to be your date or your mentor? Or begging a stranger to be available 24/7 to reparent you?

"You gals got any questions for us?" Annabel asks.

"What are the main elements of the program?" Haley says in her diligent student voice.

"Make a food plan and decide what to abstain from," Annabel answers. "Then there's meetings, a sponsor, telephone calls, the twelve-step literature, journaling, service, and anonymity."

"Never mention OA on an answering machine since you don't know if someone's partner or family knows. Except if it's a safe phone," Stan adds. I like the clandestine aura, as if we're in the CIA.

"You want to share?" Annabel asks.

"Some days all I used to eat was red gummi bears," Haley confesses. "I'd buy a bag at the grocery and throw out the other colors. Then I found a place online that sells just the wild cherry by the pound. When my fiancé accidentally opened a box filled with five hundred dollars' worth, I lied and told him it was a Christmas present for my nieces."

Buoyed by Haley's offbeat habit, I reveal, "I'm into cupcakes. Not the cake part, mostly the icing," as if I'm sharing an S & M fetish. "Is it my imagination or does hardly anybody in the other meetings mention which foods they like?"

"Major rule in the regular circuit," says Henry, nodding. "Describing a specific food could feed someone's fantasy."

I carefully place a crisp ten-dollar bill in the hat. Seems I jibe best with the godless eccentrics. But then Stan says, "A reminder that next week we switch to five forty-five P.M." Damn, I've committed to seminars from five to eight on Thursdays. I'm too much a newbie to vote on their schedule, let alone stage a mutiny. After we leave I realize I didn't get Stan's last name or number. Oh, no. I lost the only person post-Ness who'd be a good food sponsor before I can ask him to save me.

As Haley and I walk downtown, she mentions a midnight Friday AA meeting in SoHo. "How come the drunks get to hang out late but the overeaters hang it up before nine? I want a late meeting too," I say. Since they're all based on the Twelve Steps, I consider her late AA group my sixth session. Dr. Ness says that like me, most addicts are substance shufflers anyway.

At midnight on West Houston, forty people gather on folding chairs in a ramshackle theater. More men than at the other meetings, a mix of poor-looking whites, blacks, and Latinos. So there are more male drinkers and more female overeaters. Do alcoholics drink instead of eat? A few aren't sober. One's asleep. A guy rushes in, plugs in his cell phone in the corner, then leaves.

"He just needs to recharge," Haley explains.

"Hi, I'm Arnold, a drunk and a crackhead," one shares.

Another says, "I'm Terry and I have seventeen fucking years sober."

"Man, this shit works," someone responds.

The night owls are rowdy. They guzzle coffee and sodas. I'm thirsty but caffeine this late will keep me up. Overcaffeination and sleep deprivation—like after Sarah's shower—lead to disaster. At the sight of plates of free donuts and bagels, I throw two bucks into their shoebox and bail.

Several guys stand outside, puffing cigarettes. Between the smoking, bagels, donuts, and sugared and caffeinated sodas, it's my worst addiction nightmare. Haley's flirting, pleased by the male attention she's getting. Doesn't she have a fiancé? "I'm sending you to the sex and love group next," I joke, giving her Dr. Cigar's number as I put her in a cab home. I stop at a deli and buy nuts and raisins, overdoing health mixes. But at least it's not cupcakes.

On Saturday at 4 P.M., group number seven is Sugar Addicts Anonymous, SAA. According to their flyer, they've seceded from the OA union to form their own fellowship. To get there I must trek through a street fair filled with French fries and marshmallows dipped in chocolate. I go with Tiffany, my pretty black twenty-seven-year-old former *Femme* colleague, who doesn't look heavy. She's now an MTV vlogger who's been plugging my *New York* cover story on her vlog. The trick to not feeling identityless: Go to meetings with someone who knows and loves me.

"I'm Jane, a sweet junkie in a sour mood," a woman shares.

"Hi, I'm Lisa and I haven't had honey-roasted peanuts in a week."

"I'm Katrina and malted milk balls are my downfall."

"Last year, I took one bite of my husband's chocolate chip cookie and it led to me gaining seventy pounds," says the heaviest woman there.

The sugar fiends look like me: middle-aged, married white women. Alas, it descends into dull talk of higher powers, three meals a day, how to stop being caretakers and doormats. At the mention of menstrual cycles, I stick one new dollar in the envelope, nudge Tiffany, and we flee.

For my last meeting, at 6 P.M., I'm hoping the lesbian, gay, and transgender overeaters are spicier. The group meets in what resembles a kids' classroom, except for naked body art on the walls. Twenty females, ten men, no obvious trannies. Four are obese, two are too thin, most look my size and Tiffany's. Someone asks to open a window, which leads to motions, seconded motions, and votes. Clearly too many liberals in one room. I wave to the woman with fat-sponsor issues, as if we're old pals. Is she gay? Or just a meeting whore, like me?

I dig the kooky, self-deprecating intros. There's "an anal retentive Irish Catholic compulsive over-/undereating bitch," a "pissed-off recovering anorexic fag hag," and "a queer single-father Xanax-and-laxative freak." An "Upper West Side Buddhist diva dyke" who says "food is my mother, father, lover, and best friend" admits while loudly chewing gum that she calls her sponsor at 6 A.M. before she eats to "break her food intimacy bond." Dr. Ness outlawed my gum use (since it was compulsive), so watching her chew bugs me. Can one motion to ban Dentyne? Liking how they praise each other's progress and honesty, as in amiable group ther-apy, I place a five and two singles into their straw basket.

My only discomfort is the "any gender" bathroom where I pass a man standing at the urinal. As if that isn't weird enough, after we're both finished he's waiting for me at the sink.

"I know who you are," he says as we wash our hands next to each other. "But your secret is safe with me."

Before I can respond, he's gone. I wonder if he's referring to my being a self-help guru gone fat, the deceptive author of an upcoming book on how I already conquered my sugar addiction, or a publicly married but closeted lesbian whose real partner is Tiffany.

Taking inventory of the eight meetings, I see OA isn't for me. I just hate the dynamic of groups I don't lead, which remind me too much of my family. As the oldest of four kids born too close in age, I'll forever prefer one-on-one treatment, the method I push in my books. Luckily listening to the com-plexity of eating problems out there reinforces my belief that the solutions to being "food crazy" are idiosyncratic and psychoanalytic, the opposite of the "one method fits all" mode. Though my weight stays the same, maybe witnessing the potential extremes might scare me back into being sugar free and shrinking myself in a healthier way.

At home I tell Jake that in a flurry of "change my life" New Year's activity, I'm hiring a freelance Web consultant to modernize my book publicity, and I confess I've been into OA. When he says, "How cool," I assume he's heard of it. Turns out his favorite superhero, the Green Lantern, comes from "the planet Oa," home of the DC Comics blue-skinned humanoids' intergalactic police force.

That night in bed a new player shows up in my sexual dream—Dr. Cigar. We're making out and I distinctly like the feel of his big strong body against mine. When I wake up, it seems a good sign that skinny Ness is disappearing from my unconscious reveries while I'm developing a taste for his more meaty replacement. Or am I just craving something sweet?

chapter ten

her space

January 21

"You already have a ton of new friends, you're really popular," says Lori Callahan, the Web consultant I'm hiring to increase my online presence to promote the paperback of *Up in Smoke*. "Your book cover is all over Friendster, MySpace, and Facebook."

"Thanks. Did you see that girl Amy McNally from the Midwest? Her whole Facebook page is filled with my quotes. She calls *Up in Smoke* the most essential life-altering book of all time."

"Yup. You know, it's one of my top books too. It helped me quit drinking. That's why I was so excited when I found out that Craigslist ad was from you," she says. "I'm gonna put you on LiveJournal, LinkedIn, MyWorld.com, and Bebo to promote your readings, blog, and Web page."

"I'm having trouble uploading my author photos."

"No problem. I'll do it for you later this afternoon."

Instead of lunch, for our first meeting I've asked Lori to power walk around the path in Washington Square Park with me—though it's windy and forty degrees outside. I've lost three pounds being sugar free and to keep the momentum going, I need to increase my exercise. Plus, without Sarah around, I'm lonely. Sitting at the computer ten hours a day doesn't help; I could use more human interaction. Lori's a five-foot-two, charming, witty, twenty-six-year-old sprite, with short dark hair and newfound bangs. She calls herself a "nonpracticing Catholic" from Ohio, and it turns out she grew up just a few miles from where Sarah is living, which somehow makes Sarah seem a bit closer.

"What do your parents do?" I ask.

"Mom's in advertising. My father deserted us ten years ago."

This admission pulls on my heartstrings, as well as sets off a "she needs a father" alert. "When was the last time you spoke to him?"

"Two years ago he promised to come to my wedding, but he never showed up. I think it was too hard for him. He's broke and jobless and I married a wealthy banker in this big fancy ceremony."

"I'm sorry. That must have been hard for you," I say.

"I was actually thinking of writing about it. Maybe you could help me?"

I've hired her to assist me ten hours a week, but by the end of our first hour, I'm coaching her to try a book proposal called "How to Divorce a Destructive Parent" and strongly suggesting she see a male therapist, offering up mine.

By our second walk-and-talk consultation a week later, she's already met with him twice.

"You were so right, I love Dr. Cigar!" She's adopted my nickname for him. "I've never seen a therapist before. I didn't know what to expect. I felt really at ease. It's nice to talk over things with an older guy who cares."

"I think Dr. Cigar's really astute when it comes to relationships." I don't add my worry that our shared shrink isn't so up on food addiction. Lori's petite and athletic, so I bet she won't notice this gap in his bag of brain tricks.

"I told him about my fight with Tom over his insistence we stay in New Jersey because Manhattan is too expensive. Dr. Cigar says he doesn't get to decide where we live on his own."

I don't like the sound of Tom, her globe-trotting banker husband. "I agree. If you love the city, you should get a place here," I say. "What good is marrying a banker if he can't pay for a New York apartment? You could have picked a poor poet if you wanted to end up in New Jersey."

Lori cracks up. But I wonder if I want to influence where my new Ohio-bred pal resides to make up for my lack of control over where Sarah wound up.

"Hey, I convinced Dr. Cigar to join Facebook too," Lori says. "You have to check out his page."

"Why would he be on there?" I've never heard of a shrink advertising on a social networking site. Then again, I originally found him through the Internet, on my health insurance page.

"Dr. Cigar said his nieces had been trying to get him on Facebook too."

I'm still finding it worrisome that Lori's husband wants her out of the city she loves. In *Food Crazy*, I insist that your lover's job is to help feed your dreams, not squelch them. "Maybe you can ask him if you can bring Tom to your next session with you?"

"Like you bringing Jake to Dr. Ness, who told him to marry you?" Lori says. "I loved that part of *Up in Smoke*."

I often forget how much of myself I've exposed in my book and my seminars. People often come up to me asking things like, "Did you really do cocaine with a bus driver?" It takes me a minute to recall that they know my dark secrets because I've splattered them around myself.

"I'm sure Dr. Cigar won't mind if I bring my husband." She bends down to tie the laces of her black high-top sneakers. "He already met my mother."

"What? He met your mother?" I'm more than intrigued. "How? When?"

"When my mom heard Tom was going to Europe on business for ten days, she decided to come to town and stay with me. She got in yesterday at three. I didn't want to dump her for my four o'clock appointment, so I told her to come with me and meet him."

I'm amused at Lori's therapy naïveté, as if it's normal to bring your mom with you to your shrink—and not cause for more sessions on separation issues. Strict analysts allow no variations with therapy, but Dr. Ness believes anything a patient wants to bring in is significant and illuminating. In Ness's case people bring their babies, parents, siblings, lovers, friends, dogs, bicycles, musical instruments, and presents. Maybe Dr. Cigar feels the same way.

"Celia's a very young, hip fifty," Lori says. "I gave her *Up in Smoke* and she loved it. She's had alcohol issues in the past so she could relate. Though her favorite part was about sex addiction."

It takes me a second to get that Celia's her mom. "How did it feel getting shrunk together?"

I once brought my mother to meet Dr. Gold, my first therapist, when I was Lori's age. I recall wanting to demystify the process for her, as well as introduce two important women in my life to each other.

"It was cool. My mom had never seen a therapist before either," Lori says. "She told him she was having a hard time being divorced and on her own, with me across the country. But in the middle she said, 'Listen, I don't want to take over Lori's session, so I'll go take a walk.' He could tell we're more like girlfriends than mother and daughter. When she was going on about helping me with my Web consulting business, he caught that she's a bit too into being my manager. Now he calls her my 'momager.' Before she left he gave her a novel."

"He did?" Dr. Cigar never gives me any books. I'm jealous. I've given him my book (along with a box of chocolates he'd analyzed by questioning whether it was "the placebo effect, a bribe, or a vicarious thrill"). "Which book did he give her?"

"John Updike's *Seek My Face*. Do you know it?"

I don't, but want to find out why Dr. Cigar has chosen it. "What's it about?"

"An aging painter recounting her past love life. My mom couldn't figure out why he gave it to her. She's very literal. 'I'm not an aging painter,' she told me. I told her he wasn't saying she's an aging painter. She's supposed to interpret the symbolism. She said, 'I'm not so good at symbols. You'll have to interpret for me.'" Lori shrugs.

"But overall Celia liked Dr. Cigar?" I ask as we round the arch for our second lap. Time flies when I'm gossiping about my shrink. It occurs to me I'm paying Lori not to help my career, but for doing a shrink deconstruction session, sort of like a postgame analysis, the kind of thing I used to do with Sarah daily before she moved away and stopped returning my phone messages.

"Yeah, Celia thinks Greg is really cute," Lori says. "She said, 'I bet Greg has all these beautiful artistic young girls coming here, confessing all their intimacies. What a fun job.'"

"Your mom said that? How skeptical." Interesting that Lori switches to calling him by his first name, like she's not used to parental or authority figures and makes them into friends. Without knowing anything about Dr. Cigar, her mother's already undermined him by implying he's more lecher than doctor.

"Did I tell you that last week, after our first session, I bumped into Greg outside a restaurant in Koreatown? I was with my gay best friend Eli, who said, 'Man, you have a hot shrink.'" Lori laughs. "I hadn't even really noticed his appearance until Eli and my mom pointed it out."

If I like Dr. Cigar partly because of his looks, why does it bug me if others do too? "I can't believe you bumped into Dr. Cigar in the outside world. I've only seen him in the office," I say. "Unless you count seeing him outside his building puffing a stogie, which I don't."

"Ew, gross. I hate smoking. We've got to get him off cigars," Lori says. "Can't Dr. Ness do anything?"

At home, I look up Dr. Cigar's Facebook page and send a "friend request." He accepts within minutes. His picture looks good. I'm glad that he indicates he's married, a psychologist, and an NYU alumnus on his profile. But instead of saying he's looking for networking or friendship, I see that he's chosen the option "random play." This sounds like he's trawling for cybersex partners, which makes my skin crawl. I send him a note asking him to change it to "networking" because I don't want a shrink who comes across like an on-line pedophile.

"Did you get my message about changing your Facebook setting so you don't look like you're into pedophilia?" I ask Dr. Cigar at our next session, the minute I sit down.

"Yes. I switched from random play to networking. I'm new at this. I appreciate your scolding." He looks apologetic but bemused. He's in his black jeans and a striped blue shirt.

I'm wearing dark blue jeans, boots with heels, and a black sweater with a regular brassiere instead of a push-up. As I get more comfortable with him, my heels and bras are getting smaller and I'm getting shorter and flatter. "Do you see a lot more female patients than males?"

"Yes. More women seek therapy than men," he answers.

"Do you have mostly college-age patients?"

"My youngest patient now is twelve. My oldest patient is seventy."

"Lori told me she brought her mother in. So you let patients bring in guests whenever they want? Does it help with the therapy?"

"It fleshes everything out, provides corroborating evidence."

His Facebook mistake and Lori's mother's words transform my gentlemanly post-Freudian into a Lothario preying on young coeds' vulnerabilities. Worse, I'm not feeling youthful or hot so it's like I have nubile competition for his affection—girls I recruited myself.

"Haley's bringing in her fiancé tomorrow," he adds.

"She and Lori both have issues trusting men and could use an older guy to talk to," I explain.

"I get it," he says. "You need to trust me to be a good dad to your metaphoric daughters."

Later that night, I hear Dr. Ness's voice on my machine, saying, "I'll be back in town next week. I look forward to seeing you." My heart flutters at the thought of finally catching up with him in the flesh. Despite clicking with the local, loyal Dr. Cigar, I'm still not over my ex-shrink and fear the one with the worst father hunger is still me.

chapter eleven
getting off-track
February 8

"I hate having a shrink who smokes cigars. I want to get him to quit," I complain to Dr. Ness. We're on the phone but he's in New York, so I feel closer.

"What method are you using?"

"I told him he's not getting what he wants in life and it's connected to the smoking."

"Wrong technique. Ask him to quit cigars for one week so he can feel what you feel. That way he'll be in tune with you," he says.

"Thanks. I'll try that."

"So you want an appointment on Wednesday night?"

"Yes. Can I have your last slot?" I ask, suddenly feeling nervous about seeing him for the first time in six months.

"Seven thirty?"

"Okay, but let's do our session while speed walking around the park," I propose. "Washington Square is just two blocks from your office. I've lost a few pounds and think walking is helping."

"I'm a pretty expensive personal trainer." He's obviously less than thrilled.

"A relationship has to keep evolving," I use his words against him. "For two hundred dollars, you can shrink my mind and body at the same time. Freud used to go hiking with his patients in the Alps. My only apprehension is shallow. I've gained weight and feel embarrassed about letting you see me in sweatpants and sneakers," I confess. I figure confiding this vulnerability will convince him to do it my way.

"You must conquer your insecurities," he says. "Okay. Come pick me up at my office, then we'll walk."

Not the sort for cutesy pink exercise gear, I scavenge through my closet like a cheerleader trying on different outfits for her date with the star quarterback. I settle on what's becoming my uniform of black sweats with an elastic waist. I try a black T-shirt under a black turtleneck and black parka. Like many urban women, I wear dark clothes in all one color as my slimming armor.

Wednesday night it's strange to be back at Dr. Ness's work complex. When I press the security code on his door, he opens it and says, "Hi, Julia. Come on in. I'm running late," then rushes back to his inner office. I sit down on a creaky wooden chair. When the door to his old office opens, I look up expectantly. But it's only Protégé. He nods; I nod back. He seems shorter and more harried. His expression is still sour. I recall disliking him during our one meeting. Dr. Cigar's cheaper and cuter, and his Indian art trumps Protégé's cheap daisies any day.

Finally Dr. Ness comes out and says, "Sorry. Lost control of my schedule." He's wearing a down parka with lots of side pockets, leather gloves, and a nice scarf—expensive survival attire I imagine he's bought at a store for hunters in Alaska. He locks his office, then zips up his jacket.

I zip up my Gap parka, which now seems cheap and flimsy, as we take to the streets. The minute the cold breeze blows I regret my clever idea of outside therapy. I put on my gloves and wrap my scarf around my face, glad I'm in layers. "How's it feel to be back here?"

"Fine," he answers. He's clearly peeved at something.

My first thought is that he's mad that Dr. Cigar is replacing him in my dreams. But I haven't clued him in to that subconscious switcheroo yet.

"It's weird seeing your protégé again," I say.

"He's not going to be with the institute any longer," Dr. Ness breaks the news.

"I told you not to trust someone with such bad taste in art," I gloat. But for a second I feel sorry for Protégé. Imagine being stuck in Ness's space, seeing Ness's former patients, running the institute Ness founded, and being heir to Ness's throne. He can't ever win. "You just fired him?"

"I decided it wasn't working out a month ago. I'm arranging for his replacement."

We round Washington Square, passing through the marble arch, modeled after the Arc de Triomphe in Paris. Uptown friends tout Central Park as paradise. I prefer the seedier, smaller, 9.75-acre downtown version that, in the 1800s, was a common burial ground and a place for public executions before it inspired Henry James, William Burroughs, and Joan Baez.

Thinking that Protégé had big shoes he couldn't fill, I look down at the literal fancy suede-looking clompers on Ness's feet. "Those comfortable?"

"Yes, my hiking shoes are better than sneakers. I'd be fine for twenty miles," he says. "Have you really been circling around here for an hour every day?"

I nod. "But it's too tedious alone. Instead of lunch meetings or follow-ups after my seminars, I've been suggesting walking dates. I have two regulars I really like, Lori and Haley. They're young, sharp, and move fast. I've lost a few pounds this way."

"Multitasking to be time efficient?" He sounds skeptical.

"Exactly. Kills a bunch of birds with one stone. You're the one who insisted I find ways to socialize besides bars or restaurants."

"So are you going to switch all our New York appointments to walking sessions?" he asks.

"I don't know." I'm no longer sure I should see him at all. Since I'm usually a decisive person, not knowing what to do confuses me. I know exactly what I want—for him to move back so I can resume our twice-weekly treatment, lose weight, be a skinny author on TV teaching the world the difference between physical and emotional hunger, which will make *Food Crazy* a bestseller. Then I'll be vindicated that *Up in Smoke* isn't a fluke, get richer and more famous, and find emotional balance again. But he's not moving back and the long-distance is screwing up everything.

"After the *New York* cover story, Bonnie says we have a shot at *Oprah*. I've been watching the show when it gets rerun at night," I say. "You know, during my seminars, people try to touch me the way her audience touches her."

"If your clients think you're Oprah, no problem," he said. "If *you* think you're Oprah, big delusion."

"I don't think I'm Oprah. But I identify with her and want to emulate her. I always tell my clients to hang out with people you want to be."

"Everyone imagines she's their best friend, but that's just a television image. In real life she's never been married, has no kids, and only has a few true friends she trusts," he says. "Don't be fooled by the allure of false intimacy."

This, coming from a shrink who makes his living manipulating addicts to feel like he's their biggest confidant whom they can't live without. Even when he's 2,500 miles away.

"Listen, the way we've been isn't good for me anymore," I say, feeling like Barbra Streisand in *The Way We Were*, where she bids adieu to handsome Hubbell on a New York street. I'd hoped that walk therapy would shake things up, make my cerebral and chemical connection with Dr. Ness cohere the way it used to so I'd stop being so hungry. But it isn't happening. Walking beside him, I'm just as shell-shocked and starving. His legs are longer than mine and his stride is quicker; I have to rush to keep pace. It parallels what's going on internally—I'm trying to catch up with a man who can't be caught.

"How does it feel different?" he asks.

"How doesn't it?" I like walking and talking better because I can look straight ahead, not into his eyes. "Why do you seem angry at me?"

"Your request for yet another copy of all your therapy

bills really annoyed my bookkeeper." He sounds still put upon.

That minor e-mail tiff comes back to me in a rush. My accountant said we were getting audited, so I requested a consolidated bill for last year's therapy (since I deduct his sessions). Our accountant said to overnight it. Ness sent back a curt retort, insisting it would take a week. I needed records from my agent, contractor, dentist, and gyno. Nobody else complained.

"You wanted copies of your bills for your insurance two months ago."

"Isn't that what you pay a bookkeeper for?" I ask. "You told me to take control of our finances. So when Jake was in California, I was juggling our bank accounts, mortgage, insurance companies, and the IRS. I needed to prove I didn't claim any false deductions."

I now fear what I've assumed about my relationship with Ness has been falsely deduced: That he feels the same indelible psychic connection as I feel toward him. That our intense bond will last forever. That I can trust him never to hurt me.

"Maybe the real reason you're mad is that I've rebounded with Dr. Cigar?"

"So it's going well with your new therapist?" he asks.

"Aside from his addiction problems, I'm crazy about him. He's caring and cute. For a serious career woman, I can be such a dumb girl." My gigantic feet look bigger than usual in size-ten sneakers. Have they gained weight too? I look better in my slender black boots with four-inch heels. "I shouldn't need an attractive shrink, what trite criteria." I lose my balance on a stone, bumping my arm against his. Regaining my composure, I inch a bit farther to the other side of the trail.

"Physical appearances mean more to you since you quit smoking," he reminds me. "You're much more sensitive and discerning since you've given up your smoke screens."

Am I? "He has to compete with you," I concede.

Each lap is half a mile. In my mind I rehearse how I'll sever ties with him. "I've decided to take a break from you," I could say. Or, "Long-distance therapy isn't working for me." By the end of three miles I'm hoping for closure but still feel mired in confusion.

"I wouldn't say compete. Maybe supplement."

"What do you mean?" I ask. He looks more rugged out of doors, with his practical parka and hiking boots, not fazed by the weather. I picture him on his spacious ranch, driving a tractor.

"I'm not convinced we should make a dramatic decision," he says as we pass by the NYU library again. "While I'm in town, do you want my late Friday session too?"

The library's maze of zigzag stairways looks as though it was designed by a mental patient on acid, perhaps the reason so many students have committed suicide by leaping off the top tier.

"No. Give your last slot to someone else." It won't be hard for him to find another nutty Ness fan to replace me. Many of his groupies are people I've recommended. I joke that he should punch a card for referrals and offer a free session after ten, like Korean nail salons.

"Listen, I'm going to leave the session open for you, in case you change your mind," he says. "If you want it, show up. If you don't want it, just call five minutes ahead to cancel."

Walking outside with Dr. Ness is making me regress. I flash to an image of myself at three years old, walking with my slim, handsome father to Candy Cone, the ice-cream parlor in our old neighborhood. He's holding my little hand in his; in his other hand, he holds a cigarette. I'm not sure if I remember walking with him or if my memory is just from seeing a picture of us together. My early recollections of my dad are of him leaving for work while I was half asleep, then hearing him come home late, after I'd gone to bed. I spent my childhood missing him.

"I'm not keeping that session or calling to cancel. I want you to acknowledge it's over now." I raise my voice. "That's why I found Greg."

"Don't talk so loud," he says softly.

"Nobody's listening." I'm intrigued that he's self-conscious. Like any of the myopic students, drug dealers, or Rastafarian street musicians around us care. Does he think another patient might overhear? Or a colleague? Does he not want to be seen in public with the fatter, shorter me? Is this against the rules, even for a rule breaker like him?

"I think Greg Holder could be good for you."

"He's infiltrated my dreams," I confess. "He's helping me with my addiction to you while not getting me too hooked to him. Though I still don't think he really gets what an addict is."

"Addiction is a whole different universe. I'll get you the latest version of *Unhooked* if you want to show him."

"You finished it?" I'm hurt he's rewriting the book we worked on without me.

"It's a less academic version of my substance-abuse theory. But it's not ready to show yet," he relents a little. "When it's done I'll send it to you and if you like it, you can forward it to Greg."

We switch to using Dr. Cigar's first name, as if we've all become friends.

"You were the only one who could fix my food problems. But it stopped working when you left." Instead of Weight Winners' weigh-in, I need Ness to see me twice a week, smile, say I look good in his eyes. His approval feeds me.

"I don't think it was me," he says. "In retrospect, I've come up with a new theory. Maybe it was your own success."

What? He's never shared anything like this before. "What do you mean?" I always give him complete credit for getting my weight to 128 pounds while getting me off cigarettes.

"When you sold your first book, it could have been the excitement that filled you up. Not me."

"Really?" Could that be true? I picture the crowd of five hundred flooding my *Up in Smoke* book party at the glamorous Puck Building (ideal for my publishing colleagues since it housed *Puck* magazine in 1918 and *Spy* magazine in the eighties). There I danced with my "A-team" of Lilly, Priscilla, and Bonnie for hours, so blown away I forgot to put one morsel in my mouth the entire night. Ness came to congratulate me. But at our next session, he did warn me that excitement could be a drug, and that I should beware feeling too happy and high, even if the joy was natural and not substance induced.

"When I told you I was over the moon, you said Icarus flying too close to the sun was what burned his wings," I recall.

"The level of glee you were experiencing was not sustainable," he says. "It was inevitable that you'd come crashing down. That's what happens. Every night can't be a TV appearance or book party."

I play the calendar back in my mind. After months of being featured in articles, doing standing-room-only readings, posing for photo spreads, and acing television and radio spots, my book fell off the bestseller lists. The phone did stop ringing incessantly, the requests for interviews began to dry up. I sold the second book last summer but I had a quiet year to wait before it saw print. That's when Sarah and Dr. Ness broke the news about their relocations. So if my food relapse wasn't caused by losing my best shrink and best friend, I wonder if sugar is filling in for the loss of applause and adrenaline.

"Well, I certainly wouldn't be the first to chase after the thrill of public attention," I say.

"Nobody can keep up that much exhilaration. All acclaim is suspect because it takes you out of yourself," he tells me. "But no matter what, you always have to return."

"I think being so close to you and having your approval was what made the difference. It was powerful, like getting my father's love for the first time," I say, wanting him to keep the power that he's trying to give back to me. I notice it's 8:30 already: We're running late. I stare at him, not knowing where we go from here. "Are you getting in touch with Dr. Cox?"

"Yes, I saw him this morning," he affirms.

"He's back in the country? If you'd send me to your Zen protégé, why not your Jungian guru? You always say how perceptive he is."

"He moved to Chappaqua," Ness says. "I know you don't like to travel outside the city."

Since when is Dr. Cox living upstate? Does Dr. Ness drive out to see him and talk about all his patients, including me? If I'm severing ties, I shouldn't care who his therapist is, where he lives, or who I really am to Dr. Ness. As I consider letting him go, a wave of sadness hits.

"So what are we really doing here, Julia?" He catches my eye. "Just saying hello?"

"Just saying good-bye," I blurt, realizing as it comes out it's the truth.

"There's nothing more I can do for you?" he asks.

"Sure. You can fix my eating disorder so I look like Kate Moss before *Food Crazy* hits the bookstores."

"Last night after a meeting, I got back to my hotel late. They didn't have room service past 11 P.M. and no restaurants were open." I can tell he's launching into one of his personal stories with a moral I'm supposed to find enlightening.

"Nothing's open late in New York City?" I don't believe him.

"It was Midtown, on Fifth Avenue and Forty-third. Here's my point. I could have taken a cab somewhere, but I decided it was okay to go to sleep hungry."

I inspect him closely. His beige slacks seem baggy and his face looks a bit more taut. "Have you lost weight? How much do you weigh now?"

"I'm 159 but I want to be 155. I eat light all week, then have one big meal on Saturdays, whatever I want. The other days when I feel hunger, I let myself feel it. I say, 'This is my hunger.'"

Oh, no. I weigh more than my male therapist! He's been losing weight while I'm finding it. Just what I don't need to help me with my eating disorder—a manorexic shrink. "You're too thin for a six-foot-tall guy." I shake my head.

"If I build up my muscle tone, I'm not too thin. I have a new trainer, a real drill sergeant."

"How is your wife adjusting to being a caretaker in Alaska?"

He pauses. "That's a difficult question."

"You just answered it." I'm so overshrunk I can't help my-self.

"I did, didn't I?" He laughs.

"On one side I have a 220-pound fat Buddha shrink saying it's fine to overeat, on the other side an anorexic wasting away."

"A six-foot-one guy who weighs 220 pounds isn't really fat," he defends Dr. Cigar. "And I'm not anorexic at all. I just don't want to grow old with a pot belly like everyone else in my family. Don't you know I have small bones?"

"You're not small boned." Jake, Sarah, and I are all big boned. So is Dr. Cigar. "What's your shoe size?"

"Size ten," he says. "But I have little wrists. Look."

He holds up his arm and takes off his glove. Now he ap-pears younger, and frail. I envision him as a little boy deter-mined to get muscular so the bullies won't beat him up. Is he trying to knock himself off the big strong Superman pedes-tal I've put him on? He could just be drained from ten hours of appointments in the chaotic city where he no longer lives. Maybe he wants to be an average person, smaller in stature, allowed to have flaws and sensitivities, like the patients he treats and saves. After all, he's become a healer to heal him-self, like I have.

"What's new with your mother?" I need an update, sens-ing something has happened.

"Oh, I sent her designer jelly beans and she sent them back with a note that read, 'I prefer dark chocolate.' She used to end with 'you stupid idiot.' But she didn't this time. She didn't hurt me," he says. "In Colorado I found a souvenir wooden box that said 'A box for all of your dreams.' I had her name engraved on the side."

"A dream box. That's heavy. How did she respond?"

"She said, 'I'm going to put my dreams in it. My arthritis is so bad I have no feeling in my fingers anymore. I can't even drive. My dream is for the feeling to come back.'"

"Wow. It's like she wants her maternal feelings to come back for you before she dies," I say. He knows how to be the father I want because he's always longed for his mother's love. He's turned into exactly what's lacking in his own life.

I walk him back to his office and wave good-bye. I'm not sure if I'll ever return.

On my way home, I remember how safe and comforted I used to feel on this route back to my apartment, repeating whatever kooky adage Ness had written down on the back of his business card for me, as if it were a fortune cookie whose prediction would come true. I don't know if I'm missing Dr. Ness or just the delusion that he can protect me from the world—and myself.

"I'll always feel gratitude for all of your help," I e-mail the next day.

"I'm sorry I hurt you when I left, Julia," he writes back. "I never meant to."

Like semistrangers on an online dating site, we're able to get more intimate over cyberspace than we can be in person.

I do not make—or keep—any other therapy appointments with Dr. Ness. Still, I wonder if I'll ever see him again. Shutting my eyes, I imagine that *Food Crazy* will be such a huge national bestseller that my editor will clamor for all my other projects. Ness and I will rewrite and sell *Unhooked* together. We'll be on the way to sign the contract at my agent's office when we bump into Dr. Cigar. Though he and Dr. Ness haven't seen each other since graduate school twenty-five years earlier, my two Freudian fathers will hit it off, bonding in their pride over me and my accomplishments. In the movie version, I'll be back down to 128, my dream weight.

chapter twelve
father time
February 26

"Turn down that chick Muzak. I'm working!" Jake shouts.

What does he think packing for *The Oprah Winfrey Show* is? Playing? I'm out of my mind nervous that Oprah's invited the four Girl Gurus on the *New York* magazine cover to appear on her show this Wednesday. Thankfully, I'll just be plugging the paperback *Up in Smoke* and not my food-addiction book, so it won't matter that I'm still twenty-five pounds too heavy. This could be a horror show since TV adds ten pounds, I think, as I lower the sound of Mary J. Blige's "No More Drama." Walking into Jake's den, I'm dismayed to see scripts and DVDs stacked everywhere.

"The hooker's supposed to be dead but she's still moving, damn it," he says, eyes locked on the TV screen.

"Sorry. I'm worried about flying in bad weather and the lyrics chill me out."

"You mean that preachy feminist shit about bad men and the innocent women they hurt?"

"Let's listen to your Rolling Stones coots creaming over teenage girls," I say. "Why are females always getting murdered on your show, anyway? Don't men ever kill each other?"

"No. They kill women playing those femmy albums all the time," he shoots back.

His sucky mood and messy office seem a bad omen. Nick, a pal of his who is a pack rat, had so many newspapers on the floor of his place he barricaded himself inside—winding up at Payne Whitney's mental ward. I believe marriage means not letting your spouse become psycho in a pigsty.

"Can you clean up a little? Look, that stack is going to fall." I point to the top of his TV.

"You're right." Jake shoves the pile to the floor, DVDs flying everywhere.

His jumping back into an East Coast one-hour drama midseason is making him so edgy and sleep-deprived, I sympathize with Dr. Ness's move to the slower-paced Adirondacks. "You want to be buried in garbage, like your nutso friend Nick?" I shriek.

"You're one to call me nutso!" Jake shouts. "With your fucking arsenal of shrinks."

"I just have one main therapist now," I defend myself.

"You have a whole zoo-full on retainer: Ness on videocam, Cigar guy, Sarah's stolen shrink, your old one, Pamela Gold, who you sent my assistant to. Her lover Angie is now seeing Gold's shrink husband. Not to mention those idiots you tangoed with from the insurance network."

"I wasn't tangoing. I said eight shrinks in eight days was like speed dating."

"So go out with them and leave me alone." He slams his den door.

On edge and starving, just what I don't need now is a domestic meltdown with my mad mate. When the Weather Channel shows a snowstorm in the Midwest, I panic. Although I'm trying to be over him, in a total regression, I e-mail Dr. Ness. "Jake's going insane like his grandpa Alfie and I'm going to die in a plane crash on my way to *Oprah*," I write. "Can you do an emergency iChat?"

"Jake's not insane like Grandpa Alfie and you'll get there fine," Dr. Ness answers right away. "I think calling YOUR THERAPIST is in order."

I don't know whether that's a careful response proving he's been listening when I say I need to let him go, or a screw-you.

"I haven't tried Dr. Cigar for traumas yet," I answer. "My heart still goes to you."

"Tell Jake he hurt your feelings," he advises. "Be vulnerable, not combative."

"You hurt my feelings," I tell my husband. "And I'm losing my voice from yelling right before *Oprah*." I start to cry.

"I'm sorry. I'm so drained from these freezing fifteen-hour days of outside shoots. I looked so pathetic yesterday, the crew got me long underwear and a face mask."

I point to my throat so he knows I can't talk anymore. I take a pen and scrawl, "I'm sorry too. Love you."

"I'm having separation anxiety," he admits. "I like to travel but I don't like it when you go away."

He'd rather keep me in our apartment so he can pick up

exactly where he left off, like a bookmark. "Me either," I whisper, and we hug.

I try to prepare for the worst. Yet Bonnie picks me up in a limo, the plane is on schedule, she surprises me with first-class tickets, and the weather is fine. I keep quiet and drink tea with honey. With her next to me I resist the five-course meal they serve on the two-hour flight. When we land at O'Hare, a limo driver drops her off at the Four Seasons, where she's staying with the other Girl Gurus (who are taking a later plane). Then the driver takes me to my parents' house in Evanston. I get there in time for dinner. My mother puts out challah, potatoes, and pie, but the excitement fills me up so I'm able to stick with chicken and salad.

Mom is so anxious to accompany me to Harpo Studios early Wednesday morning that Bonnie lets her come with us in the limo, this one a black stretch, where Bonnie and I rehearse how I'm supposed to answer questions.

"*Up in Smoke*'s message to young people who smoke and drink is 'just say no'?" Bonnie asks.

"No. I'm not parroting Nancy Reagan's mantra," I say, sipping Diet Coke.

"What's wrong with Nancy Reagan?" my mother asks.

"Mom, she's just testing me."

"So far you're flunking." Bonnie shakes her head.

"I'm not so astute at six thirty in the morning," I concede. "Try again."

"What do you say to smokers and drinkers?"

"My message to young people who smoke and drink is that your addictions are secretly stopping you from getting everything you want in life."

"Good." Bonnie nods. "How does that happen?"

"Beer and cigarettes have an incendiary effect..."

"Word's too big," Bonnie scolds. "We need to play in Peoria."

"We're in Chicago," my mother says.

"Just an expression for Podunk, Mom. You know, like your Yiddish word *shnipishuck*. Try it again, Bonnie."

"How do addictions hurt you?" Bonnie asks, grabbing me another caffeinated soda.

"Beer and cigarettes have a sinister effect on your system that you don't realize," I try.

"Good," Bonnie praises. "How are they sinister?"

"When you have a cigarette or a drink, you're sucking in your emotions instead of allowing them to tell their own story." Now I'm waking up, on a roll.

"Any drink at all? Even one? Isn't that too extreme?" asks my mother, the redheaded overfeeder partially responsible for my obsessive oral fixation in the first place.

"That's true. Oprah's not an antialcohol zealot like you are," Bonnie says. "She was having margaritas with Rachel Day on her show last week."

"When you get rid of a toxic habit, you make room for something beautiful to take its place," I try instead.

"Okay." Bonnie pats my shoulder. "Now that's your sound bite!"

"Good sound bite. Sure you don't want breakfast? I brought extra bagels." My mom shows me the carb stash she's stuffed in her oversized purse.

I shake my head, barely able to breathe in my size-twelve black skirt and Spanx, along with a tight Bergdorf silk sweater and high heels hopefully elongating my legs. I tell myself that nobody will expect the author of *Up in Smoke* to be slender, since it's a book about giving up smoking and drinking that barely touches on weight issues. I saved those for the not-yet-published *Food Crazy*, which luckily doesn't come out until the summer.

At the studio, after an array of hair stylists and makeup artists take care of me, Ronit, Frederica, and Nancy, a producer seats us across from each other on two couches on the sound stage. I'm thrilled when Oprah sits next to me. "We have a guru group that'll fix your house, your head, your diet, and all of your bad habits," Oprah tells her audience. When it comes to introducing me, she says, "Our country's new 'quit yer boozin', smokin 'n' tokin' sage is Julia Goodman, a hometown Chicago girl."

"I made my mother come with me," I say.

She laughs and says, "Yes, Julia's mom is right here, looking very proud of her daughter. Aren't you, mom?" When the camera pans to my mother, the audience applauds.

I expect some hardball questions but the hardest Oprah throws at me is, "What do you say to people who can't afford to work with a one-on-one addiction specialist like you did?"

"I say SmokEnders and Nicotine Anonymous are free, most therapists have a sliding scale, and these horrible habits are compromising your life so much you can't afford not to try."

"That's right. You can't afford not to try," she repeats before the commercial.

Having the best time of my entire life, I'm just starting to rock 'n' roll, ready to come back after the break for a long on-air heart-to-heart with Oprah about how we're going to solve our upsetting, ongoing weight struggles, subtly slipping in the title *Food Crazy*. But it turns out we've already been on for five and a half minutes and it's all over. We're quickly demicrophoned, ushered off stage, and shuttled out a side door without an Oprah hug good-bye. Disoriented, I don't remember one line of what the rest of the group said but I float away feeling as though I'm high on the best stuff I've ever smoked.

My brother Alan TiVoes my appearance, and with the help of my webbie, Lori, the segment is on my Web site by the time we get to my parents' place. Haley has e-mailed that I "really rocked" and sales for *Up in Smoke* are rising by the second. Cyberstalking myself, I see that my paperback has indeed spiked to number fourteen on Amazon. But Frederica's *French Women Are Never Flabby* and *Further Reasons Why French Women Are Never Flabby* are three and four.

What evens out the disparity is when my father comes home from work at six o'clock that night and calls out, "How did Julie's TV interview go?"

"She was great. The best one," my mother yells, coming down the stairs.

"Alan said he recorded it? Can I see?" Dad asks.

I'm pleasantly stunned to see my dad so gung ho about my appearance. "Sure."

"But the kids screwed up the DVD player." My mother sounds upset by this, which surprises me. Usually her precious grandkids can do no wrong, while I'm the one getting in the way.

"You can watch it on my laptop," I offer.

"Okay, let's see it on the computer," he says, before he's even looked at the mail or read the newspaper.

In my old still-pink bedroom, my folks sit down on the single bed, covered by my worn rose bedspread. I sit at my desk and press the link to the video clip. They view the five-minute segment. I turn to my father, who looks enrapt as he watches me. He's nodding, playfully hitting my mother's shoulder, then laughing as if to say, "She's a chip off the old block."

When the interview is over, he says, "You were great! Play it again."

I do, wishing I could record his reaction, unable to stop watching my father watch me. Though they say the camera adds ten pounds, he doesn't even seem to notice my weight gain; nobody does. He just thinks I'm great!

"Look, Leah, there you are," he says, pointing. "You both look terrific. Julia's the smartest one." He's totally into it, impressed and entertained, amazed even. "She got the best lines in."

He's calling me smart and praising what I said? I'm so used to my father's indifference, and subtle digs making me feel less brainy than my brothers, that my first reaction is disbelief. Next it's fear, as if somebody's told me I've won the lottery but I have to check to make sure I haven't lost the winning ticket. When he says, "You were marvelous, honey, just marvelous" and kisses my forehead, my mouth is agape. I bet this is the secret reason why I really traveled all these miles in the middle of winter.

The next day, in between phone interviews, I guzzle tea with honey and suck cherry cough drops to keep my voice, playing Scrabble with my mother before my Thursday-night reading at the local Borders bookstore. Amazing what being anointed the It Addiction Girl by Oprah can do. More than a hundred old friends and classmates show up, along with my brothers, sisters-in-law, and their six little kids, who all come up to hug me afterward.

"Aunt Julie, we saw you on TV!" says my little niece Aliyah. "You were great. Grandpa said you were the best one."

"Thanks. Did you like when I read from my book, Stevie?" I ask my ten-year-old nephew.

"Not bad," he declares. "Almost as good as Harry Potter."

Even the kids seem to like me better. In the middle of winter, on a freezing night, without my husband here, I'm happy and at home. Total lovefest. And thank goodness not one person even notices my weight.

At 11:30, as I'm sitting at the kitchen table reading the *Sun-Times* article about me, my father, a fellow night owl, shuffles past me in his gray elastic-waist sweatpants and T-shirt. He takes an orange from the refrigerator. We've both had food issues since we quit our appetite-suppressing cigarette habits around the same time two and a half years ago. I'd been afraid my mother would bury him with food. But he's lost weight on his own no-bread diet. We have the same genetic addiction tendencies, so I take his newfound willpower as a positive omen from the heavens.

"Both of my partners' wives watched your show," he says. "You were really excellent."

"I didn't look heavy?" I ask.

"No, you looked pretty and sounded sharp. You were the smartest one," he repeats.

I beam, wishing a tape recorder were capturing his praise so I could carry it around in my pocket and replay it daily. "You look good too," I tell him. "You lost half your stomach."

"I dropped twenty-six pounds. I want to be 170, like when I got married."

So it's not just women who struggle to get back to their fighting weight. "I don't know how you diet in a house with so much fattening junk. Why don't you get Mom on a low-carb diet too?" Though she could stand to lose ten pounds herself, overfeeding others is her true addiction.

He sits across from me and says, "Your mother would give me up before she'd give up bread."

Easy to pinpoint the origin of my carbo-loading instincts. "Bonnie said a hundred people at the reading was a good turnout. We sold eighty copies of the paperback *Up in Smoke.*"

"It was really nice that your brothers brought their kids." He reads the *Sun-Times* article about me, peeling the orange quickly. He bites into a slice, as impatient to eat as I always am. Like if he doesn't finish fast, somebody might steal it away.

"On a school night too," I add.

"They come every Saturday. Will you be around?"

Is he asking me to stay longer? "I can switch my flight to Sunday night if you want."

"Good." He seems pleased. "I haven't seen you since Sarah's wedding. So how are you doing?"

I can't remember the last time he's asked me that.

"My career's really heating up," I say. "I'm glad Jake's done with L.A. Though I really miss Sarah."

"Has she been back in New York at all?"

I nod. "She's only been back to visit once." I let her know about my TV appearance, but she's the one person in my world who hasn't yet called or e-mailed congratulations.

"Does she like Ohio?" he asks.

"I think it's been a hard adjustment for her," I say. I don't ever tell anyone about her rough night, disappointed that it hasn't made her more consistent about returning my messages or being there for me.

"Your mom says she's due next month," he says. "Why don't you visit her?"

"I offered to fly to Ohio. Three times. She keeps saying

she can barely juggle a husband, their dogs, and her pregnancy, and they're setting up a bedroom for the baby nurse who's going to move in. So there's no room for a visitor. Her leaving the city killed me," I admit, as if the difficulties are in the past tense.

"You know, it killed your mother when the Suttons left Chicago for Aspen. She and Marsha were inseparable for thirty years. I don't think she ever got over it. Broke your mom's heart."

"Really? It was that hard for her too?" Sarah and I have been swearing since childhood we'll never be like our moms, yet we're unwittingly re-creating their exact relationship.

"Your mother resents selfish people, but being selfless is worse," my father says. "You can't be a martyr. Sometimes you have to move on."

For a guy who claims to be anti-psychology, this advice seems perceptive. Not that I—or my mother—can quite figure out how you move on from a best friend you've adored for decades. But in small ways, I am letting her go, needing her less.

I go to the fridge, which is overstuffed with cake, blintzes, potatoes, and every other kind of starch I'm avoiding. I find sliced chicken leftovers, cheese, and sliced carrots, and take them out with mustard. Now that my TV appearance is over and I aced it, I give myself permission for a little noshing. I know I shouldn't. But I hardly ever get to have a talk and nosh with just me and my father. The last time I had him to myself, we were still smoking. As the only nicotine fiends in the immediate family, I imagined we were secretly bonded by our method of self-destruction.

"How's Jake? I watched his show with the headless woman's corpse," he says animatedly, eating two orange slices at a time. The citrus squirts and I hand him a napkin.

"He's been really stressed. Working too many hours," I say. "How are *you*?" I don't want our talk to end. "Still working both jobs?" He still works at his legal practice while teaching at Northwestern Law School. I like that we both have two careers. I've inherited his workaholism, as well as his addictions, big appetite, and insomnia.

He throws the rind in the garbage, then takes the bowl of cashews from the counter. "It was so cute how all the grandkids came up to kiss you after your reading. Thank God for your brothers."

Here it comes, the theme of my childhood: Thank God for his cherished sons. But this time my big homecoming acclaim gives me confidence to confront the issue forever bugging me. "Dad, why have you always been more interested in the boys than in me?"

I expect him to ignore the question, switch subjects, or say he loves all his kids equally, as he usually does.

"Because you went your own way," he answers, as if it's so obvious he can no longer deny it. "Somebody has to continue my legacy."

Finally, after all these years, I'm getting a candid answer out of him. Incredible!

Instead of feeling hurt or upset, I marvel at his honesty. His words are vague, but I know exactly what he means. I'm the one in the family who has never fit in, who has rejected his world by not re-creating it. I used to think I'd partially imagined feeling slighted by him. Hearing him admit it, saying the words out loud, to my face, feels liberating. He seems to be admitting that my rejecting his life also slighted him.

Of course now it makes sense. My brother Scott is a lawyer at my dad's firm, with three kids. Bradley's a litigator at a local legal practice who has added two boys to the grandkid arsenal. Alan is a gastroenterologist who brings a gorgeous granddaughter to the clan. Like him, my siblings are male, conservative graduates of the University of Chicago, his alma mater. Their Midwest lives mirror his.

I'm the converse, a left-wing liberal female psych major at NYU who left home at eighteen. The minute I landed in Greenwich Village I began spilling my dirty laundry to shrinks—a *shanda* to my emotionally reserved dad. He doesn't believe in psychology, or digging through his own past—which is filled with poverty and intrusive Jewish relatives who used to "hold a tribal meeting to determine who could go to the bathroom." His mother died young from cancer. His father never forgave his only son for abandoning the family's lightbulb business to become a respected attorney.

As an urban author with no kids, I'm giving birth to books, not babies. I like that he implies my status isn't personal and the equation is easy. If I move back to town, or become a lawyer or a parent who gives him a grandchild, he'll like me better. The fact that he can appreciate my TV appearance is endearing me to him.

"You were always closer to your mom." He eats a slice of my cheddar cheese.

"But I wanted to be close to you," I confess.

"I know." He stands up, puts the nuts away, then bends down to kiss me on the forehead. "Listen, I love you and I'm proud of you," he says. Then he walks upstairs to bed.

No longer hungry, I return the rest of the food to the refrigerator. Upstairs I log on to the Internet, not even opening e-mails from Dr. Ness or Dr. Cigar. There's no need for fake fathers when I can get what I want from the original.

When my cell phone rings so late, I assume it's Jake. But it's a reporter from the *New York Post*. How did she get my cell number?

"We're running a piece on the in-fighting of the gurus behind the scenes at *Oprah*. Frederica said your food addiction book's postponed because you're pregnant and can't tour. Is it true?"

The thrill of my TV fame and fatherly praise melts with the thought that Frederica and now the entire population see me as so overweight they assume I'm having a baby. What a bitch that scrawny French woman is.

"You're calling to confirm what?" I ask, buying time to figure out how to respond. A flat-out denial would seem an admission that I'm heavy and not with child. Bonnie, who warns me never to trash anybody in the news lest it ruin my "girl next door" image, says no press is bad press. It's good the public cares about our guru quartet and my womb, right? I mean, I'm not exactly Brangelina. But how do I manipulate the rumor mill in my favor so I'll outsell that skinny French lush once and for all?

"Is your new book being postponed because you're pregnant and won't be able to tour?" The reporter is clearly trying to incite a catfight.

"My new book has not been postponed. In fact, my publisher was so thrilled with Oprah's endorsement, they've doubled the first print run," I lie, having no idea how many they're planning on printing. "The paperback *Up in Smoke* is about to be a bestseller," I add. "At thirty-eight, if I did happen to be with child, well, it probably wouldn't be a good idea to announce it this early," I say before hanging up.

As I fall asleep, I don't know if I'm knocking myself up so I can compete with Sarah, beat out Frederica, further please my daddy, or just get more book publicity.

part
three

chapter thirteen

sometimes a cigar isn't just a cigar

March 7

Rushing to therapy in the freezing cold, I turn the corner and catch Dr. Cigar in front of his building, smoking the stubby end of a stogie. Despite my cute nickname for him, I actually hate seeing him puffing on a cancer stick. It disturbs me, like coming across an ugly picture of myself I've forgotten to throw out.

"You were great on TV!" he calls out.

"Thanks." I breeze past him, wanting his praise but not his smoke, as if it'll contaminate me. "See you upstairs."

Getting out of the elevator on the eleventh floor, I bump into Mary, my agent's assistant. "Hey, we saw you on *Oprah*! Did you get the flowers we sent?"

"I did, they're gorgeous. My mom says I've really made it if you're sending me black roses."

"We had them specially dyed."

I can hear my father's voice saying, "Only in your *meshugganah* city can you get roses dyed black."

"Did you hear about all the calls for *Up in Smoke*'s film rights?" I ask. "Any news yet?"

"Lilly's meeting with a producer in Tribeca right now."

"Fabulous. Oh, I'm not here to see her. I have a new therapist, right across the hall."

"I know, Lilly told me. I hear he's a hunk. And congratulations. On the personal front."

Mary has obviously seen me in yesterday's *New York Post* Page Six, but I don't bother denying the pregnancy rumor. I wave as she gets into the elevator. Then I check my cell phone messages in Dr. Cigar's too-narrow waiting room, popping a cherry cough drop in my mouth.

"So you're the hometown girl made good," he says when he comes to retrieve me.

I follow him to his office, taking off my coat. "My favorite part was watching my father watch me on TV. He said he loved me. Isn't he supposed to love me anyway?"

"You're implying he doesn't?" He puts his feet up on the leather ottoman.

"He admitted he likes my brothers better because I've gone my own way. So if you're not exactly like him, you're an alien. Is that a brave confession or just narcissistic?" I pull my notebook and pen from my purse to take notes, as I often do during therapy. With Dr. Ness it was to jot down phrases and theories to use for my books. With Dr. Cigar it's more to catch strings of contrasting images and read them over later to translate.

He pauses. "Well, a narcissist can't stretch very far from himself. Your father's formula is 'the more my kids emulate me, the more they get love.' The goal is to be separate and cherished for yourself, not punished by the limitation of his subjective bias."

"But why did our talk make me feel so understood? It seemed generous, like he's helping me figure out my childhood."

"Well, your father respects success. That's in his repertoire and he rewarded you with candor," he concedes. "He's admitting he's had blinders on."

"Jake has a *Law & Order* episode coming up, 'Blind Spot,' where this forensic psychologist obsessed with a recent spate of killings has no idea they've been committed by his own daughter, who's become a serial killer to get his attention," I tell him. "Am I chasing fame to please my dad?"

"Better than committing murder." Dr. Cigar smiles. "Look, you're getting what you want. You've earned his praise by virtue of your earthly acclaim."

"Ness says success can be deceptive and fickle," I say, popping another cough drop.

"You're still seeing Dr. Ness?"

"I regressed and e-mailed him a few times," I'm embarrassed to admit. "Still fighting off my addiction to him. Still hurts that he left."

"Could be a bearable kind of hurt you can live with. Like a pebble in your shoe."

"More like a boulder." Does that describe Dr. Ness or my father? Or both of them? Dr. Cigar doesn't hurt at all. He's the Band-Aid. "I thought my dad's approval would heal my hunger. But since I've been back, I'm regaining the weight I lost. My throat's sore and I'm drinking ten teas with honey a day and sucking on cherry cough drops, like I need a continual fix."

"You're treating a sore throat. You're not a robot."

"You don't understand. We're talking five hundred extra calories a day in honey. And I don't mean a few cough drops, I've been popping sixty or seventy daily. Talk about self-medicating."

"You're allowed to be human."

"Please stop acting like it's a cute minor problem. I'm the heaviest I've ever been." This morning my scale said 163—3 pounds heavier than my former high score. It scares me so much I can't tell him the number. "My hunger is gigantic. An incessant, sick, spiraling addiction."

"You make yourself sound like a monster, a violent heroin addict," he says. "I find your voraciousness charming. As long as it's not killing you."

"But my appetite *can* kill me. It's endless, with the power to destroy my body, reputation, and career. Dr. Ness saw that any self-indulgence could spiral me out of control."

"So I should treat you like you have a life-threatening diabetic condition? Russian roulette with frosting?"

"Yes!" I yell.

"You have so much anxiety about food. You're frightened you'll fly too high, explode with cherry cough drops, and crash into hell."

"Don't you get that I'm out of control and can't stop eating? Being fat will make a mockery of a book that says I conquered my sugar addiction. What do you think honey and cough drops are? I try to take the advice I wrote. But what I know intellectually isn't sinking in emotionally anymore."

"What's the intellectual side say?"

"That I need an all-out assault because this is really deep. It's a family curse. My dad put on fifty pounds when he quit smoking by trading cigarettes for cookies. He's losing it now, but that could easily be me the week before my pub date."

"You're this swirl of positive energy. Then a flick of a switch turns you inside out and you're in the dark underbelly, in a death grip with your shadow side," he riffs. "Okay, Julia. Let's pinpoint your triggers."

"The hunger flares up unexpectedly. It's not predictable," I say. Before he has a chance to respond, I realize that's not always true. "I started regressing at Sarah's wedding events. So I overeat when my relatives are around. I have a few family functions coming up. My mom will be in town and we're taking her out to a fancy dinner. Then we have to go to Connecticut for my niece's birthday party. When I know in advance something special is scheduled, maybe I should just call it a free day, eat whatever I want, and reactivate the rigid rules the next morning."

"Like planned spontaneity, knowing you'll go insane, but trying to harness the ravenous chaos, flirting with the devil while keeping your clothes on?"

I scrawl his comic strain into my notebook but want him to take it more seriously. "Dr. Ness eats whatever he wants Saturday night, then goes right back to his rigid plan Sunday," I say. "But he was never really a food addict." I unzip my boots, which feel too tight; the thought of public meals with multiple members of my clan is already making me claustrophobic.

"All your struggles get acted out with your diet. What's causing the emotional conflicts?"

"I hate Frederica, who's trying to sabotage me by claiming I'm pregnant."

"She's the French guru girl? I liked her the least."

"Thank you," I say. "And Jake and I are getting audited by the IRS, which totally freaks me out."

"Do you owe them any money?"

"Not a cent. I'm so anal I've kept every receipt for the last twenty years."

"So what else is getting to you?" Dig deeper, he's saying. He's right. I have to.

"I'm worried about Sarah having a hard pregnancy in Hicksville," I list, fearing I'm all over the map today. "When I'm stressed I reach for food."

"Okay, how do we get you less traumatized by your consumption, quell the kamikaze cravings, see the frosting in the window, and assert the muscle of dramatic midzone..."

"Don't get abstract," I tell Mr. Mixed Metaphor. "It's not my imagination. Didn't you see Page Six yesterday?"

He shakes his head no.

"Well, after seeing me on *Oprah*, they called to ask if I was having a baby. I didn't want to tell them I just gained weight. So I didn't deny it. I don't know why."

"You really miss your best friend. You could be having a sympathy pregnancy."

I wave my hand in a shooing gesture, as if to say, "Don't waste my time with silliness."

"It's a real medical condition," he informs me in his doctor voice. "They call it Couvade syndrome, after the French word *couver*, which means 'to hatch.'"

"That's when *fathers* have psychosomatic symptoms because they're overidentifying with their wives," I say dismissively.

"Well, studies show the roots are anxiety about the big change coming, ambivalence about watching the woman you love become a mother, and envy that you're not able to share such a powerful experience. You've overidentified with Sarah since you were born, so that fits how you feel toward her now, doesn't it?" he asks. "Despite your overt denials, I think part of you wants to be pregnant with Sarah, the way your mothers were."

I shake my head with an emphatic no. "You're being sexist, just assuming every woman has child lust. You've been married fifteen years. Why don't you have kids?"

"When I make you uncomfortable, you change the focus to my issues and switch from patient to therapist, so you feel more in control," he observes. "Like a sneak counterattack to protect yourself from potential pain."

The guy is perceptive. "Did your wife want kids?" I'm too curious to stop digging.

"My wife had physical problems and couldn't." He's casual, no big deal.

But now I can't give up the trail to find out what's wrong with his marriage. "What does she think of your penchant for cigars?"

"She hates it," he admits. "She's a former smoker. I'm only allowed to smoke outside."

"If your habit bothers the people closest to you, that's a problem. Think about it—you're literally leaving your home, walking away from your wife, putting a smoke screen between you."

"Why is it so important to you that I stop? To reinforce your choices? To feel more secure, like you're in competent hands?"

"Yes. Otherwise I'm not sure I can trust your judgment. And how are you going to fix Haley and Lori?"

"Interesting that you switched to concern for your young protégés," he comments.

"How are you going to help us all nail what we want if you can't get what you want in life?"

"How do you know I'm not getting what I want?"

"Are you?" I confront him.

"Not even close." He laughs. "But who is? You really think you're capable of getting *everything* you want from life?"

"I'm pretty close. Great marriage and career, and I attribute my recent good fortune to quitting my addictions. When you terminate toxic habits, there's room for better things to take their place."

"I heard you say that on TV. What would take the place of my cigars?" He looks genuinely intrigued.

"Can I answer that the way I'd talk to a client?" I ask.

"Yes. Go for it. Do your addiction dance on my head."

"Okay, where's your happiness with your wife? Your marriage doesn't sound like it's thriving. Don't you want to be closer?"

"She wants to be."

"What about more success at work?"

"She wants me to make more money."

"Or having a child? Getting a better office? You're smart and good-looking, but you have the worst office out of all the shrinks I've met. You're a big reader, why not write? Where are your books?" I feel desperate to fix him, as if that'll fix me too. "Lots of shrinks less linguistically talented than you have published books. You're fifty-one. What are you waiting for?"

"Man." He seems dazed, as if my "how to quit everything" evangelism has exhausted him already. "You bring this soaring drama with you like perfume, enlivening everything, weaving me into your vast flying carpet. You're an ace at what you do—inspirational and insightful, enticing others to merge with the fast-moving traffic."

The idea of pushing himself further makes him envision a potential car accident.

"You're still smoking a cigar every day?" I ask.

"Not all at once. I go outside five or six times a day."

That's much worse. "When did you start?"

"Ten years ago. Before that I used to smoke a pipe."

"Do you see a shrink?"

"I used to have an analyst I liked," he answers. "But not in fifteen years."

"Fifteen years. That's too long. Dr. Ness sees his guru monthly," I say. "Ness once made me ask Jake to hold me for an hour every night without talking, which helped us really connect. You should try that. If you quit smoking, you'll feel vulnerable and wind up closer to your wife." I'm trying to be to Dr. Cigar what Dr. Ness has been to me, but it's not working.

"There's not one correct method. I saw a documentary about a patient who sees four therapists and each has a completely different style. They're opposites of each other," he says.

"I know. Ness was way more rigid and critical than you." I nod, noticing it's 7:15; we've gone fifteen minutes over.

"Yes, but he got you to stop hurting yourself and unlocked your talents in a way that I can't," he says with a hangdog expression, making me feel like a jerk for eviscerating his cigar affliction, and for setting up this "surpass my old shrink" contest he's not winning.

"But what good is it, if it didn't stick?"

"You're off alcohol, drugs, and cigarettes," he argues. "That stuck."

I stand up, put on my coat, and ask, "So how long before you let me help you stop sucking poison into your lungs?"

"That depends on how good you are," he says as I wave good night.

chapter fourteen
mother tongue

March 21

"Sarah named her baby Chloe," I tell my mother on Friday night as we walk to Café Arte.

"I know," she says. "Marsha left a message that she gained thirty-five pounds and Chloe was ten of them."

"Isn't that a jumbo baby?" Jake asks. "My producer gained ninety pounds with her twins. I named them Snickers and Mounds."

"Not to her face, I hope." I elbow him, feeling jolted to hear how much weight Sarah gained. I guess I never asked her specifically.

"Marsha e-mailed us pictures. Chloe's gorgeous, she looks just like Sarah," Mom adds.

I'm relieved all went well, but I can't get the number

thirty-five out of my head. How bizarre that I've put on the exact same poundage as Sarah, in the same amount of time. Freud says there's no such thing as coincidence. I recall Dr. Cigar's theory that I've been having a sympathy pregnancy. What a ridiculously neurotic reaction, since at the end of nine months, she's a mother and I'm just fat.

Over dinner at a back table near the restaurant's fireplace, I share the good news that Universal Pictures just bought the film option of *Up in Smoke*, and how making self-help books into films is a new trend that might just work because they're transformative by nature, and thus dramatic. *He's Just Not So Into You Anymore*, *Skinny Bitches Are Better*, and *French Women Are Never Flabby* are already done, and I hope *Up in Smoke* is next.

"My first choice to play me is Mary-Louise Parker," I add.

"Which one is she?" my mother asks.

"She played smart kooky feminists on *Weeds* and *The West Wing*," Jake says.

"Can a nutty Catholic do Jewish neurosis?" I wonder aloud.

"What about Jennifer Aniston?" Mom gets into the act.

"They're both too skinny. How about Liv Tyler or Kate Winslet? I like women with curves," says Jake, winking at me. He's been trying to reassure me I'm still sexy ever since he caught me crying on the bathroom floor, near the scale.

The waiter puts a basket of focaccia on the table. I usually have them remove bread so I won't be tempted, but I can't do that with company. Especially with my mother, the bread lover. I try not to stare at it.

"That decapitation on your last show was too gruesome for me," she tells Jake, tearing off a piece from the loaf and smothering it with butter.

"Alan helped us figure out which poison would kill the

Russian spy quickest," Jake says, breaking off a piece of bread too.

"He loves being your show's medical consultant." She pushes the butter and oil near him and he dips his slice.

I drink my water, chewing on the ice, wishing my salad would come. In *Food Crazy* I share restaurant war tactics for eating addicts: Spread mustard on sourdough slices. Pour pepper over the butter. Sprinkle vinegar on desserts—anything to make what's fattening easier to avoid. Jake and my mother think my weapons of attack are disgusting—though their only strategy when it comes to getting rid of carbs is to put them in their mouth.

"What else is going on at home?" I ask her.

"The kids were so cute last week. They slept over. Teddy insists he needs his Spider-Man cape on before he can eat breakfast. Stevie's reciting entire scenes from movies verbatim. Aliyah calls me 'Gammy' now and insists on wearing the pink dress I bought her every time she comes over. She looks so cute in it, I'll send you pictures."

At sixty, my mother has given up her popular party-planning business to "just be a grandma." Not her best idea, since she's been known to call in tears when Aliyah or Teddy doesn't want to visit her every Saturday. I always feel like saying, "Get another job, Mom. You can't base your entire emotional state on the mood swings of toddlers." But I'm trying not to be judgmental. After all, she toiled as an office manager to put my father through law school, and ran her own thriving company for twenty years during a forty-year marriage with four children, while I'm a feminist who can wear an "Oops, I'm only pretending to have my friend's baby" T-shirt. I can't even juggle having a husband, working at home, and feeding myself properly.

When my meal comes, I gobble up salad, eggplant, and broiled fish while she goes on about her grandkids. As her firstborn and only girl, everything I did used to fascinate her. (Or did she overcompensate because my father was so impossible?) But now I'm sensing she's tired of hearing about my work and wishes I'd have a baby, like Sarah. Grandchildren are her favorite topic to talk about; it's a language I can't speak. But I'm finally winning my father's favor, so I don't want to focus on what I can't get from her. I tell myself Dr. Ness's mantra: "Feelings are misleading." Then I try my own mantra: "Dispute your misconceptions." Neither works.

After dinner, my mother is anxious to get to her hotel so she won't be late for her friend Sheila's son's bar mitzvah the next day. A driver is waiting outside the restaurant to chauffeur her to New Jersey. Sheila, the daughter of family friends, is my age, a New Jersey housewife with four kids. Since Sheila's mom passed away, she calls mine for advice, seeing her as a surrogate parent. I hug my mother good-bye, hurt that like my father, she prefers protégés who reflect her life preferences.

"Being on *Oprah* might have impressed my dad," I tell Jake on the walk home, "but without kids I don't interest my mother so much anymore."

"You're just as myopic as they are," he tells me.

"I am not," I say. "How?"

"Most of your friends are career-obsessed New Yorkers with no kids. You lost interest in that client, Fiona, when she got pregnant and decided to apply to law school at Yale. You don't even want to write her a recommendation."

"Well, I was on deadline when she asked me to write three pages on why she'd make a good lawyer. How the hell would I know that?" But he's right. When Fiona was single and interviewing for women's magazine jobs in Midtown, I was her mentor. Yet when she got pregnant and moved on to Connecticut and law, she lost me, the way I kind of lost my father. "The New Jersey crowd will be fawning all over my mother, I'm sure."

"So? You do seminars and book signings where your fan club fawns all over you. Your little favorites are Lori and Haley, because they're the ones who want to be just like you."

"Screw you." I pinch his arm. "Stop being right about everything."

On Sunday, Jake's niece's party in Old Greenwich is overcrowded with suburban kids. I'm the only married female there who isn't a mother. In my Manhattan social milieu, skinniness is next to godliness. Here a baby bump is the status symbol. The clowns, magicians, guitar players, and balloon twisters give me a headache. I never liked kiddie parties, not even as a kid.

In addiction therapy, Dr. Ness says patients emotionally regress to the age they were when they started using their substance. When I stopped smoking, I felt like I was an awkward, angry thirteen-year-old nerd again. But my sugar problems started much earlier. I recall a Howard Johnson's birthday bash when I was five and my brother Scott was three. He was born two years and two days after I was, so to my chagrin, my mother threw us a joint celebration. I insisted on having the biggest piece of cake to get the red frosting flower in the corner. I felt overshadowed and was already reaching for extra sweetening to soothe my sour grapes.

As the Connecticut crew sings "Happy Birthday" to Jake's niece, I notice the dessert table. I become enamored with the white and purple oversized cupcakes. They're beckoning with swirls of vanilla icing, twice the size of regular cupcakes, elephantine. My fetish is in plain sight and I can take as many as I want, with sprinkles, coconut, whipped cream, or chocolate chip topping. I don't know if this is a sign from the Cupcake Gods, rewarding me for surviving the mommy-baby-and-in-law brigade, or the devil shrouded in pastel sucrose, dangerously seducing me.

Though still eating too much, I've been walking regularly and have had two weeks icing free. Yet in the throes of an addict's impulsive inanity, I hear my inner enabler argue that I've worked so hard, I deserve to be soothed with sugar. My inner self-helper shouts back: "You're desperate for love, not dessert. Don't succumb!" But I stroll over, stand in line, and put two of the plump cupcakes on my plate.

Sitting back down, I eat off the icing and adornments on top. Alas, they have a fake sugary flavor, tasting like the Valentine's Day heart candies that come in little boxes. My mother-in-law, Rose, watches me pick off the frosting with my fork, whispering to Jake. I usually don't binge in public but they seem so happily amused I smile back, not so self-conscious.

"That's the story of our relationship—she licks off the frosting, then I eat the cake," Jake jokes. He kisses my forehead, then takes a bite of the vanilla cake as his mother laughs.

Does that mean I like frivolous desserts better but he's more meat and potatoes? Analyzing the hidden implications, I worry he thinks I'm a superficial dabbler, whereas he gets the deeper core. Or that I steal the most delicious parts of life and he only gets stuck with the discards.

"I heard you have good news," my mother-in-law says before we leave, and I tell her all about the *Up in Smoke* film option.

When we get home, there's a long message from my mom. She says Sheila's son's bar mitzvah was great, and she had a riot at Aliyah's birthday bash on Sunday. Hearing this makes me crave cupcake icing. I run through my book's repertoire of strategies to counteract food craziness: Stop Sucking in Sadness. Don't Eat Your Angst. Believe Your Pain. The Only Way to Change Is to Change. Instead of consuming something I'll regret, I sit down and journal in my notebook to uncover exactly why I feel slighted over something so minor. I want my mother to be more excited over my movie option than her granddaughter's party at Chuck E. Cheese's. My book is my baby, but she likes Aliyah better? How stupid to recover from the sibling rivalry I felt toward my brothers only to re-create the competition with their children.

My brothers' kids—ages three to ten—adore birthday bashes so much that every Saturday afternoon, when they come over to my parents' house, Mom has cake, candles, balloons, and party hats ready. Even when it isn't anyone's real date of birth, the little ones request the candle-and-cake routine. They all gather in the kitchen, where my mother gives them paper party hats, pulls a cake out of the fridge, sparks the candles, and shuts off the lights. In unison they blow out the candles, sing the birthday song, and eat dessert, which my mother adorns with ice cream and sprinkles.

On the Saturday after my *Oprah* visit, I was sitting in her bright yellow and orange kitchen, reading *The New York Times*, when I was unwittingly swept up in their ritual. Catching me taking the red flower off the side of the cake, Teddy giggled, pointed, and screamed, "Look, Aunt Julie stole the flower with her fingers!" All of my little nephews and nieces found this the most hilarious antic they'd ever witnessed.

"That's gross and rude," my mother scolded. "Don't eat

with your hands, Julie! Use a fork. Now the kids are going to do it too. You're being a bad influence."

I'd just been introduced as a bestselling antiaddiction guru on national television—a role model to millions—I wanted to say. But "Sorry" was all I could muster, feeling three years old again. It figured that my family found a way to erase my Oprah-rays and instantly catapult me back to childhood shame.

Before I left the next day—though it was not my birthday—Mom brought home my own little grocery-store cake, with white frosting and red and green roses. I reminded her I was on a diet. She looked wounded, as if I were rejecting an important offering. I realized nothing would make her happier than watching me eat her present. If overfeeding was how she gave love, than overeating was the way to accept her affection. So I dutifully scraped all the frosting off with a fork and devoured it in front of her, telling her it was delicious. Then I speed-walked eight miles around the neighborhood to burn off the calories and sugar shock, calculating that I needed to jog eighteen more miles to get rid of half of it. But the last time I tried running I hurt my knees and had shin splints, and I had to catch a plane out of there.

Weeks later I still can't decide if my mother's offering was insane, endearingly sympathetic, or infantilizing. Her pushing too much food on her grandkids reminds me how she used to overfeed me. Of course, by the middle of my third decade, it's my job to control my own urges. I wonder if there's ever a time you stop trying to overcompensate for what was missing in your childhood. I once asked my father why—out of all the professions in the world—my mother become an event planner. "She was an orphan," he reminded me. "She never had a birthday party."

On Monday Jake says his family loves all the presents I bought everybody. But he adds that when his mother was asking if I had any news, she wasn't referring to the movie option. Someone had shown Rose the Page Six item, so she thought we were having a baby. She was heartbroken to learn it was a hoax. Hurt by her disappointment, I fear Sarah is my pregnant doppelganger, trapping me in a trick motherhood funhouse mirror I can't escape.

I flash to the title of my last chapter on self-empowerment: "The Only Person You Can Really Change Is Yourself." I e-mail Lori to see if she's free for an emergency double walk-and-rant session. Then I leave a message for my client Fiona, saying I will be happy to write her law-school recommendation, apologizing for the delay.

chapter fifteen
the basketcase

April 27

I know I'm in trouble when I crave cupcakes more than beef-cake.

Thursday night, after Jake leaves a message he'll be late so I shouldn't wait up, instead of feeling sad, I'm elated. I check out the Web site for Crumbs cupcakes to see if they're still open, all ready to relapse. Alas, the store closes at eight. But wait—many more entries pop up: Cupcake Crazy, Bite-Size Buttercups, Cheeks Cupcakery, Kickass Cupcaking, MiniCakeMomma, Confetti Cuties, and Let 'Em Eat Little Cakes, which boasts "all cupcakes, all the time," with recipes, confessions, four-color photographs, and "cupcake paraphernalia." Oh my gosh. Here's the beauty of the Internet. I'm not alone with my fetish. I've accidentally stumbled upon the underworld of cupcake porn.

Visiting the Beautiful Babycakes Blog, I see a picture of homemade banana cakes with cream cheese frosting, topped high with walnuts and chocolate chips that make my mouth water. I stroke the keyboard, biting my jaw as if I can eat what's on the screen. The next one shows a swirl of coconut icing topped with yellow and white Peeps bunnies. In honor of Easter the deli across the street has decorated cupcakes in the window with pink and green frosting. Though it's been more than a month since my last frenetic sugar fest at Jake's sister's kid party, I dial the deli, embarrassed to ask the Cuban guy on the night shift how many Easter cupcakes are left. I order all six, overtip, and devour the candy coating first, then the vanilla-flavored bottoms.

I wait up for Jake, but when he finally appears at 2:15, I don't want to touch him or be touched. I wish he'd go away so I can have more food delivered. I remember Henry from OA, who banned consuming more than a whole chicken and hiding out in chocolate. I need to abstain from my very Manhattan obsession of ordering in from nearby delis and eateries that deliver around the clock.

I go to bed feeling too full. I dream that Jake asks if I'm having an affair with Dr. Cigar, but I can't answer because I don't actually know if anything sexual is going on with me and my shrink. I hope it isn't, knowing—even in dream logic—that a good therapist would never touch a patient. I wake up in the morning unsure of what my subconscious is questioning. I guess it's whether I can trust Dr. Cigar's judgment—not with my sexual appetite but with my hunger for food.

At our appointment on Friday, I confess all: the cupcake

relapse, the food-porn Web sites, my dismay that Sarah has yet to acknowledge the obsessive amount of baby presents I've sent her. I insist that having a kid does not excuse her from sending me a thank-you e-mail within a month. He calms me down by reminding me that for a first-time mother, having a newborn can be overwhelming and all-consuming.

Then I share last night's dream, not ashamed to reveal that I think my head is putting him in my bed. I add my interpretation that it's a positive step that he's replacing Ness in my reveries, though I still rely on Ness more when it comes to addiction.

"He's your militaristic rabbi and I'm the fat Buddha singing 'Don't worry, be happy,'" Dr. Cigar croons. "He's the high-voltage electric messiah and I'm the blue-eyed god of love."

"From a song?"

"From the Peter O'Toole movie *The Ruling Class*."

"You're right, I don't need a blue-eyed god of love saying it's cute when I overeat. I need a food-and-exercise Nazi to rein in this obsession," I say.

"Okay. I'll get with the program. Exercise helps, right?" he asks.

"I've been walking a lot with Haley and Lori, but I'm afraid it's not that aerobic. Should I try spinning or kickboxing?"

"Yes, rejoin your old gym." He tries to muster up a military attitude, but then dilutes it with a weak-sounding "Why don't you?"

"I stupidly only like to exercise in public when I'm thin and least need it. When I was younger I'd rush to the gym in a leotard, tights, sneakers, and no makeup. But as I get older, it's trickier to navigate around my vanity. Last time I was walking with Lori around Washington Square Park, I bumped into the woman who hired me to do seminars at the Self-Help Society. Now I'm afraid I'll run into my editor or publicist or book critics."

"You feel you have to live up to your thin author's photo?" he asks.

I nod, thinking lately I need to wear high heels, a tight skirt over Spanx, and a Wonderbra beneath a low-cut top exposing my cleavage to even get a "you look nice" from my doorman.

How tragic to be haunted by my own slender, perky young image, taken only two years earlier, on the back of my *Up in Smoke* book jacket—like *The Picture of Dorian Gray* in reverse. By the time my wit and brains have caught up with my face and body, I need my double chin airbrushed. I'm relieved that I nixed my publisher's idea of having a big picture of me on the jacket of *Food Crazy* in favor of showing Freud eating a cupcake, getting icing in his beard. Imagine if I had to constantly confront my glossy slim face with my real pudgy *punim* in bookstore windows across the country.

Then again, most aging females in the media spotlight have conflicts keeping up their looks. I read that while running for office Hillary Clinton and Sarah Palin fretted about their diets and traveled with stylists and hairdressers. The amount Palin spent to appear lovely seems justified to me. Hell, even Palin impersonator Tina Fey admitted she didn't get famous until she dropped thirty pounds on Weight Winners. Fey's multimillion-dollar book advance makes my desperation to drop thirty-five seem downright rational.

"I'm doing a book signing for the paperback *Up in Smoke* at the Wall Street Borders on Tuesday. At this weight, I'm thankful I waited to write about quitting sugar in *Food Crazy*," I tell Dr. Cigar.

"You've helped so many people quit smoking and get sober. You're a one-woman self-improvement machine."

I look down at the colorful rug on his floor. I can easily discuss my innermost demons and sexual dreams—with him as the macho hero—but I'm embarrassed by his compliment. "Well, I'm trying to sell books, so I'm being manipulative. And a control freak."

"I think you're generous and pretty cool," he says.

This line makes my heart pound and sink simultaneously. Someone with my overblown addictive personality should not be paying this guy to flatter me. It's obviously not helping me set food limits. I miss having a ruthless shrink to remind me of the dangers of megalomania and self-delusion. Ness once warned me that "surrounding yourself with sycophants will turn you into Mama Cass." Hearing the echo of his harsh criticism makes me feel protected from my worst traits, like he still has my back.

"On my way home I'll pick up a schedule from my old health club," I say.

"You should check out the gym down the hall," Dr. Cigar throws out. "They do private training sessions."

"I remember you mentioned it." He made the one-stop shopping joke at our first session, which sealed the deal. Tall, cute—and a good sense of humor, I recall thinking.

"Come on, I'll show you," he says.

I gather my coat and bags and follow him down the hall to a door with a sign saying NIMBLE HEALTH-FITNESS-LIFE. He turns the knob, but it's locked. When he knocks, nobody answers. "They must have left for the day. I'll get you a card and brochure."

"Thanks." I'm nervous standing this close to him. Is it because I've just divulged he was in my sexual dream? Sitting across the room with him in his leather shrink chair and me on the couch is safer. I ponder what would have happened if we met when he was a graduate psychology student and I a freshman hippie psych major with a cigarette dangling from my mouth. Would I have taken him to bed? No, at that point—when I went for bad boys—I would have rejected a guy like him as too nice.

Over the weekend a client celebrating his one-year anniversary of being smoke-free sends me an Easter fruit basket that comes with candy, crackers, and cookies. I appreciate the sentiment and thank him. But really I abhor receiving edible gifts. It's like an alcoholic getting bottles of booze. When it's happened in the past, Ness has advised me to view it as a hand grenade to get out of sight. I've given home-baked Christmas cookies to my doorman and thrown a box of Valentine's Day chocolates in the garbage. I'm about to toss out this latest unsolicited temptation when Jake sees it and says, "That looks great. How come nobody ever sends me stuff like that?"

"What about that production assistant who used to bake for you?" I remind him.

When he came home with her huge sheet cake, I asked him to never again show up with baked goods, and next time leave the cake on set. When he said I was overreacting, I reminded him that the underling who made it for him was 300 pounds and that he always says no matter how talented, women like her can't get a career in TV/film unless they downsize. I couldn't help but add: "Don't let her dictate what food is in your house, against the wishes of your wife."

Sometimes being self-protective means sounding like a selfish psycho-shrew.

I'm lucky I originally met my hunky husband at twenty-nine, when I was a hot, skinny, albeit chain-smoking *Femme* editor not as obsessed with food or exercise. Two packs of cigarettes a day were effective appetite suppressants. Before the no-smoking laws, I had a little corner office with a window where I could puff away. Eventually Jake made a huge push to get me to stop smoking and partying, offering to pay for my addiction therapy. Neither of us knew that would lead me to become a born-again Ness-quoting prophet—or that the side effect of my smoke-free sobriety is stringent food patrol. But once the lid is off Pandora's box, all my gargantuan ugly hungers slither out.

Based on my tendency to devour everything in the house in manic moods, I can keep around only low-cal foods I can resist. Jake hates my rigid restrictions. But as workaholics, we spend a lot of time apart. We can go out to dinner or get anything delivered within half an hour, I argue. After I dropped down to 128 and became friskier in bed, he accepted my wishes, and gave up his secret stashes of nuts, cheeses, Life Savers, and candy bars.

Now I stare at the bags of cookies inside the cellophane—lemon, peanut butter, and honey—not even my favorite flavors. "I have to get rid of this."

"Don't throw it out." He grabs it. "I hate when you do that."

"I should make myself sick to be polite to someone I met once, who won't even know the difference?"

We've had similar fights when my mother sends him the white-chocolate-covered pretzels he loves. He can eat one a week. He has that type of personality. His restraint gets on my nerves.

"You have to stop scavenging through my belongings for snacks," he often yells.

"You have to either sleep with my mother and get as fat as my father was, or get all the junk food out of this house," I threaten.

"So it's either you or white-chocolate pretzels?" he asks. "Tough choice."

"You have another office. Keep your food there," I suggest. His new work space at Chelsea Piers has a minifridge. He has at least a cubicle at every TV project he works on—where catered feasts abound. He likes to flit back and forth between the locations, never telling me where he'll be, as if his goal is to be unreachable. But he prefers to eat with me.

Meanwhile, by following my diet, he's lost fifty pounds since our wedding. Currently at six foot four and 230, he still isn't slim. When it comes to curbing my appetite, Jake's never the voice of reason. Though he reluctantly goes along with my strict food rules, his favorite words are when I whisper, "Let's go get some pizza." After we jointly decimate an extra-large cheese-and-pepperoni pie at a local pizzeria, I feel obese, greasy, sick to my stomach, and want to crash alone. He's gloriously happy and ready to get it on.

"Save me the lemon cookies and pears," he adds, looking at my yellow-ribboned basket longingly, as if I'm a mean mommy taking away his Hanukah present.

"You can't afford to buy your own cookies and pears?" I ask.

"Free food always tastes better," says the well-paid director. He takes the box of lemon cookies with him to his den.

I relent, telling myself he's right. I should keep the present. I've invited people over after my reading on Tuesday, so I can save the basket for company. I wrap it back up and stick it in the fridge.

. . .

Late Saturday night, while Jake sleeps, I tiptoe to the kitchen, rip off the cellophane, and eat every strawberry candy, along with the entire box of peanut butter cookies. I can hear the story of the wife at the Sugar Addicts Anonymous meeting confessing that sharing one cookie with her husband leads her to gain seventy pounds. I go back to bed angry at Jake, sleeping fitfully. I awake at dawn, unable to get back to sleep.

I spent thousands on therapy to understand my insanity and have already clearly learned that this is my limitation. Jake made me quit cigarettes and marijuana—not only because it's unhealthy, but because he hates the smell of smoke. How dare he not understand that I can't handle junk food in our house. Staring at his back, I work myself into a rage about letting him talk me into keeping the unwanted gift basket.

"Don't tell me to keep crap in the house I need to get rid of!" I scream, waking him up.

"What? What happened?" He turns over, rubbing his eyes.

"We should have thrown out that junk food. Instead I listened to you and ate cookies and candy and now I feel ill. I told you when I quit smoking that I can't keep sweets at home or I'll eat all of it at weird hours."

I get up, go to the refrigerator, and like a madwoman grab the fruit basket, march to the hallway, and throw it down the garbage chute. In a huff, Jake puts on his jeans, takes the box of cookies, and follows, tossing them out too. Then he marches back to his den.

"There. Are you satisfied?" he shouts. "I didn't even get to eat one of your damn cookies! Now are you happy?"

"You can't make this about me denying you sweets," I yell,

holding back tears. "Don't be like my mother and Dr. Cigar and ignore what I'm telling you. You have to understand that in certain manic moods I become a raging addict. I have a disease I have to get under control or it will control me." Perhaps for the first time, I realize I really do. "I'm sorry I'm not a normal person." Now I'm sobbing. "If I was normal, I'd probably be having babies instead of books."

He holds me, strokes my hair, and says, "If you were normal, you wouldn't have me."

chapter sixteen
the replacements
April 30

"Can I ask you something?" Haley asks. "Is Dr. Cigar enamored with you?"

"Why do you ask that?" Haley's the one enamored with me—especially since, on my recommendation, the editor who replaced me at *Femme* just printed Haley's article "The Yoga Guide to Guys" in the latest issue. She's a good walking partner since as a personal yoga teacher she's so limber and fast. On our first trek we do twelve laps around the park, six miles, while she asks my advice, shooting off rapid-fire work and love questions, the kind of tête-à-tête I find fascinating. Plus, she's spilling the inside scoop of her sessions with Dr. Cigar, so sharing a shrink adds intrigue.

"He asked about my connection to you. Last session he

said, 'So tell me what Julia's like at her seminars. I bet she's right in the hub of the whole New York scene.'"

I'm not sure if this is cute, comical, or crossing a boundary. Yet as the boundary-crossing queen, I just focus on what's important. "Is he helping you?" I ask.

"Yes. Even though he said he was overbooked, I did what you said and kept asking him for a steady appointment and he caved. Like you say in *Up in Smoke*—to get clean, don't take no for an answer. Everyone is either part of the problem, or part of the solution. I want him to be part of my solution." She's overly enthusiastic. I feel tired just listening to her, the way my shrinks must feel around me.

"How cliché. I need to get some better lines," I say, as we pass the Washington Square Arch on our first lap.

Sometimes I wish I was still circling the same path with Dr. Ness. But I'm phasing out our video chats, and it's nice to take on his role and play the maven to my younger clients. Having bright youthful acolytes seek my counsel has the added benefit of making me feel useful, as though my struggles have at least added up to a little wisdom worth imparting.

"I agree with you that Dr. Cigar has to quit smoking," Haley says.

Poor guy. It looks like he's going down in history with that moniker.

"He's such a warm, kind man," she adds.

"So kind," I echo. "Ness was much more critical."

"In *Up in Smoke* I thought Dr. Ness came off too harsh, like your father. You're used to a critical paternal figure. Repetition compulsion," she says in a quiet voice.

"Hey, that's insightful," I praise. Is she repeating a psychoanalytic connection from my book or has she come up with that on her own? "What else do you think?"

"It seems like you're too much of a perfectionist, with a distorted image of yourself. What if you've incorporated Ness's mean voice into your head?" Haley muses. "I mean, you actually look great. Pretty and vibrant."

"Thanks. But I'm thirty-five pounds overweight because of obsessive behavior," I explain.

"Everyone has food craziness," she says. "On a bad day I can still consume a whole box of those red gummi bears."

But she looks so skinny. "How much do you weigh?"

"I'm five foot seven, your height, and I weigh 123."

"That sounds underweight," says the thirty-eight-year-old obsessed with weighing just 5 pounds more than 123.

"Well, I have small bones." She shows me her wrist, small like Dr. Ness's. I put my chubby appendage next to hers; it's twice as big. "What size shoe do you wear?"

"Seven," she says. "Three sizes smaller than you—and your friend Sarah."

In *Up in Smoke* I reveal that Sarah and I both wear size-ten shoes. When Sarah read it, she responded, "Keep my Bozo feet to yourself." I apologized for using her for material, but reminded her that she saw an early draft and that she had first refusal rights.

I can't believe Sarah still hasn't thanked me for all the little-girl gifts I've sent. She hasn't even responded to the message I left making sure my presents arrived. I know she's really busy with the baby, but it's been like this for nine months. Ness didn't return my last e-mail either. It's like I'm stuck on a Tilt-a-Whirl where Sarah's and Ness's responses are controlling my internal switches, lurching my heart around.

"I used to be heavier. When I'd go out drinking, I'd wind up eating candy late at night. But now that I'm sober, it's more under control," Haley is saying. "Oh, did I tell you that my fiancé, Zach, is seeing Dr. Cigar separately?"

"That's good," I say. Lori and her husband are doing couples therapy with him, so I'm pleased my current therapist is now juggling the whole quartet.

"Do you think it'll get Zach to stop being a commitment phobe, the way Dr. Ness made Jake marry you?" Haley asks.

"Ness believes if both people get stronger, the couple gets stronger." It's as if I have a *Bartlett's Familiar Quotations* filled with Dr. Ness's words lodged in my memory bank.

"After meeting Zach, Dr. Cigar said the relationship isn't the disastrous mess he expected," she reports, and we both laugh at his amusing verdict.

"He has such a funny way with words," I say. "I'll have to get him to write his own book."

"Can I ask you something?" Haley still prefaces our talks like this, as if she has a million questions she wants to pose and is shocked she's allowed the chance. It's like the glee I feel when Dr. Cigar and Dr. Ness confide their personal secrets.

"Fire away."

"When Jake refused to get married and you two broke up, how long before he proposed?"

"Are you sending Zach packing?"

From what she says about her off-and-on suitor, I hope she gives him an ultimatum. "You can be ambivalent and still make a decision" is one of my adages. Or is it Ness's? They often blur in my mind.

"Jake and I split for two months but I really left," I say. "You have to actually leave: You can't fake it. I get the vibe you want to skip the step where you learn to take care of yourself—emotionally and financially."

"That's not true. Zach isn't supporting me." She's defensive. Her pale skin turns red when she feels cornered. "I pay part of the bills."

"When I told you to get your own place, you said you were too old to get a bunch of roommates in Brooklyn and do the suffering-artist thing again. That's like me saying I want to lose weight without exercise and eating less. Change is painful, but an endless cycle of staying stagnant is worse," I say in my guru voice, adding a pithy quote from Freud's colleague René Laforgue. "The only remedy is to break everything."

"I am," she argues. "I'm making progress."

"You've been living with Zach for four years, letting him pay your bills while you're still complaining he won't get married. Where's the progress?" I'm playing provocateur, the way Ness likes to.

"Zach asked if I'd join him on his business trip to Boston this week but I said no because I had to work," she spits out. "And this Writers House agent who saw my *Femme* article called about making 'Yoga Guide to Guys' into a book. Isn't that what happened with you?"

"Yes. That's excellent. You buried the lead." I'm catching on to Haley's personality—on the third mile she lets slip the most important news.

As I'm about to make a pit stop at the Washington Square Park rest room, an unshaven guy who looks in his forties stops her. He's wearing a baseball cap backward and holding the leash of a big dog.

"Hey, Max!" she calls, and the Great Dane jumps on her. Seems like an ex-boyfriend, though it's unclear whether Max is the guy or the dog. "This is my mentor, Julia Goodman," she says.

"*The* Julia Goodman?" he asks. When I nod he says, "Cool."

Hoping he won't say I look older and fatter than on TV, I

duck into the ladies' room, not crazy about big dogs or this hulking ex. If Zach's becoming a fellow Dr. Cigar groupie, I'm voting for him. When I come out, Haley waves good-bye to Max and we continue circling to nowhere.

"Who's the old lover who broke your heart?" I venture.

"How could you tell? Are you psychic?" She looks amazed.

"I had a bunch of self-destructive relationships when I was your age, so they're easy to spot."

"Max was an addiction for two years. The equivalent of heroin." She steals the line from *Up in Smoke*, where I compare each toxic substance I was hooked on to a specific bad boyfriend. "He's the film guy I went out with after college."

"Why are you still wasting your time on him?" I ask, guessing she is, but hoping she isn't. "So Zach's out of town and before you decide if you two are breaking up or doing therapy together, don't tell me you're already hanging out with another guy?" For a sexually open liberal, my conservative streak comes out when I feel protective, especially when my young clients confess horror stories filled with drugs, orgies, bulimia, cutting, or bad guys who seem dangerous.

"We're just friends." Haley's tone implies otherwise.

"Except he still wants to fuck you. And I bet he's married."

"Divorced," she concurs. "Though he lives with his new girlfriend. But nothing happened with us yet this round. We're just platonic now."

"Stay away from Max—and his dog," I advise. The way the animal jumped on her is proprietary, as if he knows her, or the owner is using his pet to play out *his* fantasy of jumping her.

"Well, Max came on to me the other night. We kissed, but then I left. When Zach called from Boston, I told him the truth—that an old lover expressed interest, but I slept alone." She looks pleased, as if this notion is poetic.

I roll my eyes. "That's not honesty, that's mind games."

"But it really happened," she says.

"You made it happen to make Zach jealous. You're not being emotionally authentic. Hanging out with a new guy when you're not finished with the old guy is hedging your bets, so you don't have to feel lonely," I declare. "If you're not getting what you want from Zach, make a clean break. You can't just substitute one human being for another. It never works. They're just not interchangeable."

As we walk by Fifth Avenue, I look up the street, realizing that I've been lying to myself about the same kind of love overlap. Instead of really quitting my old shrink and getting over him, I'm seeing his substitute while maintaining sporadic contact with Ness to avoid fully mourning his loss. Furthermore, since I've been incapable of cutting any internal links with Sarah, I'm using Haley and Lori to fill in the friend puzzle, jumping into instant intimacy, as if their combined spirit can supplant the absence of someone who's been my lifelong sister.

How hypocritical of me to accuse Haley of trying to outrun emptiness when that's exactly what I've been attempting to escape myself. Alas, all of my bait-and-switch strategies have been dishonest, which is why they're making everything worse. As I'm slowly finding out, there's no fast replacement for the important people in your world. When they leave you have to feel pain, if only to honor what they've meant.

chapter seventeen

changing furniture

May 22

Consulting *Food Crazy*'s affirmations, I vow to quit chasing after people who are unavailable (like Ness and Sarah) while allowing my hurt to surface and tell its own story. I stop phoning and e-mailing my unresponsive former pillars, trying to recapture the attention they used to lavish on me. It feels marvelous to refuse martyrdom and listen to my emptiness. Of course, the second I befriend my loneliness, my actual friend surfaces. "I'll be in New York for a doctor's appointment Friday" is Sarah's message. "I'm bringing Chloe. Want to meet her?"

Sarah's coming to town! I get to see her and her baby! She sublet her old apartment, so where is she staying? Not in Jersey again, I pray. If she wants to stay with us, I could make room for Sarah and her daughter. But I don't have any baby equipment. Should I run out and buy a crib, high chair, and playpen from Babies "R" Us?

So much for moving on. I return her call instantly and she picks up, like old times.

"I'm seeing my old ob-gyn to check out my cesarean scar," she tells me. "It's become infected."

Yikes. I hope she doesn't go into anatomical detail.

"Andrew's coming too."

"Oh, good." Funny, I'd forgotten her other appendage.

"While I'm at the doctor he wants to show off Chloe to the people at our old firm."

"Where are you staying?" I ask. "Want to stay with us?"

"My subletter's away for the week so we'll be at my old place. Are you free Tuesday at three? Want to visit uptown?"

"Free and clear," I say, not hesitating to move appointments with Dr. Cigar, Haley, and Lori to the next day. Substitutes can't compete with the real deal.

By Tuesday, I'm in automatic Jewish *bubbe* mode, forgetting I'm getting over Sarah, leaving too many messages, buying her and Chloe presents and picking up a bouquet of Korean deli flowers, then hopping a taxi to her place on Ninety-ninth Street and Riverside Drive.

"Hey, Julie, how are you?" She comes to the door in sweats and a T-shirt, looking pretty.

"I'm good. Did I wake you?" I'd guess she's my weight, though hatching a kid is a much more noble excuse for stomach flab than too many cupcakes. In fact, packing on only thirty-five pounds for pregnancy is a triumph, whereas my thirty-five-pound icing paunch is borderline pathological.

"I was napping. Haven't really slept in a month. Come on in. Andrew and Chloe will be back in an hour. She's wearing the black outfit you got her. It's so hip. Only in New York would they have boho baby black. Sorry, I look like hell with my huge belly and droopy boobs. And droopy hair."

"Shut up, you look like Scarlett Johansson." With lighter highlights in her shoulder-length hair and her big beautiful blue oval eyes, she kind of does. She's so worried about changes in her body she doesn't appear to notice mine.

"What cool purple roses. Thanks. There's still a vase around here somewhere." She roots around the cupboards in the kitchen, baby formula and bottles stacked in the sink.

Before her engagement, she broke through the walls to open up the room, inspiring me to do the same to my kitchen. I also copied her stainless-steel refrigerator-stove-microwave-dishwasher theme. It's as if we're still little kids and anything she has—Barbie dolls, a locked diary, love beads, Nancy Drew books—I'm entitled to and vice versa.

"Just cheap bodega flowers," I admit.

"Your favorite, the color of schizophrenia," she teases.

We used to joke that we know each other so well because we bonded in utero, while for exercise our mothers took long walks tummy-to-tummy during their first simultaneous pregnancy in Illinois. This was before they could afford help, workaholic fathers never home. Over the next five years, both baby machines were also blessed with three perfect boys. In Jewish tradition, the ultimate trifecta. A blessing on your head, all the Goodman and Sutton relatives shouted from the rafters. *Zol zein mit glick.* (It is with luck.)

Our moms' happy minihelpers were us, the tall-for-our-age, gawky, big-mouthed, big-footed, dark-haired daughters. Grandparents, rabbis at temple, neighbors, and strangers at Farmer Jack's grocery constantly stopped to remind Sarah and me how lucky we were to be the only little girls in the successful Goodman-Sutton legacy. The oldest, the firstborns, the apples of our daddies' eyes. But cleaning up after three kid brothers when we were kids ourselves wasn't so fun.

Our mothers insist it wasn't gender bias but the odds that made us feel inauspicious and outnumbered. Imagine three loud, messy minipeople with penises taking over the spotlight, leaving us eternally dethroned. When Sarah and I adopted each other, we swore we'd never be pregnant four times together. Turns out, not even once. Despite three and a half decades of overwhelming overidentification, a baby is the one thing she has that I don't want myself.

I scan her classy urban abode, the tall windows revealing breathtaking views of lit-up skyscrapers on all sides. We've spent countless hours here analyzing our addictions, our guilt for fleeing the Midwest and rejecting our mothers' feminine roles, the series of sucky studio apartments and even suckier suitors we've survived. Not to mention the multiple shrink sessions it takes to finally feel entitled to reside in regal residences, along with getting good husbands in the bargain.

Sarah's living room now sports a portable playpen in the center and baby toys strewn all over the floor, but none of her old furniture. I didn't know it had all been relocated too. The only things that are the same are the TV and the kitchen appliances. The short-term renter has only a small beige settee, folding table, and fold-out chairs. I miss Sarah's old leather couch and recall the jolt I had the first time I saw Dr. Ness's protégé's redecoration of his office. I'm like a rigid OCD patient who flips out at any slight change. Ironic for someone who makes a living demanding instant transformation in everyone else.

Sarah and I sit side-by-side on the little beige love seat. With more weight on our big bones, it takes us a while to fit comfortably, finally leaning against opposite sides and putting our large feet up near each other's faces.

"Everything went okay with your doctor appointment today?"

"Yep," Sarah says. "Want to see my scar?"

I really don't. "First open my presents." I hand her scented soaps and lotions, a satin shoe carrier, different-size Asian bags and minipurses—a travel kit I've assembled that implies: Keep coming back to visit.

"Thanks," she says, nodding but then distractedly returning all the little gifts to the yellow Pearl River shopping bag they came in. "We sublet this place to save some money. But I don't like being here without my stuff."

"Me neither." I'm still hoping she'll be able to talk Andrew into moving back here.

"We're putting it on the market so we can buy a bigger place in Ohio."

This bad news feels like a punch in the gut.

"I tried to talk him into buying a house in Williamsburg."

"Great idea. Get a house in Williamsburg!"

"Ms. Greenwich Village a Brooklyn fan? Have you ever been to an outer borough?"

"Well, the other choice is Cleveland," I say.

"He just really wants to stay in Ohio. He's happy there. What can I do?"

"So things are better with you guys?" I ask her.

We've never really revisited the problems she relayed during that horrible phone session in December.

"What do you mean?" She's avoiding the subject, as if she now resents my knowing what she's been through. Hey, I didn't campaign for the job as intervention counselor. She's the one person I don't want to be the guru to.

"Are you sure?" You could always come back here without him, I don't say.

"We're fine." She looks at me strangely, as if it's uncouth to throw a one-night relapse back in her face. Then she says, "We're trying to get pregnant again. That's why I've stopped breast-feeding. Dr. Wiley says if it doesn't happen soon, we'll try in vitro."

I'm floored. I know she's turning thirty-eight, but she just had one baby. It seems too soon for her to already be making another. Or is it just me who can't handle a second bundle? It feels like I just keep losing her—once to her husband and twice to motherhood. There are all these people between us now with more rights to her.

"Are you sure you're not…"

"I'm not pregnant!" I snap, agonized that Sarah thinks I'm that fat. "I just gained weight." The same amount that you did, I'm too embarrassed to admit.

"I didn't notice at all. But Katie read in the paper that you…"

"Oh, that was just a stupid press mistake." I'm relieved that's the reason she's asking.

"I thought you might have changed your mind."

When I shake my head no, she looks even more deflated than I do.

"Are you sure?" she presses.

"Listen, I'm so happy you're happy," I say. "But I love being a bestselling guru. I've never enjoyed anything so much in my life."

"You can be a self-help icon and a mother. All the celebrities are having babies now."

A roster of role models runs through my mind—Oprah, Suze Orman, Dr. Robin Smith, Deborah Tannen. None of my favorite successful female self-help sages have kids. Martha Stewart has one offspring, but no longer has a husband. Intense passion in work and love is what I want.

"I'm better off not," I tell her.

"You're already decided? You won't have any regrets?"

She looks at me hopefully, wanting to convince me to jump on the baby bandwagon with her. But I'm still haunted by her relapse, which really shook me. In actuality, it's liberating to not spend my adulthood as a mother or caretaker. Instead, Jake and I take good care of our careers, ourselves, and each other. If—as my book proclaims—it's never too late to have a happy childhood, the trick to my youthful glee rides on *not* re-creating my past or DNA with children.

Yet just for Sarah I say, "It's not over until it's over," leaving room for lots of interpretation.

"Are you afraid of the gaining-weight part? Is that why you don't want to get pregnant? It's not that bad, really. If that's your block, I get it and you guys could adopt. Or did you ever consider using your egg and his sperm and paying somebody to carry your baby for you? It's only twenty grand; you can afford it now. Since you said you put on a few pounds, you could just go to a spa to lose weight, come back with a baby the surrogate birthed from your egg and Jake's sperm, and nobody would have to know."

Whoa. Sarah's inquest seems like payback for all the intrusive inquiries and unsolicited analysis I've inflicted on my clients and shrinks. I'm not sure I owe my best friend the unadulterated truth right now, especially if it deflates her while she's vulnerable. I'm proud of her for giving herself what our mothers could, but I can't—or won't. So I settle for whatever little deception might help her get what she wants.

"Yes, we still talk about all the baby options," I lie. "But it's not on the front burner. At this point I'm focusing on Jake and my new book. Hey, did you eat today? Don't you need food? Should we order in?"

She finds the menu for a nearby Japanese place and orders us a bunch of brown-rice sushi rolls and edamame, insisting on treating when the delivery guy arrives. I turn on her TV to watch what Jake calls "a chick show" where two ambitious girlfriends in New York—a fashion designer and a magazine editor—are complaining how they can't find men who can handle their success. All talked out, we watch the show while laughing and eating from each other's plates with our fingers.

Then Andrew comes in with Chloe—a gorgeous baby with blue oval eyes just like her mother's. She's wearing the black baby karate pants I got her, with a pink top.

"What happened to her black shirt?" Sarah asks him.

"I changed her," he says. "All black is a bit much for a baby, don't you think? I want people to know she's a girl."

I cradle her, playing with her tiny fingers and toes, asking myself again if I want one. Miraculous as she is, I just don't have the mommy gene. As if reading my mind, Chloe spits up all over her pink shirt. And me. Grossed out, I hand her back to Sarah.

"When are you visiting us in Ohio?" Andrew asks, handing me baby wipes.

"First you have to invite me," I say, suddenly not all that upset they haven't yet. "Listen, I should get back downtown. I have an appointment."

"I puked all over my wittle pink shirt just for you," Sarah coos in baby talk. "Thank you for the cool duds, Auntie Julie.

Nice to meet you. I'll see you soon." She holds up Chloe's hand. "Now we go bye-bye."

"Bye-bye," I say, waving back.

After almost a year of overeating to sidestep my sad-ness, I finally feel ready to let go of my old best friend and my old best shrink. I speed walk all the way downtown in half an hour, sweating and crying as I soar past each crowded street corner alone.

chapter eighteen
the least secret life

May 31

Lori, who calls herself my "right-hand webbie," has been instructing me to approve all "friend requests" of people who appear sane, so I soon have tens of thousands of pals I've never met on MySpace, Friendster, LinkedIn, and Facebook. On Saturday, along with webstalking myself to check the paperback *Up in Smoke*'s Amazon numbers (I'm 284), I visit the social networking sites to publicize my readings and seminars and gauge my popularity hourly. The bombardment of friendship inquiries from around the globe makes me feel hip and happening.

On Sunday Amy McNally, my biggest Facebook "friend"— more like obsessive groupie—posts on my wall that she attended every one of my events when she lived in New York, though I barely remember her. She's starting a fan club in her new home of Tucson, Arizona—launching GoodmanGirl, her blog about me. She links all of my podcasts and TV and radio appearances, and posts pictures of herself wearing T-shirts with my adages: "Believe Your Pain," "Get Real and Feel," "Don't Light It, Fight It," "Say No to Substances & Yes to Yourself."

She also sends me a personal message that she's coming to Manhattan for business the next day and it would make her day-week-year-life to get an hour alone with me. I fear she might be too nutty and am about to beg off, when she says she's recently seen Dr. Ness in Phoenix. What? Seeing as a patient or spotting him like a paparazzo? How does she know where he lives or what he looks like? She promises to tell me "the whole scoop on Dr. N's Southwest practice." I haven't had a video chat or phone session with him in a month and am successfully weaning myself off of our cyberconnection. But I can't resist her tantalizing offer. I tell her to meet me for lunch at my diner at 2 P.M., dying to hear about my old shrink's new office and city.

When Amy walks in, I go to shake her hand but she hugs me. She looks twenty-five years old, my height, and chubby—I'd guess she's my current weight of 163. She has short chestnut brown hair with bangs like mine, and is wearing all black clothes.

"I can't tell you how incredible it is to meet The Julia Goodman! After I quit smoking and drinking using your methods, I bought twenty copies of *Up in Smoke*, for all my friends and relatives. I brought a few for you to sign." She takes out copies of the hardcovers. She's schlepped them from Arizona? Doesn't she know the paperback is lighter? Selfishly, I don't remind her since I earn more royalties from the hardbacks.

"Okay, sure. Thanks." I hate to admit I find this more endearing than insane. My vanity, along with my curiosity about Dr. Ness, is clouding my judgment. "Is Tucson close to Phoenix?"

"Few hours' drive," she says.

A new waiter comes to take our order since it's George's day off. I get my usual—diet soda and my idiosyncratic chef salad. Amy orders a bacon cheeseburger, fries, and regular Coke, which (irrationally) pisses me off. If I have to diet, how come she doesn't have to?

"Why did they push back the pub date of *Food Crazy: How to Stop Your Sugar Cravings* to the fall?" she asks.

"They didn't. What are you talking about?"

How does she even know the new subtitle we just added? Bonnie has made me swear I won't say the whole title in interviews yet. "Never mention a book they can't yet buy when there's one already in the stores," she advises. Studies show if readers can't purchase what they want, they buy something else and often won't return for yours.

"The description's on Amazon and your publisher's online fall catalog," Amy says.

"It's up there already? I haven't even seen it yet." So Bonnie has sworn me to secrecy while blabbing to the cyber set herself! "But it's supposed to be in the summer catalog."

"Coming out September 20. I advance ordered and they told me I'd get them on September 15. I wrote it in my calendar. Must piss you off they don't tell you this kind of stuff."

"No, it's not a big deal," I say, annoyed with Lilly. What good is having a big literary agent if she doesn't track what's going on with your book?

"So is Dr. Ness in *Food Crazy*? Did he help you edit this one too?"

I nod my head yes, but she's talking like we're all on intimate terms. "Have you met him?"

"Oh, I'm his patient," she casually lets drop. "Didn't you know?"

I find this extremely unnerving, as if what she's really saying is "Oh, I've been sleeping with your ex. Didn't you know?" The waiter brings out sodas and straws and I take a sip. I love to share Dr. Cigar with Haley and Lori, but Dr. Ness is a different story, especially since he left. Although if I'm no longer seeing him, it's not really sharing him, right?

"When did you become Ness's patient?" I ask, trying to match her casual tone and cadence.

"Right after I read *Up in Smoke*. It's been almost a year now." As she sips her cola, I wonder if she knows how many calories she's chugging.

"In Arizona?" I assume that's where they recently met.

"I started seeing him in New York, before he moved," she says cheerfully.

I feel as though a younger rival is not only having an affair with my ex-boyfriend but rubbing in that they've been bicoastal and closer than he and I ever were. "How did you find him?"

"Through your book, of course." She seems surprised I'm not aware of this.

"But I used a pseudonym for him."

"I found him in ten minutes. I'm a Google stalker," she says. "Literally."

"On Facebook it says you're a computer consultant." I let her know I checked, as if somebody would post "ax murderer" or "pedophile" on their profile to give you a heads up.

"That's my official title. But really, Fortune 500 corporations pay me big bucks to dig up dirt on potential CEOs and other high-level employees. I get the name and resume of someone they're thinking of hiring, and I can uncover the real story in twenty-four hours. Kind of an Internet detective."

"You told Dr. Ness you read my book?" I want to unravel this mystery myself.

"Oh, gosh, yes. I talk about you all the time. He said he's had hundreds of calls from people who figured out he was the addiction specialist in *Up in Smoke*. He never told you that?"

"No, he did," I pretend I'm in on this. "He's my mentor. It's my duty to spread the word."

"Does it bother you that I tracked him down through your book?"

"No, it's great. Anything that helps you stay clean and sober." Wanting to be a good guru, I stay in self-help mode. But if I'm responsible for that many referrals, he owes me a commission, or a discount. Still, I have a more pressing itch. "What's Dr. Ness's Arizona office like?"

"Bigger than his New York office, five hundred square feet. Lots of plants, fake but real-looking. Brown leather couches. Mahogany desk." It's strange how she intuitively knows how hungry I am for details. "Dim lighting. He spray-painted the light fixtures brown. It looks like there's coffee spilled on the ceiling."

I have found someone in the world who has an even worse Ness fixation than I do! "What else?"

"He has a huge screen for videoconferencing on his desk, which spooked me. Here I thought my lack of under-eye concealer wasn't detectable."

"You two do iChats?" I idiotically assumed he and I had an exclusive computer-video relationship. It's like learning a lover who dumped me has shared our special sex position with his new paramour.

"Twice a week, until I was transferred to Tucson. You sure this isn't weirding you out?"

That's the expression Sarah and I always use. Did I drop it in my book or an interview?

"Not a bit. What a terrific connection." I give her a fake smile, stung by the revelation she's replaced me on Dr. Ness's couch. "You didn't move there for him, though?" I can't help but ask, finishing my diet soda and ordering a refill.

"No, no. That was a coincidence. Well, when they decided to expand, my boss gave me a choice between Arizona and Ohio. What the hell would I do in Cleveland?" she laughs.

"Actually, my best friend moved there," I say.

"Serena in your book?" she asks. "Sarah Sutton, I Googled her too. Is she still working as an architect?"

"Not at the moment. She got married and had a baby," I explain.

"That must really be freaking you out," she says.

Bad enough she's checking out my friends and shrink. But can this Google stalker be Googling my thoughts too? She's the one starting to freak me out. For someone who prides herself on being naked and revealing in public, I suddenly wish I could be anonymous again. I wonder if this is how Jake and my family feel when they complain that being written about exploits their privacy.

"I think it's fantastic," I say. "Sarah's husband and baby are making her really happy."

"In your seminar, you said 'Love doesn't make you happy, you make yourself happy.'"

"I also said 'Hunt down your own happiness,' and Sarah's finding domestic bliss as a wife and mommy." What bullshit.

I'm afraid Sarah's throwing away all her training and a great career. But whenever I suggest she do part-time consulting or a freelance design gig, she gets annoyed and switches the subject.

"Dr. Ness and I had this big double session last week..."

"You do two sessions in a row?" I ask. He never once offered me a double.

"Yes, it's a hundred-mile drive so he's been very accommodating with his schedule."

He wasn't ever so accommodating with me. He was usually late and often tried to talk me into earlier sessions.

"I was going on about how jealous I am that he told you all of this really personal stuff about his family. He never divulges any intimate details about his life to me. I think you're his favorite," she admits.

Since his New York practice apparently consists of *Up in Smoke* fans, I damn well ought to be. But I find her admission endearing, as if the trophy wife is admitting to the original, "I can't live up to your image."

"Well, he's known me a lot longer," I throw out.

"You guys are still tight?" she asks, looking up at me sheepishly.

"Yup. Like Oprah and Dr. Phil," I lie. Actually that might not be off base since the tabloids say they're having a big falling-out over competing doctor shows.

"He opened up to you about personal things he's never even mentioned to me." She takes a bite of her cheeseburger, getting ketchup on her chin. I point and she wipes it away with a napkin.

I pick at a few strips of turkey in my salad. "Remember, I was interviewing him for my article and then my book."

"Is that why you changed so many facts about him?" She

slathers more ketchup on her fries. I'm about to warn her about carbs but don't want to call attention to my own food issues or weight gain, which thankfully she hasn't mentioned.

"I changed names, that was all," I say.

"What about making his older son into a daughter?"

"What do you mean?"

"In *Up in Smoke* the shrink has two daughters. But he really has a younger daughter and an older son. Did he ask you to change it so you'd be protecting his kid's identity or something?" she asks.

"No, he really has two daughters," I insist.

She shakes her head. "He has an older son. I Googled his name and Yale. Sam Ness is a junior. He's the only Ness there."

"He never told me his older daughter's name. Could Sam be a shortened version of Samantha?"

"It said 'Samuel Ness' in Dr. Ness's father's obituary."

"His father died? When?" I'm confused. He talked about his father all the time, as if he was still around. "There was an obit?" How could I have missed it? "I read the *New York Times* obits daily."

"It was in the *Lincoln Journal Star* last year. Google Nebraska and Theodore Ness at the same time. I brought some documents to show you." She pulls a folder out of her briefcase.

"You did?" Why would she schlep our head doctor's dossier across the country?

"I knew you'd be interested."

"I am." She wants to win my affection by spilling Ness's secrets and it's working. Our impulse disorders are overlapping. "Let's see."

She hands me a few pages. The first article says that "Theodore Ness" is survived by his children, including Michael Ness, and his grandchildren, one listed as "Samuel Ness."

"Why was his dad's obit in a Nebraska paper when the Ness family's from North Dakota?"

"They weren't from North Dakota. They grew up in Lincoln, Nebraska. I found their school and tax records. I wondered if he asked you to change details so nobody could track him down."

"Are you sure?" I ask, now completely hooked, like we're fellow addicts sharing a needle.

She nods yes and hands me a thicker stack of different documents.

"I've looked up Dr. Michael Ness on the Web," I admit. "But none of this stuff ever came up before."

"I do this professionally. I get a hundred thousand dollars a year to dig up dirt that nobody else can find." She vacuums up the rest of her fries. "If everyone knew how to do it we wouldn't stay in business."

"Is it legal?"

The waiter takes her empty plate. I nibble a slice of cheddar cheese before giving him my plate too. George gets upset when I don't finish my food but in a rare twist, I've lost my appetite. Has that ever happened before? I almost like it.

"The info is all in cyberspace. You just have to know the secrets of how to access it." She hands me an old-fashioned film still of a pretty, dark-haired, wide-eyed girl next to the monster-clad actor Boris Karloff. "I'll have a slice of apple pie with whipped cream," she orders. "Want some?"

If she's this much of a hog in public, what does she consume at home? She seriously needs to read *Food Crazy* to find out what's not feeding her that should be. If only I could fix what's not feeding me. Meanwhile, I'm preoccupied by the photo of the familiar-looking young woman. "Who is this?"

"That's Dr. Ness's mother in 1931," she says.

"Really?" Now that she says it, I see the family resemblance. Dr. Ness has large brown eyes, small nose, and high cheekbones.

"That's when she was an extra in *Frankenstein*, her only movie," Amy tells me.

"An extra? Her only movie? What do you mean? She was a famous actress."

"Nope. That was it for her."

"I'm sure you're wrong," I argue. "Dr. Ness made it clear she'd starred in hundreds of movies until her alcoholism destroyed her career and all her marriages."

"Not true. She gave up acting to be a wife and mother."

"She had four children and Dr. Ness was the youngest?" I ask, doing the math in my head.

Google Stalker nods. "Yeah, that part of your book checked out. But not the part that she'd had four husbands or was an alcoholic who lost touch with her kids. According to the county records, after she divorced Dr. Ness's father she only remarried once and they stayed together until the guy died. I found these fundraisers and wedding-anniversary parties where all the kids showed up with their spouses. Here, look." She gives me other documents and small-town newspaper pictures confirming what she says.

She slurps up her apple pie without guilt while I look over the pages. I'm confused and queasy. Oh my God, Dr. Ness has lied to me about everything! I'm stunned. And hurt. And betrayed. And all of a sudden nervous, since I repeat everything he's told me about his past word-for-word in *Up in Smoke.* Many of the articles about my book in major papers make reference to the shrink revealing the substance problems of his own wacky family. Though I've changed his name, if Amy can find out the truth by Googling, others can too.

I wasted so much worry that future readers of *Food Crazy* will think I'm a fat fibber if I'm not skinny. Now I'm way more petrified that past *Up in Smoke* fans will discover these discrepancies and assume I've falsified details of my earlier recovery too. It's like James Frey's *A Million Little Pieces* mess. Or the time the coauthor of *The Rules* got divorced. This will be worse, like learning Dr. Ruth is really a virgin, Suze Orman is declaring bankruptcy, or Deepak Chopra is a homicidal maniac. If Ness has been fraudulent, that makes me his partner in fraud.

When discussing my ex, the Sociopath, Ness once surmised that my former boyfriend made up stories to keep me by his side, then convinced himself the grandiosity was true. But when my exalted onetime shrink was faking his background, I was a loyal follower with no plans to ever leave him. And Ness has too much self-awareness to stumble into sociopathy, doesn't he? So what could be his motivation to lie to me?

Much more important, if the guru who has mended my addiction problems turns out to be delusional, then I've been cured under false pretenses. That could mean my smoke-toke-and-alcohol-free sobriety, financial gains, and marital success no longer count. Although I've been clean and sober for almost three years, on some level it might mean I'm not really fixed! I'm afraid all my healing and supposed wisdom will unravel like the tall tales he's been shoving down my throat.

· · ·

After lunch I run home and e-mail Dr. Ness about my lunch with Google Stalker, asking why he's told me he's from a different state, his mother has been an alcoholic in many well-known movies with a whole bunch of husbands, that his father was alive, and that he and his first wife have a daughter, not a son. The gender of his oldest child bothers me most because he's shared elaborate stories about her. I hear them echoing in my head. How she's cried after he's shown her up at tennis but he won't let her win. How she's refused all therapy. Has trouble adjusting to Yale. "She," always she! I'm sure because I've written down "she" in my journal and mention his older daughter in *Up in Smoke*. I never make mistakes like that and he has never corrected the pronoun.

I leave messages at all of Dr. Ness's numbers, telling him it's an emergency, begging him to call back as soon as he can. Not wanting to believe Amy, I Google Lincoln, Nebraska, and find the Nesses, who it turns out have lived there for a century. I look up North Dakota and can't find anything with the right names. I'm so stunned I can't stop punching dates and locations into the computer to uncover what other false data he's been dishing. My level of frenzy is exaggerated—as if I've caught my husband happily ensconced with his second family that I never knew existed. I e-mail Ness four more times, demanding answers. I'm becoming Google Stalker on steroids.

A few hours later his response pops up in my inbox. "Yes, I have a son at Yale. Perhaps your psyche turned him into a her since you identified with my older child."

"You said daughter. That was real," I write him back. "You transsexualized him yourself! You called your mother a raging alcoholic so that's what I wrote!"

"I think she was, but when she got sick ten years ago she had to stop drinking. It's a subjective term. Once you suffer from alcoholism, AA says you're always an addict in recovery."

"No. You drink or you don't," I type back furiously. "There's honesty and there's lies!"

"Julia—in philosophy there's no objective reality," Ness answers, dryly. "What's real is what we perceive. The idea has deeply influenced my views. For you, my Yale child became a she because you identified with that person. That's as it should be. For you, that child should be a she although, according to literal and subjective reality, it is a he. My mother became more horrible to you because you fear she hurt me. The exact story of what happened isn't important. What's significant is that she's an extension of you."

"That's pseudointellectual crap." I pound the computer keys. "Yes, you were a father figure. But I overidentified with your daughter because you talked about her. Why say you're from Dakota when you're not? That your mom was a famous actress in many movies when she was just an extra in *Frankenstein*? That she had four husbands when she was married twice. How would you feel if you thought your shrink Dr. Cox lied to you? What the hell happened to leading the least secretive life?"

Dr. Ness doesn't answer. I sit at my computer for hours, hoping he'll continue our fight, but he doesn't. I try another few e-mails and phone messages, but he's gone.

When Jake comes home late that night, I spill the saga.

"It's not that big a deal," he says.

"What do you mean?" I'm shocked. "The guru I trusted most, who insisted the way to be happy and successful was to lead the least secretive life, invented a whole life for himself that isn't true."

"It's just some minor details. He probably wanted to be a role model for you, and for his life to neatly fit his theories. He's just human, and has a ton of patients who each need to hear different angles of his story. Plus, he might have been trying to protect his privacy."

"I don't know why he would do that when he knew it was going to see print."

"The pillars are tired of being written about" is Jake's verdict.

"What the fuck does that mean? You're identifying with him and taking his side?"

"Well, it's intrusive and bizarre to have personal details about yourself, your bad habits, and dialogue you really said spilled in somebody's book. I don't like it. Neither does your family."

Aha. So this could be punishment for my past indiscretions in print. *Six Characters Seeking Revenge on an Author.*

"Maybe he was trying to keep some of his own story for himself," Jake adds.

Dr. Ness has mentioned that he's rewriting *Unhooked* on his own. "But he could have told me this is off the record or that he's saving that material for his project. Or he could have said it's none of my business."

Jake looks at the papers on my desk, picking up the black-and-white picture of the pretty seventeen-year-old future Mrs. Ness in the film still Google Stalker gave me. "Who's the cute girl next to Boris Karloff?" he wants to know.

"You wouldn't believe it."

He stares at her carefully, then glances at me and says, "She looks just like you."

part
four

chapter nineteen
foreign exchange

June 3

My time is running out to shrink myself thirty-five pounds before my pub date shrinks my career to smithereens.

With the deceptive Dr. Ness still not returning my messages and thus banished from my brain, and Dr. Cigar's advice unable to help me drop an ounce, I am ripe for a new diet guru. So I perk up when Erasmo, a young nutritionist I know, sends me a link to his blog, Bite Me. It's filled with amusing articles he's written: "Gummi Bears Do Not Count as Fruit," "100 Tricks to Cut 100 Calories," "Convoluted Claims of Popular Diets," and an "All-Star of the Day" column featuring a picture of kiwi, shrimp, or oatmeal that he interviews as if it were a celebrity. I call him to share my latest nonnutritional nightmares, then beg him to be a non-OA version of my new food sponsor. I bet a good-looking, slender, vain, gay twenty-seven-year-old Latino Manhattanite will understand my complex food craziness. Erasmo agrees to do it for free if I help him turn his blogging project into a book, declaring that my dropping the big three-five I've gained in the sixteen weeks before my pub date is "totally doable."

Upon questioning, I learn he's my height, five foot seven, and 146 pounds—thinner than I am—and he's never been heavy, but too skinny. He eats trail mix all day to keep weight on. I want to shoot all the scrawnies out there who consider this a problem, along with faux smokers who puff one cigarette at parties. He lives with his rich boyfriend in SoHo, where he's the chef of the household, cooking wheat couscous, quinoa, and meat substitutes, while cutting out unhealthy crap like artificially flavored frozen yogurt.

"Uh-oh, what's wrong with frozen yogurt?" I ask.

"It's processed with garbage like corn syrup, citrates, phosphates, and other chemicals," he says. "Can't you tell how phony it tastes?"

"No, it's one of my favorite food staples," I admit.

"How unsophisticated is your palate!" He sounds incredulous.

Good—I can use a discerning critic to replace that rat Ness. As in a phone session with a new potential therapist, I relay my weight, exercise, and addiction pathology. Erasmo barks orders: Drink water instead of diet soda, no fake sugar, eat more vegetables, make all fruit—except for dried fruit—free foods, quit salt altogether ("restaurants add too much sodium, which will make you look bloated in pictures and TV"). Smart way to motivate a vain author into submission: the vanity diet.

"Can I eat the icing off cupcakes once every two weeks?

Or once a month? Since it's my favorite craving." In my frazzled Ness-less state, thinking of losing anything else is too painful.

"Will you ever be able to eat the icing off of one cupcake, enjoy it, and then stop?"

"No," I confess. "I usually eat frosting off of three or four cupcakes. Once it was nine."

"Then do you feel satisfied and call it a day?" he probes.

"No. Then my craving gets more intense and I want chocolate or candy."

"If you're working with me, you have to swear you'll quit the junk foods that trigger your extremes," he declares. "Let's just not go there."

Dr. Cigar lets me justify not letting go of junk food. But Erasmo's right, I just have to stop going there. It feels like I'm being ordered to give up a close friend—after I've already lost cigarettes, alcohol, diet pills, my beloved shrink, and best childhood buddy. Deprivation overload.

"Okay," I say, assuming he'll next nix the deli salad-bar salad I just tried—with olives, artichokes, cheese, chicken, nuts, and chickpeas. But he approves wholeheartedly.

"Eat that every single day. Those are healthy carbs and protein. If you enjoy what you're eating and feel full, you won't feel out of control later."

But later I'm invited to a fancy champagne toast at Bergdorf Goodman that my publisher is throwing for my fellow girl groupie Frederica Follet, the very one who has finked on my fatness to the *New York Post*. And who is so skinny her nickname is Filet. Why are they going all-out at a fancy shmancy overpriced uptown boutique for such a tacky book? We share an agent and editor, so I'd have to see my whole team—whom I've been avoiding since the pregnancy rumor hit Page Six.

But Priscilla—the coolest, least-demanding editor on the planet—e-mails that she expects me to show my face. Damn! How to do that while hiding my extra flesh and not filleting Frenchie?

I buy a new Spanx girdle that I squirm to fit over control-top pantyhose, then put on a flattering black skirt with black hose, black low-cut top, five-inch black heels that kill my feet but will hopefully detract from my padding by adding height. I curl my hair to cover half my face, try contour blush to define what's left of my cheekbones. I'm afraid I'll be so anxious I'll end up overeating in public, calling attention to my bigger bod. I decide to stick to protein but Erasmo e-mails that fruits and vegetables are better.

"Beware nuts!" he warns. "They're high in protein but a cup of almonds is 800 calories."

For that amount, I can have icing off two cupcakes.

At the soiree, dozens of chic bony New York women mill around—all wearing black, ruining my camouflage by contrast. Even in dim lighting I'm obviously the heaviest ebony-clad chick here. I nervously chomp on carrots and celery. Frederica's in all black too, but she's three inches taller and thirty pounds thinner than I am. She's posing for photographs, so I don't have to be all kissy kissy with her. The Spanx elastic waist over the tight hose top are both digging into my stomach and I'm about to teeter-totter out when Priscilla and Bonnie spot me and rush over.

"Julia, how are you? I haven't seen you in months. Except on TV. You were stupendous! I was joking that you've been avoiding me." Priscilla hugs me. "Don't you look glamorous?" She's pretty but in a reserved, understated way, wearing silver-rimmed glasses, a gray skirt, and flats.

"Thanks. I've been dying to see you and catch up." I stand

up straight, sucking in my tummy. I decide not to bring up the change in my pub date, feeling too fat to fight. "Just been so busy with work."

"New project?" Priscilla prods. "When do I get to see it?"

"Lilly said not to mention it to anyone yet," I whisper, having no idea what my next book will be. *Off the Couch: A Shrinkaholic Quits Therapy* or *Clean Break: How to Quit Quitting Things*? "Of course you'll be the first."

"We have first option, so you don't have a choice," she jokes.

Bonnie, in her usual navy blue pants outfit, looks me up and down, trying to figure out what I'm hiding. "Your outfit's a bit overdone," she whispers. "Frederica's the glamorous Frenchwoman. She's Ginger. You're Mary Ann, the girl next door, remember?"

When it comes to classic TV, I see myself as more Agent 99 on *Get Smart*, not the drippy Mary Ann. "I'm on my way to a black-tie charity function," I make up on the spot. "At the museum." I stand tall, holding in my stomach and pushing my hair over my jowls.

"That skirt style isn't so flattering," Bonnie says. Little does she know it's very slenderizing. "Did you see your guru sisters Nancy and Ronit? Want to get a picture?"

I want to throw up. "I'd love to but I'm actually late. Another time?"

"You can't go yet. We have great news for you," Priscilla announces. "Frederica is endorsing *Food Crazy*. She gave us a great blurb that we're putting on your cover!"

"How fabulous of her." My heart sinks at the thought of that French faker endorsing me. Everyone knows we have the same agent and editor so it's clearly logrolling. She hates me as much as I hate her. What a sly move on her part—doing our publisher a favor, remaining their little darling, while getting a free ad for her book on my cover.

"You're bumping Suze Orman's 'Julia Goodman's one smart cookie'?" I ask, dejected.

"Suze's the money mentor and there's already a financial book with the words 'smart cookies,' about making more dough. Frederica's the food sage." Bonnie gives me an annoyed look, like I'm an ingrate not to be thrilled. "Much more crossover audience."

"What did she say about *Food Crazy*?" I'm sure it's some passive-aggressive snipe like "She's the American version of me." My pantyhose are so tight I can barely breathe.

"Okay—are you ready?" Bonnie asks.

"'Fearless, canny, clever, sexy,'" Priscilla recites, as if it's a magic code that will unlock the door to megastardom.

It's actually pretty good. For *Up in Smoke*, the quit-smoking guru Allen Carr only gave me the boring "Smart and entertaining," and everyone was overjoyed to get that.

"She gave you *four* adjectives!" Priscilla emphasizes.

"That was nice of her," I concede, bending down to pull my hose up a bit. But my nail causes a snag. Oh, God, I've torn the hose under the Spanx and the rip is running all the way up the back of my leg. I stand up straight, smiling, leaning against the wall, pretending nothing's wrong.

"There's the guest of honor now," Bonnie says as Frederica comes over and kisses both of my cheeks. "We were just sharing your great blurb with Julia."

"Thank you," I suck in to say.

"No, no, no, ees my pleasure." Frederica drips phoniness. "Julia, was big mistake from reporter on Page Seex. She says you are having baby and I says, 'I don't know, would be good, no?' And next day came out bad in paper."

"Oh, don't worry about it," I say, thinking she's an author on this country's bestseller list but she can't figure out English grammar yet.

"Excuse me, are you Julia Goodman?" a tall young woman in a blue dress interrupts to ask.

When I nod, she swoons. "I loved your book. I took your 'How to Quit Anything' seminar last year. I quit smoking and drinking that day. It changed my whole life!"

The timing couldn't be better if I staged it myself. "I have a new book coming out," I say.

"You can advance order it online," Bonnie throws out.

"I will. The minute I get home," Fan Girl giggles.

"Okay, we'll leave you to your public." Priscilla beams in approval. "Let's do lunch soon."

"Great." I wave as they start to walk away, hoping nobody will try to hug me so I don't have to move.

"Next Tuesday?" Priscilla offers.

"I'll e-mail you," I say. Priscilla is vice president of her division, busy and high up on the editor totem pole there. I'm usually honored on the rare occasions she asks me to get together but now I need to worm my way out of a brightly lit meal during the day.

"Didn't you say if we followed Frederica's advice we'd become chain-smoking alcoholics?" Fan Girl asks. "You said her book should be called *French Females Are Lushes with Lung Cancer.*"

"Ssshhh." Do I really say things like that out loud in public? Good line, sounds like me. Thank goodness she's out of the earshot of my editor, publicist, and Frenchie. "You must have heard me wrong, honey. What's your name?"

"Abby Schwartz."

With her dark hair framing pretty features and no makeup

except for red lipstick, she looks like a college-age Sarah, which (irrationally) makes me trust her.

"Listen, Abby. I need your help," I say quietly. "I'm having a wardrobe malfunction. If you get my long black cashmere from the coat check we can meet tomorrow, do a free one-on-one session and see if there's anything I can help you with."

"Really? It would be such an honor to hang out with you," Fan Girl gushes, taking the ticket and rushing back with my wrap. I throw it on, take her card, and teeter slowly outside to hail a cab, which thankfully stops right in front of me. I feel stupid, hungry, on edge. At home I take off my shoes, peel off the forty-three-dollar girdle and ripped thirty-four-dollar control-top hose and throw them in the garbage, change into a T-shirt and elastic-waist sweats so I can breathe. I order in honeydew and cantaloupe melon and plunge it all down my throat fast. I'm bloated afterward but at least it isn't icing.

The next day I e-mail Fan Girl to see if she wants to do a walking session. Unlike Haley and Lori, she's not the least bit interested in a walk-and-talk date. "Let's do lunch or dinner," Fan Girl writes back. But I just don't need any more meal mates in my life, and send her a signed book to thank her instead. Meanwhile, I have an important business meeting at my diner with Erasmo—who is gung ho about inspecting Julia's Salad.

"Four ounces of turkey, two ounces of cheese, low-cal dressing. Not bad for your main meal," he declares. "But twenty big black olives is two hundred calories. Do you adore olives?"

"No. Olives aren't my favorite." I pull a can of caffeine-free Diet Coke from my purse. "They don't serve caffeine-free sodas so I bring my own." George sets a glass with ice and a straw on the table.

"When I said quit diet soda, I didn't mean drink caffeine-free. All of it contains phosphoric acid, which raises your body's phosphate levels and extracts calcium from your bones."

"Really? I have to give up diet soda too?" Isn't there anything I can safely put in my mouth anymore?

"Yes. Switch to water," Erasmo orders me while eating an omelet with spinach and cheese, wheat toast, and home fries.

"Why do you get to eat that?" I point to the potatoes.

"Because I'm trying to gain weight, not lose, honey," he says. "What's stressing you out so much today?"

"I saw my editor, publicist, and mortal enemy last night and I'm afraid they can tell how fat I got. Even when I stick to my diet, it's like my body wants me to stay this weight." I dig into Julia's Salad, which I'm sick of.

"The 'body weight set point' theory." He spreads butter on his toast, luckily whole wheat, which I find bland. "Set comfortable weight that your body keeps bouncing back to. When you eat less you feel like you're starving."

"So I'm locked in a battle with genetics, my addictive personality, my set point, and my age—since my metabolism is slowing down."

"We need ten percent fewer calories and more exercise as we age. But you're an intensely single-minded, type A obsessive. If you put your mind to following the new diet I gave you, you'll do it." He sounds as upbeat as I do at my seminars—it's really fucking annoying.

"That added fruit you suggested is bloating me out," I say. "Maybe I should go back to Dr. Ness's plan of eating just twice a day, with no other food consumed. That's the only diet that ever worked for me. As I say in *Food Crazy*, repeating the same meals might be tedious but an addict is better off without choices. Variety stimulates the appetite. The more monotonous my diet, the less I ate. You know, you can actually bore yourself thin."

"But on his plan, you said you were always hungry and felt deprived." He pours ketchup on his great-looking greasy potatoes. Jerk.

"You say that like it's a bad thing," I joke. But then I get serious. "Look, feeling deprivation doesn't have to be a horrible punishment. Ness says I should view it as a chronic condition that can easily be controlled, like someone who has dyslexia or diabetes. You don't let it ruin your outlook. You just get the facts and treat them. The fact is that a normal amount of food doesn't satisfy me. I don't have the button that turns off when I'm supposed to feel full. I just accept that I'm a bottomless pit of emotional hunger."

"Why? What's wrong?" He looks upset, as if I've confided I have a fatal illness.

"I've always been this way. It's how I'm built. My addictive personality is like a deformity."

"Really? That's so sad." He looks as though he's about to cry.

"It's actually a triumph that by dealing with it head-on, I get such a great life. I just have to work harder than most people to keep my impulses under control." I stare at his fries. If he goes to the bathroom I'm stealing one. "Dr. Ness brainwashed me to believe my dreams came true *because* I quit my bad habits, so if I relapse the good disappears. I accept the trade-off." I want to kill Ness while quoting him at the same time.

"Even if it's not true?" Erasmo is dismayed that I'm turning his rational theories on their head. "But lots of smokers and drinkers are rich, happily married, and have nice homes."

"Not me. It's easier for me to quit something than to be

moderate." I push my empty plate away, noting he hasn't finished his fries or toast. How can he order toast and fries and not finish? "Normal rules do not apply here."

"Okay, I'm starting to get what you're up against. But I'm surprised you can't even add fruit."

"When I ate that melon you suggested, it made me crave junk food."

"So melon is your gateway drug? Damn, I've never heard that one before."

"Most addicts get clean in AA, or at a dry-out clinic. My method involves a psychoanalytic understanding of my idiosyncratic addiction patterns."

"But you were a smoker, not a crackhead. They don't have dry-out clinics for cigarettes."

"You're acting like there's a hierarchy for bad habits. Any addiction can be destructive. My sugar issues are threatening my career and hurting my head and body. Most diets are designed for the masses—it's why half the country is still obese."

"Basic nutritional guidelines work for ninety percent of the population," he argues. "You know that *Seinfeld* episode about Bizarro Jerry where everything was opposite of what you expected? With your food craziness, you're Bizarro Julia."

"Exactly! Now you're getting who I am." I pay the check.

"Oh, did you read my blog, by the way?" he asks. "Could it be a book or does it suck? Give it to me straight."

"I think you have a timely idea and a funny, distinctive voice. To turn it into a self-help book, be more topical and provocative. You should promote or trash specific celebrities, low-cal chefs, or bestselling diet-book authors. Maybe try a service piece for *Femme*, to get your brand with your name on it published. Call yourself Erasmo, Bite Me's Food Guru. The rag is monthly, so aim for Thanksgiving. Something like 'Best Tricks for Staying Trim on Turkey Day.'"

"What good ideas!" He pulls a small notebook from his briefcase and starts scrawling notes. "I could roast Rachel Day's dumb Dunkin' Donuts endorsement. And quote tips from diet/exercise gurus, like that buff lesbian Leona on HBO's *Work Me Out.*"

"Exactly! I'll be happy to take a look first, and then send it to one of my old colleagues. That'll get heat on your project. Then I'll show you how to use the clip at the start of your thirty-page proposal," I say. "So you think I should just quit the frozen yogurt every day?"

"How many ounces of the frozen junk are you eating?" he asks.

"I don't know. I don't like the taste of fresh yogurt and I'm ODing on too much fruit." I lead him outside. "Everybody wants to hit the youth market in the blogosphere."

"Are you sure it's low-fat?"

I take him to the deli, pointing to their frozen-yogurt machine. The deli guy, Amad, puts a little in a cup and hands it to Erasmo, who tastes it. "It's low-fat," he concurs. "Remember the *Seinfeld* episode where they lied about the calories of diet yogurt?"

"Have you memorized decade-old reruns of that yuppie show?" I ask. "There's this great Gail Parent novel *Sheila Levine Is Dead and Living in New York* where the heroine has a diet dessert analyzed and when she gets the results, she wants to kill herself. Why would I want to live in a world where a man would lie about calories?" I paraphrase.

"Show me the size she gets," he says to Amad.

"Sure. Extra-large mix, three Diet Coke caffeine-frees,

apartment number nineteen F," Amad recites my usual order, handing Erasmo a huge container the size of a beer stein.

"Can I take that with me?" Erasmo puts the cup in his backpack. "Okay, I'll crunch out the numbers for you and e-mail you later." Now he sounds like my investment banker. At least it looks like I've finally found a food sponsor I can brainwash into understanding me.

An hour later he e-mails, "You've been eating thirty-two ounces of yogurt for 500 calories every night. Your regular salad's about 800 and your fruit is 200, which brings you to 1,500 calories a day. Let's get rid of all olives, aim for a smaller yogurt, double your exercise to an hour six days a week, and you'll be healthier and make your 128 goal by your pub date."

How ridiculous would it be if, after all the overanalyzing, the entire solution turns out to be an eight-word haiku: no cupcakes or olives, smaller yogurt, keep walking.

"Okay, you're on," I promise, kissing olives and too much nightly frozen yogurt good-bye. It feels as if life is an endless stream of substances I have to give back to the gods of pleasure. I hear the echo of a line from a Bob Dylan album Jake's been playing, something about how just when you think you've lost everything you find you have even more to lose.

chapter twenty
just because you're paranoid

June 20

Dr. Cigar is ten minutes late. When he comes to the waiting room to get me, he shuts the door and blocks it. "Wait here," he says with an air of espionage.

The building's ancient elevator is slow and I guess his last patient, who is on the way out, must still be standing outside in the hallway. "Isn't Lori on Fridays before me?"

He shakes his head no.

"So Haley's here?" He's only seeing two of my clients, along with their male counterparts. I wanted him to stem Tiffany's minor obsessive-compulsive disorder. But he's referring her to his brother, the uptown psychiatrist, who can prescribe medication. I recall Haley mentioning a couples session with Zach—I didn't know it's right before mine. So it's Lori-Haley-me in a row, Dr. Cigar's Goodman spring lineup.

"I was afraid you were late because you were taking care of my referrals, then I thought that was just my neurotic sibling rivalry issues talking. But it was perceptive, not pathological." This amuses me. "Just because you're paranoid doesn't mean someone's not watching you."

"Sorry I'm tardy. I'm so busy I can't breathe."

I feel guilty I've overrecommended him but Dr. Cigar and I have a good yin-yang balance. I hurry him up, he slows me down. It's like the dynamic between me and Jake. My mate moves so slowly his folks ironically call him Flash, while my dad still calls me Speedy Gonzales, after the "fastest mouse in all Mexico" cartoon I liked as a kid. I stare at the salt-and-pepper tresses on Dr. Cigar's head and the beige billowy shirt making his shoulders look muscular. I just now notice that he and Jake look alike—both big Jewish guys with good hair who wear black jeans and eighties-looking shirts. So that's why I'm drawn to Dr. Cigar—not because he knows Dr. Ness from shrink school but because he resembles my spouse.

He checks the elevator situation down the hall.

"I could just say hi to her," I throw out.

"She was upset. She might not want you to see her crying," he explains.

That's ultrasensitive. Or maybe inappropriate to reveal. I think of Suzette, a meek makeup artist who took Dr. Ness's number, ended our friendship, then flipped out when she saw me in his waiting room. When I complain to Jake about scenes like this, he shares the Yiddish expression "So what are you so mad at me for? I never helped you," about how people resent do-gooders. Or he says, "Stop hooking up every loony tune you know with your fucking shrinks."

When the coast is clear, I follow Dr. Cigar to his office, then let him know I'm in a mood.

"Because of food grenades and life? Have you left the cupcake underworld behind?"

"Yes. But now I'm nervous about our tax audit, hate this new diet, which is killing me, and have four all-day seminars next week. Jake's on a work rampage. And Google Stalker says Ness is in New York. For the first time ever, I'm refusing to see him when he's in town. I'm putting my size-ten foot down."

"Brain overload. You need a break. You're professionally shrewd but personally retarded. You and Jake forget that playing ruthless masters of the universe costs too much emotionally."

"His last episode on the Palestinian-Israeli situation enraged the network censors," I say. "Why did he have to be so controversial?"

"To say 'screw you' to everyone so they'd fire him and he'd have time to chill out."

Interesting theory—justifying Cigar's lackadaisical work outlook. "After decades of struggle we're not dropping out just as we start to make it," I argue, then add, "do you have time for an extra session next week?"

"You want to hide out from Ness here? I'll be your safe house?"

"Yes." Like I'm a felon on the lam. Or joining the witness protection program—but only to shield me from the real criminal who could hurt me: Dr. Ness, the perjurer.

"I can see you next Monday at three P.M.," he offers.

"Thanks." I write it down. "I'm pissed off that he hasn't returned my calls. I was so over him until he started ignoring me. But I'm not paying him two hundred dollars to tell me why he lied. Google Stalker makes me doubt everything he ever said. Now I regret pushing Haley and Lori into therapy. Do you think it's helping them?"

"I do, though they're very different cases," Dr. Cigar says.

Lori is like me—fast, hungry, wildly ambitious. Haley is like Dr. Cigar—slow, catlike, ambivalent about success. "I told Lori to stand up to her mother and husband and advised Haley to push herself further to make it on her own."

"You have great psychological intuition. You never wanted to become a therapist?" he asks.

"I was considering going back to school. But after *Up in Smoke*, I made tons more money while still helping people."

"You're a powerful figure to your followers. Part therapist, mentor, mother, booster, friend."

Despite my rage at Dr. Ness, I can hear him telling me never to view connections with protégés as true equal relationships. It's odd, having someone I abhor whispering wise warnings in my head. His voice also cautions against believing Dr. Cigar's praise.

"It's not altruism. Playing the guru role can be selfish," I explain. "It feeds my ego and bank account, makes me less hungry, fills in the empty holes."

"With love and acceptance?" he asks. "You're creating a supportive New York family."

"Where I have all the power. I'm more the bossy father figure at the head of the table than the mom serving meals," I say. "Oh, I found a new food sponsor, this nutritionist Erasmo. When I told him my sugar issues, he said, 'Let's just not go there.' Of course I shouldn't ever shove toxic junk into my mouth when I'm alone late at night. Why didn't you just say, 'Julia—this is just too sick, stop this disgusting activity right now'?"

"The last time I was that critical with a patient, his response was 'I'm going to kill myself, you motherfucker' and he jumped me and scratched my arm." Dr. Cigar grimaces at the memory. "The time before, a woman threw coffee cups and preservatives at me and stormed out screaming. I wound up losing both of those patients."

"Really? Jeez. Well, I can handle it. The only advice that's helped me has been harsh and blunt. I do it for my clients. Saves them a lot of time and misery."

"You break through their blocks to unlock their potential," he agrees.

"I need blunt criticism, blame, and disapproval to keep me from screwing up."

"But I don't disapprove of you. You're strong, mature, at the top of your game." He smiles.

I feel weak, immature, overweight, and on the verge of letting my big mouth screw up my body and career. "I'm afraid you just don't get me."

"I do," he says. "When you quit your addictions, you gave up the luxury of a false show. Then Ness and Sarah left you prematurely with no training wheels and you felt tremendous subjective misery, split in two. Like you were screwed. Eating is your last line of defense. Without the people who helped you under the hood, you're at your most insatiable psychotic core."

"I like 'under the hood.'" I picture myself as a car whose engine is sputtering, waiting for a team of ace mechanics from a nearby service station. Then I imagine it's about pregnancy—only under the hood I'm barren. Boy, I admit it, Sarah's baby lust is really getting to me.

"At first I mis-saw you," he admits. "So quick and confident, it was a wild ride, like being in the presence of fire. I thought, This woman's flying so fast, I'll stumble and she'll cruise right over me. But you proved you weren't all speed and velocity. You filled me in, invited me belowdeck, lifting the curtain. I didn't believe the distorted nightmare X-ray mirror but you made me see past the strong rat-a-tat rhythm to your empty ravenous soul."

Can't he stay with one image for a whole sentence?

Although I want the critical truth, now I'm insulted by his admission that he's mis-seen me. Along with quitting Dr. Ness, I feel like quitting Dr. Cigar and starting over, shrunk and shrinkless. But first I want to convince him I'm not really so empty, hungry, and fucked up. Or is it me who needs convincing?

"Can I ask you something?" Haley begins on our walk-and-talk date. "How much about my past sex life should I reveal in *The Yoga Guide to Guys*?"

I ask her about her clients, old lovers, and her struggle to make a living, digging for juicy details. Most of the men in her private yoga sessions contact her through Craigslist and, without knowing them, she goes to their apartments.

"Isn't that dangerous? Cute young girl shows up with mat. Don't they ever come on to you?"

"Well, the two guys I train in Chelsea are gay and perfectly lovely," she says.

"What about the straight ones? Somebody had to proposition or grab you."

"Well, one guy in this Flatiron loft did, but in a mild, metrosexual way. I trained him twice and on the third session he greeted me naked on his couch, asking if I wanted a martini."

"That's hysterical! Did you have a martini?"

"No, I didn't have a martini." Her face flushes.

"Any other weird encounters?"

"One client was enthusiastic over the phone. When I got there it turned out he was a paraplegic in a wheelchair. We did some arm and neck exercises. I think he just wanted to be touched."

"Put that in the intro—about a yoga teacher making house calls, helping everyone achieve calm and nirvana while your fiancé is making you insane and chaotic."

Hearing the problems of clients in their twenties makes me thankful I'm older, preferring my middle-aged angst to quandaries of sexual orientation, "what will I do for a living" doubts, and unusual drug addictions. I'm becoming a mobile self-improvement session. Or else I'm Vampira, scouting for fresh blood.

After walking for two hours, we head back to my apartment. Since my muscles are tight from the eight-mile trek—my high score for recent walk-and-talks—Haley shows me yoga stretches in my living room. I do downward-facing dog, king of the dance, lotus, cobra, and half-moon poses. She corrects my stance and shows me how to get better balance. What a good teacher she is. While I used to enjoy faux yoga workouts with J. Lo and Aretha Franklin blasting in the background, Haley turns off all the music for a silent, introspective workout. When I ask if she wants me to edit her book proposal, she cuts me off and says, "You really need to stop talking and breathe."

I quietly ponder the psychodynamic possibilities of my latest triangle with Dr. Cigar and Haley. By sharing my psychedelic shrink daddy, I could be making this girl, with red hair like my mother, my new fake sister, to replace Sarah—

who has sort of replaced me with Chloe. Or since Sarah has a little girl, Haley could be filling in for the daughter I don't have. I just need to introduce her to my agent across the hall to sell her book to complete the adoption process.

Over the rest of the weekend, still steaming that my ex-shrink has been feeding me Aesop's fables, I imagine barging into Ness's office and insisting on answers, warning the other patients and therapists at his institute that what he says is half fiction. Does he fake them out too, or just me? If he denies it, I'll emulate a Puccini opera and cry out, "Falso! False as Judas!"

Interrupting my revenge reverie, there's a Facebook message from Google Stalker, who I'm starting to see as the younger, nuttier me. She wants my opinion on whether to frame the old picture of Dr. Ness's mother and send it to him anonymously. "No, put your name on it," I advise, wondering what her twisted fantasy is. To drive him insane? Or to create a mystery about his mother only she knows the answer to, which would mirror his power over her?

At the same time, I'm happy to hear Jake's show is renewed for another season, and he's inviting the cast and crew over to our apartment to celebrate. On Saturday the galleys for *Food Crazy* arrive with Frederica's quote in bold letters on my cover. Despite my angst, I love seeing my baby become a book. It's beautiful. Jumping into the proofreading process, feeling busy and productive, I don't have time to ponder the deep meaning of Dr. Ness, how his lies or his leaving led to my frosting fetish. Or it could be like AA, where I'll always be in cupcake recovery.

There ought to be a recovery group for getting over your shrink.

On Sunday with Lori, on my sixth speed walk this week, she tells me her husband has ADD. Dr. Cigar has recommended treatment with his psychiatrist brother, the fellow puffer. I find his latest sibling interlinkages exhilarating, as if we are all endlessly connected in a head game of Twister. But then Lori says she's separating from her husband and taking off for Europe with her mother, and I feel like Lori's also divorcing *me*. I don't realize how deep our bond has grown until she says she's severing it for two months. It reminds me of Sarah and Ness moving, and how impossible they are to replace or get over. Perhaps that's why I have kids on the brain. If you have children, they can't leave you—at least not until they're old enough to walk or drive away.

At 9 A.M. on Monday, I find a hundred e-mails in my inbox. One seminar attendee who has been out of town e-mails that she's "having Julia withdrawal." Jake paces between his den and the living room, negotiating his new contract. He wants me to meet him at his show's wrap party that night. Overbooked, I request a videocam appointment with Dr. Cigar. But his office computer is a PC, not a Mac, thus he doesn't have the right equipment for an iChat. When I suggest a phone session, he reminds me that I called the telephone and technosessions with Dr. Ness pale and ineffective. So I keep our face-to-face, but arrive ten minutes tardy. His door is open. I rush in.

"You used to complain when Dr. Ness wasn't on time," he admonishes.

"I know. Sorry I'm late. Here's my new baby." I show him the *Food Crazy* galley. "Despite the behind-the-scenes mess, holding it makes me happy. It's like giving birth to a child who might be schizophrenic and die in a few months but…"

"You can't help but love it anyway," he jumps in, nodding and paging through.

"Yes. I have the urge to sign a copy to Ness, writing 'Why did you lie to me?' in red pen."

"Don't. That would be inflammatory," he decrees.

Good word to use. Causing excitement, anger, heat. I have the urge to put my feet up on the fragile straw table, but instead move a more stable leather ottoman and rest my legs on it. I'm getting comfortable here, just as I'm deciding to quit.

"I should tell you that I'm going out of town for vacation for three weeks. To Thailand." He sounds psyched. "I've never been to Asia before."

"Are you taking a laptop?" Good for him for going on an adventure, though I selfishly want him to stay reachable. So much for being ready to leave. At the beginning of my courtship with Jake, I was ambivalent about him—until he abandoned me for the West Coast, where I followed, chasing him until he caught me.

"I'm sure there are Internet cafés all over," Dr. Cigar promises.

I take note of the timing, as if we have a mutual organic need to back off and get some distance. "If I'm angry at Dr. Ness, why do I still want to give him my galley?"

"He was the father at the time of conception," he says. "So you want to see him holding your baby."

While the talk of fake babies conjures up the pretend child in *Who's Afraid of Virginia Woolf?*, on Tuesday afternoon I realize

I haven't yet had my period this month. I check the calendar—I'm ten days late! But it can't be. Jake and I are pretty randy lately but I always use birth control. Pretending I'm a mommy-to-be for Page Six, I fear my body has believed my distortion. Now I'm having a sympathy pregnancy with the press version of me.

"If I'm really careful with my frisbee and the foam, I can't get pregnant, can I?" I ask my gynecologist, Dr. Lay, over the phone, using my contraceptive's nickname.

"Well, no method is one hundred percent safe, except abstaining," he says. "Have you been having sex?"

"Yes," I admit. More than usual actually, since Jake has been back from L.A.

"Has your weight been fluctuating?" Dr. Lay throws out.

"Why? Does that matter?"

"Yes. If you go up or down five to ten pounds, you need to have your diaphragm refitted or sperm can get through and impregnate you."

"Now you're telling me?" I'm shocked. "My weight can fluctuate five to ten pounds in one weekend!"

"Well, if you're late, go to the drug store and get a pregnancy test."

I plop down on the blue couch, pondering whether I've willed my womb to be with child. Freud would have a field day. If I'm pretending I've had no free will and it's an accident, that means I don't have to consciously make a choice to get pregnant. Dr. Cigar would be right and despite all my denial, I really crave a baby to be Sarah's little girl's best friend. It would be lovely, with Chloe and my kid continuing three generations of the female Sutton-Goodman camaraderie. Sarah, my mother, and my father would be so overjoyed. And I bet a pregnancy would force me to fix my lifelong food craziness, to get it right for my daughter. Overwhelmed with conflicting emotions swirling through my system, I shut my eyes and wind up falling asleep on the couch.

I wake up bleeding, knowing I'll never admit to anyone how disappointed I feel. Not to Jake, Sarah, or Dr. Ness. Not even to myself.

chapter twenty-one
out of character

June 25

"I need your advice," I tell Jake, walking into his den.

"What?" He uses his "stay out of my tree house" voice, as if girls have cooties, and I should mind my own business and keep away from his stuff.

"I've been going over my galleys of *Food Crazy*..."

"When did you get your galleys?" He sounds hurt I haven't told him. With the early copies of *Up in Smoke*, I summoned him home from work, waltzing around the apartment with them in my arms, screaming in triumph. It was the best day of my life, though I never say so because he says his best day was the day we eloped.

"They came last week."

"Congratulations." He kisses my forehead. "Aren't they a little late?"

"I told you, Google Stalker's info checked out. They did switch my pub date to September twentieth."

"That's right. I'm sorry."

"At least it gives me more time to get in better shape," I explain. "Here's my problem. I don't know whether to add an addendum to *Food Crazy,* coming clean about my weight gain, the recommendations of Erasmo's that I'm taking, and Ness's lies. Or do I rush and try to rewrite the whole book, incorporating how Dr. Ness's departure and deception affected my sugar issues?"

"Put the date you wrote it at the beginning of each chapter," he suggests, "the way we sometimes insert datelines at the start of our shows to clarify the time sequence to the audience. Leave the book the way it was when you wrote and sold it. You can always do another episode, I mean sequel."

That's the perk of picking a partner with a good sense of story structure.

"Smart idea, thanks." Now I kiss his head. "It's weird rereading what Dr. Ness told me. I don't even know what he was making up off the top of his head."

"Want to watch an early cut of my next episode?" he asks.

"Sure," I say, hoping it'll get my mind off my deceptive shrink.

I sit on the couch watching the show, with Jake's arm around me. The lead detective is reconciling with his schizophrenic mother on her deathbed. He's yelling at her to stop lying to him about the past. Like the detective, I wonder if Dr. Ness's mother's elusiveness and insanity are genetic and that makes him elusive and insane too.

. . .

"I'm worried that my dynamic with Dr. Ness mirrors the way he pathetically sends undeserved gifts to his long-lost mother," I tell Dr. Cigar at our next session. "They haven't seen each other in thirty years."

"Providing the perfect model of dysfunction?"

"Unless he's been lying about that too?" I shrug. "I heard Lori's leaving her husband and you referred him to your uptown doctor brother. Another subplot thickens."

"He doesn't take any insurance, but her husband's a banker so he should be able to afford three hundred dollars an hour."

"Your brother is more arrogant than you are." I can already tell. "You should try arrogance. You equivocate too much."

"Everyone likes a dictator," he says dryly.

"Sylvia Plath said every woman adores a fascist."

"You and Ness both have that combo of arrogance and charismatic power. He zeroes in on the problem with his X-ray eyes and you emulate him, turning your laser beams on me."

"How's that?"

"You sear off illness, ectomize the problem, excise the tumor. Like the flange on the side of your kidney that's causing irritation and gets zipped off in an outpatient setting. You burn off impurities, surgically remove the trouble spot, really getting in there under the skin. Not like a bully but exuberantly."

I bet sneaking in the word "bully" means he sees me as bullying. Because I make him be more ambitious by taking more patients? Hound him to quit cigars? Dr. Ness once told me I was his most taxing patient of all time.

"Stop saying I'm like Ness. I'm honest and literal—the opposite of Ness!" In the next episode of Jake's show, the star finds out his biological father might have been a serial killer, the reason why he's become a homicide detective, his nemesis.

"I meant it in a good way," Dr. Cigar defends himself.

"You can be authoritative too. If I demand it, you'll give me your opinion."

"With younger patients I offer more advice, especially the little birdies starving for any directives, rules, or summations to help parent them through their lives of quiet desperation," he says.

I recognize the Thoreau quote. "You should be more forceful and critical with big birdies like me."

"I sprinkle bon mots of wisdom through our sessions," he says. "But you parry them back with your speed-of-lightning tennis racket. Boing boing boing."

I jot that down, wondering if subconsciously I choose shrinks based on their verbal dexterity so I'm never bored. Or I can steal their lines. "You have such a colorful way of speaking."

"It's associated with art, but it's not literary. Not standard processing," he lets me know, as if this is a serious problem he's given a lot of thought. "It's more like a neurological quirk or a learning disability."

"ADD?" I ask, back to diagnosing my doctor instead of vice versa.

"I was hyperactive as a kid, and depressed, but never diagnosed with ADD."

"Like Tourette's syndrome? You can't help but spit out a string of nonlinear sentences?"

"I have to struggle to talk like a civilian. My vernacular comes out impressionistic, sly words sneak beneath the radar. Might be unconscious. I don't naturally speak in paragraphs."

"Haley says it's hard for her to keep up with you," I recall. Lori, nonlinear herself, follows with no problem. Like me, they both find his speech patterns enchanting.

"It can sometimes confuse or offend."

"Or entertain and enlighten," I say. "Have you always spoken like this?"

"It's what made it hard to forge an identity when I was young. What made me stumble."

"Really? I like having a shrink who talks in Beat poetry." I envision him as a vulnerable little stuttering boy while his classmates made fun of him.

"Yes, I'm trilingual. English, Spanish, and metaphoric," he quips.

"What if you're just artistic?"

"Some people pretend they're artists for secret reasons, to cover up that they can't color in the lines or use correct punctuation. I dip too deep into the unconscious."

The trait I'm most drawn to in him is actually his handicap. I recall Dr. Ness once saying that our wounds come from the same source as our power.

"I think you're too blocked to unblock me," I let him know what I'm really thinking. "On Erasmo's food plan I've already dropped six pounds. And all it took was careful attention to how many calories I was eating."

"Well, he's a nutritionist," Dr. Cigar says. "I'm not."

"But you can't pick and choose which problems you want

to help your patients overcome. On some level I don't think you want to help me quit my sugar addiction or lose weight. You'd rather keep me stuck where you are." I decide right there I'm leaving him—sooner rather than later.

"If I unblock you, you might run ahead too fast and I won't be able to keep up?" he asks rhetorically. "I'll be the one with the broken leg who gets left behind?"

That's his whole argument?

That night I walk seven miles with Tiffany, who isn't happy with Dr. Cigar's brother and wonders if Dr. Cigar's schedule has loosened up.

"Check back with him next month. He may have a Friday six P.M. slot opening soon," I say.

On Monday morning, my accountant calls to report that the big audit meeting with the IRS agent has gone well. Thankfully, everything I have deducted—including all my addiction therapy with Dr. Ness—turns out to be legit. I don't owe anybody anything.

That afternoon, when I click on the computer, there's a letter from Dr. Ness. It has been three whole weeks since I left the last angry message for him. My heart is pounding as I read it. I feel as though I'm about to learn something essential, as if I'm an adopted child discovering the circumstances of her birth.

> *Julia, I was out of town and just received all your messages. I'm sorry you're hurt. I never meant to hurt you. My goal has always been to assist you any way I could, by getting you to*

quit your addictions, and enhance your career and marriage.
When you asked personal questions, I tried to answer in a
way that might heal you.

I think of my answers to all of Google Stalker's questions, where I changed details to come off like a better role model, along with my response to Sarah's baby inquisition. I was lying to both of them with good intentions, as Dr. Ness lied to me.

At the beginning you were just taking notes in your journal.
You never said our sessions were on the record. When you
complained you were wasting your life fixing other people's
articles instead of getting your own bylines, I encouraged you
to write yourself. When your agent asked you to expand your
piece into Up in Smoke, *I was happy you sold the book, it*
took off, and your hard work was rewarded.

In my profession, literal facts never matter as much as
subconscious feelings. You said your article was about how
you were conquering bad habits that were limiting your life.
I had no idea you were quoting me and using my personal
story until you showed it to me in the magazine. When I read
the pages, and then your book proposal, it felt exactly right.
How to recover from substance abuse, from your perspective.
In the chapters you gave me, you used anecdotes confessing
to the emotional distress and pain behind ending your own
addictions, which seemed excruciatingly honest and moving.
You changed my name to protect my identity and because I
wasn't anywhere near as important as the theories and strat-
egies you extrapolated from our work together. After your
book came out, it helped many other addicts quit, an admi-

rable feat you should take pride in. I'm so proud of you and wish you only the best.
    Michael

I read his letter, confused that his version is plausible. Oh, fuck, though I don't want to, I find myself believing him. He's definitely helped me get and stay clean and successful. I recall being afraid my addiction book wasn't dramatic enough since quitting cigarettes isn't like getting off heroin or selling my body to buy crack. Being on the nicotine patch and doing talk therapy to stop smoking cigarettes could be seen as too boring. I wonder if Dr. Ness exaggerated his background to make my pages juicier so they would sell? If he did, it worked, since his wild and wacky disclosures are what made my introduction and first-person anecdotes so unusual. I never asked him, "Is this one hundred percent true?" Indeed, I egged him on and never took the time to fact-check carefully.

Now that I know he's puffed up his past, I have the chance to edit out all the falsifications in subsequent editions of *Up in Smoke*, but I make no move to take them back or update. Hell, I'm not even planning to mention the little fact that I've porked out in *Food Crazy*—a book about how applying his addiction strategies (along with others) makes me skinny. Thus I'm complicit in this deception. Meanwhile, his explanation seems unsatisfying. What I really want from him is much more personal.

"Your e-mail feels evasive and shrinky," I respond. "You didn't say whether you care that I've quit seeing you or if you miss me." I think of the scene in *To Sir, with Love* where the female student writes a love letter to her male teacher and he responds by correcting her grammar.

The next day he replies: "Me? Shrinky? Not how I see myself. Yes, it was weird not to see you when I was in New York. It was unusual and there was certainly a space in my week that felt empty—where is Julia? But then I knew why you weren't in my office where you are always welcome. You've been a special, thoughtful, generous patient I'll never forget."

Damn. It's easier to paint him as an elusive, prevaricating prick. Especially when Dr. Cigar is leaving for his Asian adventure. I feel confused, angry, and disappointed with both of my head doctors. But instead of ruining my diet with sugar, I scrawl my rage into my notebook. Then I print out my latest back and forth with Dr. Ness and show it to Haley after our walk the next day. The benefit of hooking someone up with your shrink is that they actually care about the minutiae of your analysis of your analyst.

"Truthfully, his response feels phony and defensive. He doesn't really address whether he lied to you or why," she says. "He implies it doesn't matter as long you end up clean and successful."

If I'm currently a mess, and his leaving and lying exacerbates my food craziness, I fear that means our past addiction therapy was a failure. Or that it only has a shelf life of a few years. Or that it can continue to work only while we're in the same city. Then again, I haven't relapsed on the big five (cigarettes, pot, pills, alcohol, and gum), everyone I know has bouts of overeating sometimes, and my book has no doubt enhanced my world, career, and bank account.

"Did you believe his letter?" she asks.

"It's not like he did anything intentionally illegal or immoral." Am I sure, or am I trying to convince myself that we're not coconspirators?

"When he answered if he missed you, it's like he only told you what you wanted to hear."

It's certainly nicer when people shower you with the validation and praise you crave. But that happens so rarely. "I always tell clients not to expect people to read their mind, and to learn to ask for what they want," I say, confused as to why I'm defending him.

"Interesting that he ended by saying you could always come back to his office, reaffirming you're still his patient," she notes. "You let him get the last word."

"Good insight," I tell Haley. "You know, the cliché is that all shrinks have emotional issues and they pick the profession to heal themselves."

"Julia, can I ask you something?"

"No, you're not allowed," I kid.

"When are you going to get Dr. Cigar to walk with you?"

Funny, she follows my shrink sagas the way I used to follow Dr. Ness's mother's antics, as if we're both addicted to real-life soap-opera installments. "I've asked him twice. He says he'll try it sometime. Want to come over and do yoga?"

"No, I have to go meet Max," she says out of nowhere, adding, "he's invited me to spend the month at his house in Southhampton. I have to pack."

"The Max I met?"

"Yeah, my ex. The one with the dog."

I stop walking and stare at her in disbelief. "Max, the cad who hurt you and lives with his girlfriend while still trying to get you in bed? That's the man you're going away on a trip with?"

"Boy, there's a reason you're not known for your subtlety." She tries to make light of it.

But when I'm exercising so much and dieting so rigidly,

I'm edgy, with less patience for polite banter or phoniness. "I'm serious. Why the hell would you go away with that creep?"

"I already said yes."

"Is he planning to keep his girlfriend in Manhattan, keep you out there, and play musical beds? You're too good for that. I thought you're in therapy trying to work it out with Zach."

"I don't want to talk about this anymore." Her face gets red, like she's about to cry.

"Haley, don't go. It's a bad idea and you know it."

"Julia, you don't get it. It's over with Zach. I just moved to a Brooklyn shithole with roommates and roaches," she argues. "Max owns this huge estate, right on the beach, that's practically empty. We're just friends and…"

"You don't need his summer house. You're doing so well—staying sober, working on your book, being in therapy. Don't regress now." I can't stop when she's making such a bad mistake.

"I'm not your client anymore!" she yells. "Quit haranguing me with your tough-love bullshit!"

"It's not bullshit. It's been working for you."

"Well, it's not anymore. Everything's not black and white. We can't all have perfect marriages like you do!"

"I just want to talk about it," I try.

"I can't talk to you anymore. Just leave me alone!" She runs off, leaving me stunned, standing in the dirt.

Walking home a bit shell-shocked, I think of Dr. Cigar's story of how being blatantly critical caused a male patient to yell, "I'm going to kill you, motherfucker," and made a female client throw coffee cups at him. I hear Dr. Ness reminding me not to confuse my relationships with young protégés with true equal friendships, and accusing me of attributing qualities in myself to other people before I really know them well. For a minute I fear my blunt self-help approach is fatally flawed. I must be a lousy maternal figure to my fake daughters since they're both deserting me. What if Lori and Haley never come back? I'm undeniably hurt. Although compared to missing Ness and Sarah, I can't help but feel that this isn't even a scratch.

chapter twenty-two
out of order
July 2

"Are you anorexic? Do you binge and purge? Have you ever abused laxatives? Are you obese? Have you had stomach staple surgery or liposuction? Are you addicted to diet pills? Are you bipolar? Have you been hospitalized for depression? Are you suicidal? Do you have obsessive-compulsive disorder? Is this an emergency?"

I answer no to the questions in quick succession on the phone with the lady at the Rendow Institute of Eating Disorders. She makes my usual intrusiveness seem quaint. Erasmo, who is finding the emotional outbursts caused by my complex consumption issues a bit over his head, suggested I try an expert here to psychologically supplement his new nutrition guide. But I guess cupcake compulsion leading to counterphobic delusions of pregnancy doesn't count for anything. On the bright side, I haven't had an icing pig-out in more than a month, so hopefully that substance has shuffled on.

I explain my problem to this Rendow person and that, since I'm down to 149, I'm just looking for assistance in shedding 21 more pounds in ten weeks to speed shrink my body back to slenderness for *Food Crazy*'s pub date. Alas, my lack of eating craziness confounds her. She says "Please hold" twice, and finally promises that someone will call me back but she doesn't say when. At the midnight AA stag-fest meeting the most serious addiction mavens were men, while more shrinks from the fair sex majored in food malfunctions. Which is better for me?

Wanting a doctor who has worked with addicts, I call Westchester information to get the phone number for Bryan Cox, Dr. Ness's Jungian guru. If he's that good, and has a session available, it will be worth it to get the train to Chappaqua, I decide. But taking a page from Ness's impoliteness, he doesn't return my call. That afternoon, the Rendow-recommended Kathryn Dorman does.

She's an eating-disorder specialist on West Eighteenth Street, ten blocks from my apartment; a bit farther than Dr. Ness and Dr. Cigar, I note. Her only open slot is Monday at 8:30 A.M. I wonder how far out of my comfort zone I will go for a new food guru to fix me. Even my former *Femme* bosses used to let me start my day at ten.

"That's very early for me," I tell her. "But just this one time."

"I appreciate your flexibility," she says, which makes me almost like her.

Hanging up, I examine my error in picking Dr. Cigar as my head doctor. Instead of finding a woman pro who comprehends complex eating conundrums, I inanely sought a cute downtown male to crush out on to get me over Ness. When Dr. Cigar said he had experience doing behavioral work with impulse disorders, I assumed that covered my compulsive eating and lingering addiction issues, yet I never checked the definition in one of my old psychology texts. Now when I do a computer search for "impulse disorders," what comes up on PlanetPsych.com is self-mutilation, domestic abuse, pathological gambling, pedophilia, trichotillomania (recurrent hair pulling), dermatillomania (compulsive skin picking), kleptomania, and pyromania. Wow! There are so many manias out there I'm happy to have missed.

It's telling that a psych major and therapy junkie like me has misdefined my own problem. My obsessive desire to clone Ness must be causing the cross wiring. Sexism is lingering around here too. Sarah used to think it was idiotic for a proud feminist like me to prefer male physicians, still wanting a daddy figure to diagnose and save me.

While checking out the Rendow Institute online, I read an article that says thirty-five million American females in this country currently suffer from eating disorders. I recall OA, remembering I'm far from alone.

"How much do you weigh?" I can't help but ask Dr. Dorman, sitting across from me in her blue pantsuit. She looks average, between a size six and eight.

"That's a rather personal question," she says.

But 8:30 A.M. Monday is too early for me to putz around with small talk. In my first meeting with this attractive brunette Chelsea psychologist, I've already shared the condensed version of my past and addiction history, my mental ménage à trois with my two male shrinks, and my "what I was doing there" story, ending with my ten-week goal to get back into shape. I'm impatient to extract data to determine if she has any diet-guru potential. She's forty-five, a graduate of Yeshiva University, and stands five foot six, one inch shorter than I am. She doesn't exercise much, she says, has never had serious weight issues herself, so I can't discern deep motivation for her career focus. Since she comes off as calm and rational, I guess it's a practical decision—millions of women with this disorder can mean millions of paying patients.

"You prefer the blank-slate approach?" I ask.

"Not necessarily," she says.

No strong feelings either way. Nothing rebellious or unorthodox. She seems less dark and damaged than I consider myself, Dr. Cigar, and Dr. Ness to be. Easygoing, cheerful people rarely hold my interest. Unless she's hiding something.

"So you can handle answering personal questions?" I need to know.

"I already told you my age, my height, school, and exercise habits." She sounds defensive. "Why do you want to know my weight?"

"You're an eating-disorder specialist," I say. "Dr. Ness is six feet tall, weighs 157, and thinks I should be 128. Dr. Cigar is six-one, 220 pounds, and thinks I'm fine the way I am. I have a theory that every expert I speak to will project their own weight range on me."

"I'm 138," she coughs up.

She weighs ten pounds less than I do now, but ten pounds more than my goal. If I decide to see her, I assume she'll push me to settle for her size when I want to be smaller. I realize— with frustration—that after all this time I'm still spinning like a whirling dervish looking for Ness's replacement, but at least now I'm open to shrinks of the fair sex, whom I should have tried in the first place. For someone who finds that instant gratification isn't fast enough, this process is certainly going slowly.

"Since your area is eating problems, does that mean you see mostly young women?" I ask.

"Yes, I see more women than men," she says. "Not necessarily young."

"I read that out of seventy-two million dieters in this country, forty-four million are females. Why so many? Getting relegated to the kitchen makes you want to eat all its contents in one sitting?"

"Yes, that or starve yourself," she surmises. "It's difficult to find balance. There's more pressure for a woman to be thin than a man. Women still feel defined by their looks and body."

"I'm guessing you'll say I look fine, to eat three meals a day and a big breakfast. And repeat the clichés: Trust my body, eat when I'm hungry, fill up with fruits and vegetables."

"I usually do recommend eating intuitively," she concedes. "Three meals a day, two snacks. Be consistent, trust your body. Though my approach is more psychoanalytic than behavioral. What's worked in the past for you?"

"Dr. Ness was sharp, behavioral, almost dictatorial. Dr. Cigar's approach is loosely psychoanalytic, but I fear he's looser morally, and too weak for me." I look around her office, which is airy, neat, decorated in pastels, feminine and light.

"But if you're still entwined with both of them, you're obviously not trusting your own judgment."

"Well, Dr. Ness used to say that an addict's impulses are always wrong," I tell her. "Since I'm here now, I'm obviously considering making a change."

"After your tag team of male doctors disappoints you, you run to a woman?" She raises a pretty eyebrow.

I wonder if she has a problem with men. Then I wonder if I do.

"Eating problems start with your mother, right? My mom was an orphan and an overfeeder. My dad was a chain-smoker who gained fifty pounds replacing cigarettes with oatmeal raisin cookies."

"And in your late thirties, why are you still letting their habits control you?"

Touché. Good, she has balls, albeit polite ones. Dr. Dorman reminds me of my first shrink in the city, Dr. Gold. If she wasn't retired, I would go back to her. "You're on staff at Rendow?"

"No. They just refer clients to me on an outpatient basis," she says.

I surmise that I've flunked Rendow's food insanity test and thus they have to go outside to find someone to deal with noncutter-nonanorexic-nonbulemics. "Any prognosis yet?" I ask.

"You're a confusing case. Bright, productive, happily married to a man you adore. You seem too insightful and accomplished to be so preoccupied by minor weight fluctuations."

"But my entire career is at stake here. I can't promote a book on conquering my sugar addiction if I'm a chubby closet sugar fiend." I guess she's taken in by my strong appearance, like Dr. Cigar. My parents were the same way. Growing up, when one of my brothers had dyslexia, a bout of stuttering, any behavioral problems, or bad grades, my mother would immediately get them help in the form of a tutor, a psychologist, or a speech pathologist. Since I always had good grades, spoke well, and looked fine, nobody probed the twisted insatiable hungers lurking inside.

"Your entire career is not at stake. You're already success-ful and nobody has the power to take that away," she decrees. "You could accept that you're an average-looking self-help guru, like Oprah, Dr. Phil, Suze Orman, or Emme, the plus-sized model who writes books on real beauty. You're very well spoken, sharp, and poised for someone with the raging problems you claim to have, that's all I meant."

"Most patients come in here flipping out?"

"Yes, more apt to appear troubled, panicked, disconcerted." She nods. "With you, I'd want to find out why being thinner matters so terribly much. What does this magical 128 number mean to you? Is looking good in the TV spotlight for your book tour just an excuse for self-hatred? Are you struggling between two parts of your identity—the married, middle-aged working woman with healthy priorities versus the slen-der, young, hot femme fatale you used to be?"

Middle-aged? Used to be? Ouch! "Wait. Can't I be both?"

"Yes, people are complex," she says. "We can explore the overlapping roles."

"You seem kind of mild and normal for me." I want to see if being my typical provocative self will freak her out.

"Why do you think so?" She's poker-faced.

"Average weight, staid, middle-of-the-road opinions. No heretical stances. No eating disorders in your past. No addic-tion issues," I list.

"I've had my struggles," she says.

"Never been married?"

She points to her bare ring finger and shakes her head no.

"Straight or gay?"

"Why does that matter?" she snaps, as if I'm homophobic to ask.

When a single client of mine used a dating service to find a suitor, but then that relationship didn't work out, I advised her to get back out there again and try a different type. Maybe I should reopen my speed-shrinking contest until I land a better contender. For a second I wonder if I should speed shrink with the other team.

"My lesbian friends are much less concerned with being thin," I tell her.

She rolls her eyes, then says, "I'm straight."

"Where are you from? Have siblings? Parents divorced?"

"Parents together. From Philly. One twin brother who just got married. That count for any dysfunction?" she laughs.

"I guess I'm used to shrinks who admit to being emotionally damaged."

"You want someone as blunt, harsh, and extreme as Dr. Ness," she comments. Or is it a question?

"Well, I don't need to pay someone to be nice to me. I have enough pals and fans," I say. "I want a critical eye. Dr. Ness was really discerning."

"You also said that Google Stalker made you feel he was less than honest. I think you just want the old Dr. Ness back. But I can't live up to your image of him. Nobody can." She shrugs. "Not even him."

I know it's true because I feel like crying. "It's understandable, since his addiction model worked best for me," I say defensively. "Quitting junk food altogether, like cigarettes or drugs. Few choices or tempting fate."

"I've done addiction work too," she insists. "But I don't usually have a blunt, aggressive style. That's not who I want to be."

Now she sounds defensive, but it's my fault. Any future shrink I hire has to contend with the ghost of Dr. Ness. He's ruined me for the entire profession.

"How much do you charge?" I ask.

"My fee is one hundred and fifty dollars a session."

I write her a check, thinking she's between Dr. Ness, who charges too much, and Dr. Cigar, who asks for too little. A moderate older female might be able to help fill in the last piece of my food puzzle in time for my pub date.

"I have an evening time opening up," she offers.

"What insurance do you take?" I ask, sad to give up Dr. Cigar who—despite his deficiencies—I am close to.

"United Medical Fund."

"That's mine." That means she'll cost twenty-five dollars a session. Good sign.

"But I'm not taking any more patients on the insurance plan right now," she adds.

"Why not?"

"Because I limit the number, as most doctors in private practice do."

I don't want to pay full price for services that may not work. I take her business card, but unlike Dr. Cigar's and Dr. Ness's cards, hers shows no e-mail address. Bad sign. I've become so tech dependent, I need a shrink who is into cyber-consulting. On my way out, I hand her one of my promotional postcards for my seminars, which lists my phone number, e-mail address, and Web site.

Although I've let Dr. Cigar know I'm checking out Rendow, walking home I feel fickle, as if I've been cheating on him with Dr. Dorman, especially if I can convince her to change her mind and accept my insurance, thus making it easier for me to dump Dr. Cigar. It seems like it would be a divorce, where I'd have to choose between my figurative mommy and daddy. I've already choked trying to choose between my faux fathers, Dr. Ness and Dr. Cigar, and worry I've entangled the latter with my two fake daughters, Lori and Haley, still triangulating in ways I don't intend.

It's clearly time to escape all Freudian family reenactments, grow up already, and make decisions on my own by seeing myself as the final authority.

The next day Dr. Dorman surprises me with an e-mail follow-up. So she's computer savvy after all. She attaches articles on beauty myths, fat phobias, and a dysmorphic disorder where women have wildly distorted body images. She's trying to be helpful but nothing she sends speaks to me. I'm highly functioning, happily married, capable of slimness, and not about to be talked out of my craze to see my body speed shrunk before my second book's birthday.

It appears that the most original, radical, shocking stance I can take is to love myself while still wanting to weigh 128.

chapter twenty-three
the walking cure

July 13

Friday the thirteenth seems a dangerous day to fire your shrink. I worry Dr. Cigar knows I'm going to give him his walking papers and won't show. But here he is, waiting by the Washington Square Arch in his linen pants and green summer shirt, his leather bag slung across his broad shoulders. With his longish hair and scruffy beard, he looks like a hunky middle-aged hiker in the Himalayas. He smiles at me warmly and I melt. I don't have the heart to just blurt out that we're over. I decide we'll walk first, chat, then at the end of the hour, I'll break it to him gently. But his goofy-looking shoes don't seem sturdy enough to go the distance.

"What kind are they?" I point.

"Rubber-soled white Crocs sandals." He looks proud.

"Can you walk four or five miles in them?" I stare down skeptically. My feet are well cushioned in black Nike walking sneakers with silver streaks on the side. Their box is labeled BLACK LIGHTNING.

"I've walked many miles in them. Though not speed walked, more like strolled."

Dr. Cigar has agreed that I'll pay his twenty-five-dollar normal price for this hour walking session. My only condition is that he can't smoke a cigar while we trek around. I wonder if he lit up on the way to meet me. I can't smell any smoke on him. Is that why he looks uncomfortable? In the old days, if anybody told me I couldn't have a cigarette, I would leave.

After a lap I'm glad his long legs are taking giant strides. "Good, you walk fast," I praise, as we make it around the regal NYU Law School buildings. A few young joggers in running gear pass us by. "You walk a lot?"

"Not in circles. I prefer going somewhere."

"Freud used to hike with his patients," I argue. "Shrinks who do walk sessions say it speeds up therapy."

"Because exercise is a mood improver?" he asks. "Exercise your glutes and exorcise your demons at the same time?"

He's so funny and cute, I'm losing my resolve to break it off today. Maybe I'll insist we hold more sessions outside, forcing him to help me get in shape. Is this a test I'm conscious of? I want him to fight for me, to work me out, to win me back to his couch.

"I read a study saying physical activity allows more access to right-brain thinking," I say. "Plus, consider the metaphors. Lying on the couch implies you're sick. Going outside and stretching your legs is healthy and active; you're getting somewhere—physically and emotionally." I don't mention the warning that the practice could backfire for clients with boundary issues or for those who are competitive with their therapist. I don't excel at setting limits, and I have a tendency to compete with my shrinks—over who is guru-ing whom. "You're a behaviorist, right? Don't you want patients to set goals and accomplish them?"

"Man, you sure walk and talk fast at the same time," he says. "More like ranting or purging."

"That means it's not aerobic enough," I fret. "My heart rate's higher when I'm swimming. You don't bike or swim?" I ask. "Or do weights?"

"Nope. Just walk," he says. "I have to lose a few pounds. I read a study that showed every year out of college you gain a pound."

His looks aren't the problem; I like the gray specks in his newly grown beard. It's his defeatist attitude that bugs me. "Don't use statistics to avoid blame for your weight gain."

"I just find it reassuring that research shows it's biological."

"That means you have to work harder to stay thin like I've been doing. I'm now 144, on my way down—16 more pounds to go," I announce.

I feel much better, lighter, but more volatile and still a bit nervous for him to see me in my workout clothes—black sweats, a tight black Lycra top with a built-in bra and a light-weight, half-sleeved black hoodie that hides the excess jiggle still under my arms.

I recall Dr. Ness questioning if my getting slender and sexy again feels dangerous for me, especially since I want to keep my marriage monogamous and stable. When I was single and liked my figure, I showed it off constantly. When

I don't like my body, I'm less likely to take off my clothes. So staying heavier is like built-in birth control, a way to protect myself from straying.

"Are you back on Dr. Ness's do-or-die food plan?" Dr. Cigar asks. "Just having Julia's Salad for late lunch every day, low-fat frozen yogurt at night?"

The guy isn't a good diet coach, but he is a good listener. It's nice to chat with him in the open air, even if it's smaller talk than usual, hiding what I'm really thinking.

"I'm trying some of Erasmo's variations. Yesterday I had baked salmon and vegetables, lower calories than Julia's Salad," I say. "On Wednesday I added a brown rice sushi roll and edamame. Last weekend I allowed myself microwave popcorn."

"Popcorn's not fattening," he comments.

"The way I usually eat it, it is—the whole box, three bags full. Last weekend I had blueberries with Cool Whip Lite on top."

"Again, not that many calories."

"Bad advice. You forget who you're talking to. I ate all the blueberries and the whole container of whipped cream, six hundred calories."

He doesn't respond. I bet he's tired from traipsing around in the sweltering air after a long day of hearing everyone's dark inner conflicts. Or his feet hurt from the lack of support. We hear off-key folk music coming from a guitar player.

"I've been eating more, but no candy or cupcakes," I report. "I'm exercising six times a week. If I have an extra meal, I'll swim the next morning and then walk at night. I want working out to be my new addiction."

"Still doing outdoor office hours with your acolytes?"

"Yeah, I have a whole new roster of walkers." I stop by the

short metal fence to do the stretches Haley's shown me. I pull my legs back behind me one at a time while elongating my arms, feeling sad that she—and Lori—no longer call or e-mail me very much. A few pigeons swoop down to eat crumbs on the ground. "I hear Haley's piece 'Yoga Guide to Guys' is leading to a book. And did you know that Lori sold an article to *Femme* about sunbathing nude in public and posed for a photo with no clothes on? It's running next month."

"No. I haven't kept in touch with Lori or Haley since they went out of town. I said no to both of their requests for phone appointments." Unlike Dr. Ness, he doesn't do long-distance.

"When I tell my protégés to get naked, I mean it metaphorically," I joke, then worry that Haley or Lori might be in trouble. Though I am trying to give them both space, I wonder if I should call to see how they're doing.

"If Lori asked you whether she should do the photo beforehand, would you have approved?" he asks.

Good question. "Last time we spoke and she brought it up, I told her she's beautiful and it's her decision to make. She e-mailed that she has weight issues and wants to do it because when she's ninety she'll look at herself and think she had a great figure. Interesting that a slim, athletic twenty-seven-year-old has body issues." I kick a few stones out of my way, deciding not to call either of them, though I'd respond if they contacted me. I need to stop trying to fix other people while I'm still broken myself. "I keep hoping working out will get rid of mine. I swam a hundred and twenty laps this morning, a whole mile. I don't lose weight swimming, but it's good for getting toned," I tell Dr. Cigar.

His eyes glaze over.

"You don't really want to help me get in shape. Do you?"

"Not really," he confesses.

"Why? You have to tell me your opinion," I demand. "That's what I pay you for."

"You look fine and your weight talk is superficial and trite. Your overeating was the presenting problem when you came in, but it doesn't merit such obsessive attention. It shouldn't rule your life the way it does. The amount you flip out about it is misguided and wrongheaded." He stops to take a breath. "Like you're screaming 'I'm blind, I'm blind!' But there's no optic nerve damage."

"Good line," I say. Not that I agree. I'm not a superficial girl vying for *America's Next Top Model*. I'm a food addict who needs to stem unending compulsive behavior. Imagine telling a patient struggling with an illness, "Get over it so we can talk about something interesting." Still, I like how emphatic Dr. Cigar sounds, more engaging than his passive, wishy-washy voice. "Why didn't you say that before?"

"I thought I could help you in more important ways. But you're really strong in your convictions," he answers. "You're doing so well, running your own impressive parallel universe. It's hard to go against a guru."

"I need my own gurus for the truth. I've been asking you for criticism since we met."

"You do take perverse delight in being challenged, and outwardly beg for it. You're brave that way." He nods.

A tall, attractive Latina girl in a halter top stops Dr. Cigar to ask directions to the D train. He slows down to answer. "It's just three blocks west," he says, pointing.

"That way?" She smiles at him, lingering.

I take a few steps forward, wanting to lose the interloper. When he catches up, I say, "Sometimes I still hope that Ness and I can be friends one day." He turns back and waves good-bye to the lost girl. He's such a flirt. I'm jealous he isn't flirting with me.

"You two will never be friends." He sounds sure.

"Never? Why not? I stay close with former clients."

"He'll be a special mentor, but someone who can always piss you off and make you insane."

"Haven't you ever gone to former patients' readings or recitals?"

"Sure. To be supportive. But the shield has to remain up. That's the beauty. Your old shrink is a special VIP, but never the chum who does lunch or the movies."

Is he talking about me and Ness? Or me and him in the future? "Why not?"

"You don't want to break the taboo. The delicate contract sanctifying the relationship could collapse; magic slippers turn to clay feet. It's like a therapist sleeping with his patient."

"Have you ever slept with a patient?" I blurt out.

He looks taken aback by the question. "Why are you asking?"

I'm confused that he doesn't answer right away or just say "No, of course not," like I expect him to. "Because I want to be able to share all my intimate secrets with you," I tell him.

"What are you afraid of?" he asks. "That you might want to cheat with more than cupcakes?"

"I haven't touched another guy since the day I got engaged to Jake."

"But what happened before your engagement and your born-again passion for your husband?" he asks. "Sexual chaos with bad lovers and cocaine with bus drivers."

"Right." I break off a branch from a nearby tree, stripping it of leaves one at a time. "That's why I need to trust my therapist. Dr. Ness was a moral compass. I thought he had a faithful marriage, gave money to charity, was devoted to his family." My shoes feel like they're getting heavier; it's harder to march on.

"Maybe you're still shocked I'm not him?" he asks. "Look, I applaud his effort to create a better planet with his super-hero resolve. But I never aspired to be your messiah."

"Not being ambitious is your rationalization to remain weak, smoke your stupid cigars, and stay unhappy." I toss the bare branch and step on it.

"That's intriguing and might be right, but it's not your job to be my therapist!" he says loudly.

"Well, you certainly need one. You said it's been fifteen years since you've been on the couch. And during this time you've never been content with your marriage—or your work—and you're a goddamn shrink who helps people with work and love. Don't you believe in your own profession?" It's such a no-brainer I want to bean him on the head.

"Why is my personal life your business?" He looks drained, as though he wants to bean me back.

"Because I really believe if you can't fix yourself, you can't fix me."

"That's not true. In a class of thirty therapists, you look around and think: These shleppy losers can't help anybody. But they can. They're not handicapped by their humanness," he argues. "It's this amazing transubstantiation."

"Doesn't that refer to bread and wine as the flesh and blood of Christ?" I'm looking straight ahead and not into his eyes, now fearing he's screwing around with a patient. Have I misjudged his integrity from the start? After Ness proved himself untrustworthy, this is a total deal breaker.

"It's the conversion of one substance to another," he ex-plains. "So a therapist can be immoral while helping you be more moral. You're a self-help guru with all kinds of insecurities and problems, but that doesn't get in the way of you helping others."

"But I don't want an immoral therapist. I need somebody to look up to. I wouldn't have sent you my fake daughters if I didn't think you were above reproach. I wouldn't let you near them if I had any inkling you'd touch a patient. Or that you sleep with anyone but your wife." I recall Lori's mother commenting on what a fun job he has, with young females confessing all their sins, implying he's a lecher.

"You're saying what I do in my marriage could blow your worldview. You're the self-appointed Moral Majority deeming no other lifestyle can exist. You're a right-wing conservative like your father."

I ponder if that can be true. I've missed Dr. Ness and my dad so much, I could be subconsciously emulating them to fill in the void.

"I'm not that judgmental. Everyone has self-destructive tendencies. Sarah was smoking and drinking pregnant, and I still love her. I've forgiven friends who've broken the law or screwed around," I defend myself. "But you just said this can't ever be a friendship. A doctor has a sacred role and takes an oath to do no harm."

"I've never had an affair with a patient," he finally says.

"Good." I'm relieved. "Why couldn't you say that right away? When I asked Dr. Ness, he was unwavering about the importance of fidelity."

"I'm made of different material than Ness. Everything isn't black, white, and safe, Julia." Dr. Cigar takes a few breaths. "Look, you need to believe your nutty rules work—if you touch one cigarette or one lover, they'll throw you out of TV guru-land. I don't want to threaten your system. But you break boundaries, go right up to the edge, and then you run away."

He's right. I pick male shrinks I find stimulating to be the good father while I play the psychobabbling Lolita. Then I expect a promise they'll never cross whatever line I set. Ness once surmised that it's because I have a basically good dad—yet his affection disappeared when I started growing breasts and getting my period at ten. That was too early to become a woman and lose your father's love. Why did he stop being affectionate and telling me I look pretty? Did it make me feel lonely, like something was wrong with me?

I speed up, getting a few steps ahead of him. I note this is all surfacing while I'm breaking the rules, leaving the protective nest of his office, exposing us to the real world in Washington Square Park—a raunchy counterculture haven of nonconformity.

"Look, I'm trying to be paradoxical," he says, catching up. "You're afraid of your hunger? Good, go eat some cupcakes and look that dumb icing death in the eye. You won all the gold stars, so what's the next threat to Barbie's dream house? You're so awed by your newfound success you fear someone will take it away and steal your identity. What if there's another booster rocket under there?" he asks. "You don't need a perfect body or therapist or any more pillars to harness that fire."

His arm brushes against mine; I move farther away. I hear the echo of Dr. Ness telling me about an obese patient of his who gained weight to hide herself and avoid being seen as a sex object. Is this true or made up? If I get in shape and look hot I might want to screw around like I used to.

"You know, Haley didn't let me talk during yoga. She said I had to learn to be quiet and hear myself breathe. Dr. Ness said I was afraid of silence." With that I shut up for a second to inhale a few times. I check my watch to see it's 8 P.M., which means we've been walking quickly for almost an hour. I'm physically revved up, but spent from the heavy emotional workout. I stop at the corner of Waverly and University Place. I don't want to say good-bye to him yet. "Want to go another round?"

"No. No." He looks exhausted. "I want to sit down. Change of venue's disorienting." His face is red. "Feels like you pulled me into your scene, making me come to your office."

"Listen, I don't think it's working out with us." I force the words out.

"You wanted to break up with me outside?" he asks.

"I don't know. I'm sorry. I thought I'd feel too self-conscious walking with you," I say. "But I don't."

"You look beautiful in your sleek black Lycra, stretching your long legs like a ballerina."

Another poem that melts me. "You're a little uncomfortable? No?" I ask.

"Well, it's hard to sound presidential while panting," he admits, and we both laugh.

Then, while still standing there, he leans over and kisses me, right on the lips.

He tastes like smoke.

chapter twenty-four
changing cycles
August 22

"Hey, Alan. Do you have a sec? I have a problem and need your advice," I say to my kid brother over the phone on Friday.

"What's the matter?" he asks.

"I'm sure it's nothing, but..." I'm embarrassed divulging intimate female trouble. But I trust his medical judgment. Indeed, I feel closest to him when there's something wrong with me that he can heal over the phone.

It figures that after the inappropriate kiss, and my subsequent decision that my mental health requires getting rid of all my mental-health experts, a physical problem arises. I rein in my embarrassment to tell Alan that my monthly visitor will not leave this month. The timing is bizarre. Earlier in the summer I was ten days late. Now I'm closing in on my goal weight, and Lori's e-mailing someone she knows at Gawker to imply I'm recovering from miscarrying, which they'll use for an updated gossip item. It appears as if my fake pregnancy is confusing my body into a real miscarriage.

It's the sixteenth day in a row I'm bleeding. This has never happened before. I've been steady as clockwork since my period first started in fifth grade. Okay, lately I've been a little early, and just that once ten days late, but I've never been this out of whack. Dr. Lay's on vacation and hasn't answered my e-mails or returned my messages. Since I'm usually physically as healthy as an ox, my mind goes straight to metaphor. I've always felt too much, talked too much, wanted too much, eaten too much. Now I'm bleeding too much.

For a control freak who hates surprises, this unexpected onslaught is throwing everything off. Instead of power walking six miles six days a week as usual, I've become listless, either canceling, copping out in the middle, or moving more slowly. I sleep longer, don't go swimming, don't want Jake to touch me.

"I looked up erratic menstrual bleeding online and it said it could be hyperplasia," I share my self-diagnosis with my brother. "One article said it's more likely to occur in women whose weight fluctuates."

"Hyperplasia is just abnormal cells. But you should have yourself checked out," Alan scares me by saying. "Get an ultrasound, Pap smear, and endometrial biopsy."

"Really? Why? What else could it be?"

"They need to rule out uterine cancer and fibroids," he says. "Get a blood test too, to make sure you're not anemic. You could need iron tablets."

When it comes to health issues, my brother is overly protective. He often tells me to fly to Illinois when I need tests, as if no physician in the state of New York could possibly know what they're doing. "You never really know a doctor until you've been in the operating room next to him," he always warns.

"Would they need to take vials of blood?" I ask squeamishly.

The longer we speak, the more fragile I feel. I've always been afraid of shots, invasive procedures, surgery, and hospitals. The only reason why I'm not afraid of Dr. Lay is that he pens bestselling women's self-help books and talks about his publishing deals while examining me so I don't notice what he's doing.

"A pinky test might suffice," my brother says.

I'm not above fainting from that small a needle prick. "This could explain why I've been so tired?"

"Your metabolism could be slowing down. Maybe it's early onset of perimenopause or a hormonal imbalance and you need replacement therapy," he says. "If you won't stop bleeding, they might have to do a D and C or, in the worst case, a hysterectomy."

I'm clear I don't want a baby, but the thought that I might never be able to have one is daunting. I respect all the Goodman men's complete inability to sugarcoat (like Dr. Ness), but sometimes I wish Alan would. When Jake's late father was in the hospital and Jake asked my brother his prognosis, Alan said only, "Uh, boy." That was the moment Jake knew it was all over.

"Okay. Thanks. Love you," I tell Alan quietly.

"Love you too," Alan says. "Why don't you call Mom and talk to her? Some of this is genetic."

When I phone my mother to ask, she says, "Don't be nervous. I've had weird periods before. I went through menopause early."

"How old were you when your periods were erratic?" I ask.

"From thirty-eight to fifty," she recalls.

"Damn it all to hell. Just as I'm getting thinner and emotionally balanced, my internal rhythms go batty," I say, laughing.

"As long as you're healthy," Mom says. "Don't worry. We're from strong Russian stock." I flash to the day I told her I lost my virginity at sixteen. She cried for two weeks, then invoked her maiden name by concluding, "Well, the Weiss women were always hot-blooded." I've always taken that to mean I'm high-spirited, not a hemophiliac.

"So what did your brother say?" Jake calls to ask.

"I need a bunch of tests. I might get bad mood swings."

"You're so moody anyway, how will we tell?" he jokes.

"Aren't you wondering how this is going to affect you?" I ask.

"I already figured out this means I'm not getting laid this week."

As if a never-ending menstrual cycle isn't distressing enough, that night my lower left molar starts to ache. I e-mail my longtime dentist (cyber address: PaulTooth) that the sensation is like tinfoil wrinkling under my gum. He says to come in the next morning. Although I promiscuously juggle multiple therapists, with the rest of the medical profession I play hard to get—avoiding M.D.s and dentists for years at a time. So if I'm rushing to see him, PaulTooth knows it's serious.

At his Upper East Side office on Saturday, he takes X-rays, then calls an endodontist ten blocks away and hands me the address, saying, "Dr. Suskin's expecting you." Tooth doctor number two takes more X-rays and concludes my tooth is abscessed and I need an emergency root canal.

"It might take two or three visits," Dr. Suskin explains, as he holds up a long needle.

"Listen, you have to do it in one sitting. I already know I'm never coming back."

He looks at his watch. "If we can start in half an hour, I'll try to do it all this afternoon."

Petrified, with thirty minutes to kill, I walk outside for a final feast in case I don't survive, or can only eat soup for the next few days. Passing a pizza parlor, I have a craving for a whole pie with extra cheese and pepperoni. Then I wonder if they have an uptown Crumbs. But I realize that being an overpizza-ed pig will make me feel worse, and I don't want to die letting the world know I'm an icing addict until the end. I picture being in one of the autopsy scenes on Jake's show where they can tell what a person's last meal is.

"Detectives, come here, you won't believe this," Female ME says.

"What is it, Rodgers?" Male Cop asks.

"This woman's stomach is coated with chocolate frosting."

"You think it's a clue to our suspect?" Female Cop wants to know.

"Could be kinky." The ME shakes her head ominously.

"I get that. It seems we've got the cupcake killer on our hands," Male Detective says, right before the commercial.

Just in case, I eat a boring salad.

Thankfully, Dr. Suskin has a nurturing personality and his first name is Alan like my brother's, which I find calming.

PaulTooth has obviously warned him about me and my taste for what Jake calls "chicky music," because he has headphones and his iPod ready with a selection of songs by Gwen Stefani, Mary J. Blige, Alicia Keys, and Madonna. The next set, filled with raunchier Rolling Stones hits, helps more. It takes five hours, ten novocaine injections, laughing gas, and me loudly humming "19th Nervous Breakdown" five times in a row to drown out the hideous drilling sound. The nurse shuts the door so I won't scare the other patients.

As Dr. Suskin drills and shoots more anesthetic into my gums, I close my eyes under his protective yellow glasses. I'm replaying "(I Can't Get No) Satisfaction" while reliving what happened with Dr. Cigar in the park a few weeks before, which I've been trying to repress. After our kiss—which in retrospect seems an almost innocent little lip-lock, with no tongues or other touching—I ran home. Feeling confused and angry at myself, I called Dr. Gold. Though she's basically retired and only consults part-time, my first shrink always phones me back right away. I told her the story of the smooch with Dr. Cigar and why I think it's all my fault, since I'm the one who insisted we meet at the park and felt jealous when he was being flirtatious with the girl who asked directions. Ending our therapy was making me emotional about parting. Maybe he was intending to give me a European double kiss on the cheeks and I felt compelled to literally kiss him goodbye?

"E-mail him a polite note that you're terminating therapy, don't see him again, and from now on make a rule to only see therapists in the office" is Dr. Gold's advice.

"How can I make sure this never happens again?" I hear myself ask.

"Regular checkups," says Dr. Suskin.

I open my eyes, realizing where I am, and that I'm now talking to my current tooth doctor, not my former head doctor.

"You have to floss daily. Brush three times a day. Drink water instead of soda, and avoid anything with white sugar," he continues answering the right question, which I'm asking by accident.

"You mean like cupcake icing?" I eke out.

"Cupcake icing would be the worst," he confirms.

Talk about a sign. Or is it a conspiracy? My sugar addiction is damaging my potential book PR, body, mind—and now even the roots of my teeth.

At home I take the first round of what's prescribed: an antibiotic three times a day, two Advil every four hours, and two Tylenol with codeine. I haven't been on any drug or had a drop of alcohol in the three years I've been clean, so all the anesthetic, nitrous oxide, and pills turn me into a zombie. I feel like a weak, spacey, vulnerable mess, bleeding from both ends.

I e-mail Jake a post-op follow-up that I'm fine, insisting he stay at work as late as he needs to finish reediting his new episode—ironically involving a "ripped from the headlines" story on poisoned Chinese toothpaste. When Haley e-mails that she's back in town and wants to walk, I let her know I'm under the weather. She sweetly offers to bring over chicken soup. I'm glad she's no longer upset with me but I want to be alone. I spend the hot, humid night reading a stack of newspapers and magazines, stumbling on articles about illness, aging, and death. After quitting all therapy, I've been feeling strong and independent. But in my overmedicated stupor, I worry that my capacities are decaying, along with my fertility and tooth enamel. I recall Freud's theory that dreams of teeth falling out are about losing power.

I barely hear Jake crawl into bed at 4 A.M. but he's gone by the time I wake up on Sunday. My stomach is killing me. When I e-mail my brother, he says to stop taking all the medicine, drink water, don't exercise, stay home, and chill out. Next Dr. Lay checks in from his Caribbean vacation. He doesn't sound worried, though we make an appointment for next week and he suggests birth-control pills might regulate my cycle. He reminds me that I have a signed copy of his book, *The Women's Body Bible*, which I reread. My preoccupation with shrink shopping is switching to being in the market for the right medical doctors. No matter which subset I'm phasing in or out, I can't escape human dependency.

Dr. Ness used to say I should make more room for suffering and let myself fully experience sadness. I turn off the lights, light a lilac candle, and open the windows, as if to invite everything sad to hang out with me inside. But since I've heard back from Alan and Dr. Lay, and ceased the medication, something odd happens: I feel fine. I'm better and clearer, relieved that I'm not dying of a mysterious illness. In fact, I'm actually lucky and grateful. My two-fanged physiological maladies shock me into lucidity. Many women my age can't afford good health care, and have draining full-time jobs while bearing responsibility for children or infirm parents. They're coping with being single, divorced, widowed, or stuck in lousy marriages by using unhealthy substances to escape their pain. I have to pull it together so I can help them.

I remember my first pivotal session with Dr. Ness, where I complained that I couldn't stop smoking, was fighting with Jake, and was sick of the years at my low-paying job fixing other people's prose. When Ness asked if I'd ever been suicidal, I said no, but "I'm scared that I could die tomorrow and never have gotten anything I wanted." He asked, "What do you want most?" I surprised myself by quickly answering, "My own byline."

Now I'm the author of two books, have three years of clean living, a warmer marriage. Just the other day I walked into Jake's den, noticed the garbage overflowing in his can, and wanted to call him a slob. I heard Dr. Ness's voice warning me never to criticize my husband. Just as I advised Sarah's wedding guests, I said, "You're lucky you're sexy because otherwise I wouldn't put up with this pigsty."

Jake smiled and pulled me near him for a kiss, having heard only "You're sexy."

I imagine Dr. Ness's wife criticizing him incessantly. I wonder if he's enhanced my world in a way he can't balance his own. Even if his stories are fables, I'm sure that he's been a true healer to me. And although I hate Dr. Cigar's weakness for women, I accept the profuse apology he e-mailed, along with a promise to see a shrink himself. I suppress my urge to send him to Dr. Ness.

If I have to judge how Ness and Cigar treated me in the book of life, I know they've been ultimately well intentioned and kind. Is it the lingering effects of the painkillers that make the past year seem surreal? I'm not sure if Ness has been my guardian angel, or if our interplay has been more sinister, like Dorian Gray and his portrait. If my trip is like Alice in Wonderland's, Cigar seems the Mad Hatter and Ness the disappearing Cheshire Cat. Their meanings keep shifting in my mind like a kaleidoscope. All of my shrinks always tell me to let the conflicting colors coexist, and today I can.

Rain smashes against the windows and the sidewalk below; the thunder roars. I take a shower and don't weigh myself. I pick up the silly Post-it note that says 128 that I left on the scale, hold it over the kitchen burner, and torch it. When

I'm hungry, I order myself a bowl of chicken soup, replacing Diet Coke with water. My food and weight issues, along with the desperation to look perfect on TV, suddenly seem less important. If I'm not slender by September 20, I should add an addendum to my book, telling the truth: I'm fine the way I am. I'll stop putting energy into myopic quests to improve my appearance. If I never get any richer, sexier, or more slender, I'm enough. I make a pact with God: If you let me be okay, I'll let me be okay.

I don't hear Jake come in, but I wake up facing the window with his limbs wrapped around me. I whisper, "I'm so lucky to have you." He points to the happy photograph of us that Ronit the House Whisperer made me put in the red heart frame on the dresser and says, "It's the picture's fault." Lying there close to him I'm serene, as if I've discovered in his arms free daily therapy and an antidepressant all in one.

Getting up, I'm relieved to find the bleeding has stopped, along with the rain. My tooth pain is gone too. My energy level spikes, right in time for my next "How to Quit Anything" seminar, which starts that night at 6 P.M. Going online to check the registration list, I see fifty new names. I update the packets I plan to hand out and go make copies. Getting the mail on my way back, I see a flyer in the lobby for lessons from "Karl the Kickboxing King." This buff male boxer, whose cute picture is on the card, offers to train novices for $125 a session, at an apartment in my building. How convenient. One-on-one kickboxing would burn a ton of calories while jump-starting my metabolism. Exercise is organic and good for me, I tell myself, taking down his number.

Back upstairs, checking my AOL, I read an ad for a "Reset

Your Body" program run by an organic dietary guru who helps you detox, stabilize your blood sugar, lose weight, and stem carbohydrate cravings. It meets at a school of "Core Integration" in Chelsea. A little New Age granola sounding, but I can use a minidetoxing from all the meds. I still have four weeks before my book publicity campaign. The initial meeting is free tomorrow and I don't have plans. While reserving a seat, I check my e-mail and Facebook, my latest addiction.

There's a missive from Sarah, who says the good news is she's pregnant again. Already! I'm about to be depressed when I read the bad news: The fabulous Rabbi Wald, who married her the summer before, was killed in a car accident.

I'm still metaphorically sitting shiva for Sarah, but I'm thankful it's not a literal loss, just long-distance. Knowing she's grieving for her childhood clergyman somehow makes me imagine how I'll feel if my own rabbi-like figure, Dr. Ness, dies. What if something happens to him while we're still estranged? On a whim, I write him a long e-mail, forgiving him for the lies and evasions, saying that I've come to understand how he might construct stories to help someone get out of pain. Any technique you use in the service of the noble goal of healing is okay as long as it works, and his methods mended broken parts of me. I ask how his wife is doing in Arizona, about whether he's reconnected with his mother. I confess to ending it with Dr. Cigar, adding that maybe I'll see Ness again when he's next in town. He could try to make one of my readings. If he tells me a time that's convenient in advance, I offer to plan a book event around his schedule.

When I finish, I read over my missive. It's gushing and purple. I delete it before pressing Send, thinking this is what he's taught me: I can have impatient outpourings, inappropriate feelings, and extreme cravings—for the wrong people or the wrong substances—but I don't have to act on my impulses. I'm so sure he'll be pleased that his lessons are sinking in that I have the urge to e-mail him again to explain how I no longer need to send him the letter. Instead I turn off my computer and run outside, totally pumped to teach a new batch of sage-seeking addicts how to get cleaner, leaner, and meaner, like me.

part
five

chapter twenty-five
starstruck
August 25

Now that I'm on a weight-loss streak, completely finished
with psychotherapy, and glad all shrinks are out of town
until Labor Day, Dr. Ness's Jungian guru, Bryan Cox, finally
returns my calls. I phone him back with the intention of
leaving a message that I'm no longer looking for a new therapist. Cox surprises me by picking up his phone.

"Michael Ness gave you my name? Okay, I'll be in the city
this Friday. I can come to your place at six. My fee is one
hundred and twenty-five dollars. What's your address?"

He speaks quickly, even faster than I do. I'm surprised
that he charges less than Dr. Ness. Does Dr. Cox know that
for two years my old time slot with Dr. Ness was six on Fridays? It feels destined. Ness used to discourage me from

calling Cox by saying I'd have to schlep to Westchester, so I'm stunned that Dr. Cox is offering to come to my apartment. I've never known a shrink who makes house calls. How convenient! Even better than e-therapy is a live person coming right to you. You can get anything delivered in Manhattan, so why not door-to-door analysis? Since Ness admires Cox, I already trust him. Plus, I'm dying of curiosity.

"Few questions," he says. "What's your birthday? What's your husband's birthday? Where were you born? What time?"

Wondering if this is for an insurance form, I look up the times and locations for him. "Good. You can ask me anything important on Friday," he says by way of good-bye.

After I hang up the phone, those questions seem bizarre. I flash to a skirmish I had with Dr. Ness a while back when he asked me to edit his institute's newsletter. I suggested he take out a one-line reference to astrology that made him come off too quirky and unprofessional. "Keep your eccentric hobbies to yourself" was my advice. He argued by quoting a Danish astrologer from the 1500s who said, "By looking up I see downward." I responded, "By admitting this in public, I see space cadet." The subject never came up again.

But now I wonder if Cox is a serious follower of Carl Jung who studies the subconscious through art, mythology, religion, and the stars. Has Cox influenced Ness to take an intergalactic view of the world? How flaky! Then again, I'm a Greenwich Village optimist intrigued by confessional poetry, Freudian dream analysis, and Jewish mysticism, as well as a pusher of all kinds of silly self-help strategies. I tell myself it's not my place to cynically knock anybody else's spiritual intrigues.

On Friday, I figure Cox will be late, like Ness always was, especially because there's a summer storm outside. By five o'clock I worry that Cox will cancel and that I'll never get a chance to lay eyes on Ness's head doctor. When my buzzer rings ten minutes early, I open my door to find a cute be-spectacled sprite who looks younger than I am. He takes off his shoes and raincoat and hands me his umbrella before I can even put my hand out to shake his. He goes right to the couch and sits down, pulling from his briefcase two pages filled with complicated planetary maps.

"Do you want to record the reading?" he asks.

At this second it hits me—he hasn't come to analyze my complicated psyche. He's here to read my celestial chart. The infamous Bryan Cox from Chappaqua whom Dr. Michael Ness has always touted as a "brilliant Jungian" is his astrologer. Wow. Ness deceives me again. On second thought, he never used the word "psychoanalyst" to describe Cox; he called him his "advisor," "guru," or "guide." I assumed Cox was a shrink, and Ness never corrected me. Another sin of omission? No wonder Ness keeps coming up with excuses for me not to call Cox. I'm flabbergasted but try not to show a reaction. I haven't seen Dr. Ness in months, and it certainly isn't Cox's fault that I've jumped to the wrong conclusion about his profession.

I never pay much attention to my horoscope. But know-ing Cox's bent makes me hungrier to understand my one-time mentor's mentor—regardless of his bent. I'm feeling stronger and emotionally distant from Ness. It's time to get real and unmask my old shrink for the quack that he is, like pulling back the curtain on the Wizard of Oz.

"No, that's okay. I don't have a tape recorder," I say, not knowing how this is going to work. Do I take my place across from him? Obviously I don't lie down on the couch. I decide to sit next to him. He doesn't appear to mind.

"What do you want to know?" he asks.

He holds out a page that says "Julia—Inner Chart" and "Julia—Outer Chart" and "Geocentric Tropical," which has a circle filled with numbers, little moons, arrows, and squiggles. I take a peek at what's labeled the "Twelve Sidereal Zodiac Signs" and "Ascendant-Descendant Axis and Midheaven-imum Coeli Axis" across from it. The glyphs look goofy, but I'm attempting to listen, remain open-minded, and not discount his assessments as inane or nonintellectual. Still, I'm just not the type who consults the cosmos for guidance. I'm way too grounded in reality to take this seriously.

"What does this stand for?" I gesture toward a sequence of numbers he has underlined.

"That shows rage, abandonment, and betrayal," he says.

"Really? Where?" I inch closer, staring at the mathematical symbols, playing along, amused by his lack of small talk. And I thought Ness was intense. I just can't believe that the shrink who taught me self-control believes that an astral system is actually controlling the universe.

"Right there." He points to a squiggly symbol. "You're in the middle of a twisted triangle with major heartache."

When Cox mentioned important questions, sexual psychodramas weren't at all what I had in mind. I'm in such a good mood that the idea is completely laughable—except that it feels weirdly familiar. In college I was involved in a few dark relationships with lovers who weren't faithful, and I'd obsess over what would happen. Would he desert me for someone younger or prettier? Was he having an affair? Telling the truth or deceiving me? I haven't felt that kind of terror in years.

"Who is the triangle with?" I want to know, guessing some fellow author like Frederica is sticking voodoo pins in a doll that looks like me.

"There are angst and stress concerning the male in your life," he responds, pinpointing a second circular inner chart he's brought.

The male in my life? "My husband's not abandoning or betraying me. He's back from L.A., where he was working, and said he's not doing another show there again. No angst or strife at all." It can't be my husband—can it? What's he really up to all those nights I can't reach him on the set?

"Well, I see a manipulative, controlling, passionate, intense, critical male central to your life who is betraying you," Cox says calmly, as if there's no chance he's wrong, pointing to symbols labeled "Geo Lon."

"That's not my spouse."

"What other men are you involved with?" he asks pointblank.

I immediately think of Dr. Cigar, the only other male I've kissed since I met Jake. "I recently stopped seeing a male shrink. But he's not the least bit manipulative or controlling. He's sweet and passive, albeit a bit misguided."

Cox shakes his head, as if I'm missing something. "You haven't been seeing anyone else?"

Then it dawns on me who Cox is talking about. How stupid that I don't immediately put together that it's the guy I stole him from.

"It has to be Michael Ness," I say. "When he left New York last summer, I felt very abandoned."

"How do you know him?"

I used Ness's name as a reference in my original phone messages to Cox, but I never divulged that I was his patient.

"He was my shrink for a few years," I admit. "But it's over. We broke up."

"Oh, that makes sense now." Cox stares at a different

circular line of numbers. "That's why he's a substitute for your angst, a container for your anxiety. He's your evil twin, your addiction."

"You never spoke to Ness about me?"

He shakes his head no.

"He was my addiction specialist. He helped me stop smoking and drinking."

"Yes, I see you're a woman of horrible habits." He's following a line of numbers on my chart. "You were living out your dark Pluto side through addiction, gambling with feelings of control. But after you got rid of cheap substitutes to anesthetize your sensuality, you had a reawakening. Pluto loves torment, burning, and death."

"I was very dependent on Ness, so when he moved, it did feel like I had to mourn his loss." I wonder how honest I should be, but decide that lying—or omitting the real story—is counterproductive. "Then we had a big fight because I felt like he deceived me. I wanted to kill him."

"Yes, I can see his demise right here," Cox says. "You recently killed him off."

"Isn't it bizarre that the powerful man in my chart isn't my husband?" I ask.

"No, it's actually ingenious," he says. "With all your Pluto, you're drawn to the tumultuous underworld. For you, love masochistically must be connected to abandonment and betrayal. So you've found a safe way to play out your erotic desires. This way your home, bedroom, and life are harmonious and drama free."

What's with all this Pluto? "I thought I'm an Aquarian." I recall a long-ago definition for my ilk that I liked. "Feet firmly planted on the ground but eyes gazing toward the stars."

"That's your sun sign. Your moon is in Pluto. Pluto people need a taste of poison."

"Ness is poisonous for me?" I hate how accurate that feels.

"Your penetrating, frustrating, unending obsession with him stimulates your imagination and creativity," Cox says. "He's the poison that cures you."

Mind boggled, I grab a notebook to take notes. This seems ludicrously extreme. But I am ludicrously extremist, with a powerful connection to Ness I can't shake. I entertain the possibility that this is why he could get me clean while unlocking my creative blocks in such a short time span. In *Up in Smoke* I quipped that I finally managed to get rid of the bad boys in my life and marry a sweet, nurturing man, only to pay Ness to be the "bad boyfriend." But I thought it was just a joke! How fascinating that astrology—which I don't believe in—might provide the language to explain my complicated long-term link with my beloved therapist better than common sense or psychotherapy.

"Why are you using present tense when it's over between Ness and me?" I ask. "As you saw, I killed him off."

"He gets resurrected. You'll have to learn to let him die again."

I feel exhausted at the thought. "Why does he reappear if I'm doing fine on my own?"

"Your mood is overly determined by those around you. You have no self-reliance. You can't find answers within yourself and you have a need to be controlled," he explains. "Your Virgo rising craves someone discriminating and critical. In the Aquarian way you thrive on soulful pain; that's your story, the healing fiction becomes your obsession. You're a complicated person, and Ness is drawn to the complexity of your suffering. He's an efficient, reliable, controlling presence who likes having power over you. He has a terror of his own demonstrative messy angst. You suffer theatrically, in style, and he needs that theater; it feeds him. Look in your eleventh house," he adds. "It's crammed with planets."

I'm unfamiliar with the terminology but like the poetic sound, still trying to wrap my head around Ness having an astrologist instead of a therapist, let alone him being resurrected as the poison that's curing me.

"So I'm his doppelganger? That's all that's between us?" I'm disappointed with that dynamic but intrigued that astrologists apparently have no client-patient confidentiality rules.

"No, there's love there too," Cox concedes. "He's still your magic charm. But you'll have to banish him to death and remourn him."

"When does this happen?" I want to know, as if I can mark my calendar for another tumultuous death and shiva.

"When you no longer feel a need to be abandoned."

"How long have you known Ness?" I venture.

"Why do you want to know?" Cox asks.

He's answering my question with a question, just like a therapist. Come to think of it, this question-and-answer session isn't so different from my interaction with Ness. I still want to be controlled by a father figure who'll map out my destination and assure me everything will be all right. I'm still craving a new guru to help me figure out what the hell was going on with my old guru.

"What sign are you?" I ask.

"That's none of your business."

Funny that of all my guides, my stargazer is the only one with no boundary issues.

"Anything else you want to ask about your future?"

"What about my best friend, Sarah?"

"I see many women here, one from a long time ago who's on her way out, while some new female blood arrives."

"What do you mean, on her way out? She doesn't ever wind up moving back to New York?"

He points to the corner of my chart. "The Saturn/Venus shows deep disappointment, a big break from the past. But the Uranus/Venus conjuncture means out with the old, in with the new. The women more recently added to your life are the ones who come through for you. I see fresh, younger faces."

Does he mean Haley and Lori? My book team? "But how do I live without Sarah?" I need to know. Although she's been gone more than a year, the idea that she won't be a big part of my day-to-day world again has never occurred to me.

"You don't have a choice. You get sick of martyrdom, so you move on."

Odd, that echoes what my father told me the last time I was home. "How do I do that?"

"You're coming to a dynamic phase where you live and breathe work. That's what feeds you. All your Sagittarius makes you more ambitious and extroverted." He holds the page of my planetary activity up to the light. "See, there's an eclipse coming. The gods of publishing, public speaking, and communication shine on you. Next month you'll enter the most significant, exciting period of your professional life."

I haven't told him I'm an author with a new book coming out, have I? Do stargazers Google?

"My second book will do well? Better than my first?"

"Much better," he says. "It's going right to the top of your chart."

I don't know if he means my terrestrial chart or the one for bestsellers.

"Just beware more personal betrayal, get a thicker skin, and chill out. Your impatience can hurt you."

Here he and Dr. Ness are in sync. He hands me the pretty circles filled with asteroids and lunar nodes and shuts his briefcase, signifying our session is finished.

I write him a check, pondering Ness's connection to Cox, which now doesn't seem that insane. One person's poison can be another's cure, and sometimes they coexist in the same body. Since I'm forsaking my dependencies on sugar, Sarah, Ness, and Dr. Cigar, I might just be shopping for a different impulse disorder. Or is it a male savior I still haven't given up on? Suddenly remembering that Ness sees Cox once a month, I wonder if my speed-shrinking search isn't really over, after all. Instead of getting my head shrunk, should I be considering a contender who analyzes the cosmos?

"You don't need to see me again." Cox reads my mind, as if the decision has already been made and is not up for debate.

"When Ness called you his Jungian guru, I thought you were a shrink," I admit, handing him his payment.

"I was," he says, finally revealing something personal. "But I found it too limiting. Astrology is the original psychology. Freud reductively based his work on the Oedipus myth to fit his own pathology. Astrological theories encompass all mythology."

Man, that's an unexpected angle to consider. I write it down. I wish he would stay and explain my star patterns to me some more. Is there anything I can do to change the course with Sarah? When will Ness resurface so I can kill him off again? Will I lose my final six pounds to make my goal weight in time for my pub date?

Alas, he grabs his coat, hat, and umbrella and makes his way toward the door.

"I see you making strides outside, more sweating, less hunger. Lot of Uranus/Venus, which is very proud and vain. You're coming to a skinny phase," he says quickly, before I can even ask.

chapter twenty-six
setting the pace
September 19

"I finished wrapping three shows today," Jake announces as he walks in the door at nine o'clock Tuesday night. "I've been in the editing room for hours. I need some air. Let's take a walk around the park."

"Are you serious?" I'm surprised. "I have to get up at five A.M. for the *Today* show." I'm excited that I've been invited to go on the show as a solo author to talk about tomorrow's official debut of *Food Crazy*.

"I know, I've already set all three alarms. But you said you're not going to sleep early or you'll wind up awake half the night like last time."

"You really want to take a walk?"

"You go there with everyone else," he says. "Do I have to be your protégé or shrink to get a walking office hour with you?"

"Okay, I'm up for a late walk," I tell Jake. "Let's do it."

For once in my life I have kept my mouth shut and not mentioned Dr. Cigar's kiss, though I wonder if Jake surmised that something happened when I abruptly quit seeing him. On the other hand, I did divulge my secret session with Ness's celestial charter. When I told Jake that Cox had seen "a controlling, manipulative, critical man" who'll keep betraying me, my husband cut me off midsentence by saying, "That has to be Ness." When I called Dr. Ness to thank him for the card he sent congratulating me on the publication of *Food Crazy,* I told him what Cox said too. He buoyantly jumped in with "That has to be me!" If Ness is my evil twin, why aren't I equally poisonous to him, I asked. He laughed and said, "Julia, do you really think the universe could possibly be that symmetrical?"

I rush to put on my new size-medium tight black Juicy sweatpants, which happily fit my now 128-pound body perfectly, and the Lycra top that shows off my newly sculpted arms. We make our way through the lobby hand-in-hand, a nice breeze hitting us as we step out of the revolving doors. A late stroll with Jake strikes me as inspired.

"So why did you decide to get off all therapy?" he asks.

"It's time to stop analyzing and start living," I tell him.

"Well, remember, you already have the solution to all your problems—me."

"Yeah, I know, you've done wonders with me," I quote my father's line.

Independence used to be my goal. But I've come to believe the struggle of life is actually finding the right people
to walk beside you. I know my mother has done wonders
with my father, saving his life when she married him. And
after a rough first year, Sarah does seem much happier married than she ever was single. Dr. Ness has a theory that
there are only three ways a person can truly change: when
someone close dies, with good therapy, or through good
love. Good therapy led me to good love, and trusting Ness
implicitly helped me transfer that raw trust to my husband.
I'm not bitter about my experiences on the couch. I'm just
kind of over it.

"Do you need me to go with you tomorrow?" Jake asks.
"Or is that brash publicist going?"

"Bonnie's not brash, she's funny and honest."

"She makes you look quiet and subtle."

"Would you want a shy, meek head of publicity?" I ask
him. "I'm lucky she likes me and my book. She's picking me
up in the limo at five forty."

"I thought you go on with Meredith Vieira at seven thirty.
That's when I set the TiVo."

"They're doing my makeup and hair first," I say. "Bonnie's
rehearsing me on the way there."

"Nervous?"

"Only about having to be charming and presentable so
early in the morning." As we walk by a New York University
dormitory, we pass a cluster of students. "Did I tell you Google
Stalker's moving to New York and applying to grad school at
NYU?"

"So she can stalk you up close and personal?"

"She signed up for my next three seminars. And she sold

a piece on *Food Crazy* to my replacement at *Femme*. It's coming out next week."

I stare at two fresh-faced long-haired girls in jeans and T-shirts having a smoke on the steps. I imagine that's what Sarah and I looked like at eighteen, right off the bus from the Midwest. My NYU psych professor recommended my first shrink, Dr. Gold, who had a sliding scale, charging me only twenty-five dollars a session. I told her I worried that being a career woman meant I'd never marry. She said I could have a great career and a great husband, and years later wound up dancing at my *Up in Smoke* book party. I recall that she liked Jake from first mention.

"He doesn't smoke, he doesn't drink, he doesn't party," I complained after our first date.

"You're listing all of his assets, right?" she asked. "I like the sound of this one. Go out with him again."

Twenty years after I landed in this part of the city, I'm oddly thrilled to be accompanied by Jake—as if it's an exotic treat to take a walk on a Tuesday night with my partner. He looks tall and rugged in his worn black jeans, green button-down shirt, and black sneakers.

There's a noise by the bushes and he asks, "What's that?"

"Probably just a squirrel."

"An urban squirrel." He points to a big fat ugly rat eating a leftover cupcake in a pile of garbage on the ground.

"Yuck. See what happens if you eat carbs," I joke as we walk faster, inching farther away from the rodents and closer to the curb. "Where are you taking me for our anniversary?" I ask. "Paris, or Venice?"

"I already told the producers I'm taking my wife to dinner next Saturday night and won't be reachable. No CrackBerry or cell phone," he offers. "Let's go somewhere special. How about Peter Luger's?"

"Great idea. We'll schlep to Brooklyn so I can watch you shove a whole cow into your mouth, along with hash browns, onion rings, bread, and beer at nine P.M."

"Yeah, you're no walk in the park either," he teases. "Don't tell me, we have to do the early-bird special at your favorite diner like eighty-year-old *alter kockers* in Florida because of some new weird food plan you're on."

"Hey, I'm back down to my goal weight right in time for my book events. So don't even think about getting in the way of me and my diet."

"How come the thinner you get the more headaches you give me?"

Emoting and making him crazy—instead of myself—is part of the weight-loss method that wound up working for me. I've gobbled up the combined wisdom from all my gurus, as if I needed a brain buffet. Along with Erasmo's lower-calorie food plan and walking office hours six days a week, I'm back to Dr. Ness's psychological dictums that are dotted through my books—letting myself be more intense and finicky, not eating to suppress emotions, learning to tolerate more hunger, and depending on human beings, no matter how erratic they can be. If the choice is to cry, scream, or eat, I cry and scream. Funny that Jake barely notices my weight—or emotional—fluctuations except when they directly affect him. His concerns are whether he gets food and affection when he wants them, and how much my diet and workout routines inconvenience him.

I admit returning to my slender self is making me more edgy, bitchy, and needy. I know several heavy women in happy relationships and a bunch of slim neurotics who are single and miserable. It's as if my whole gender has a misguided notion of what men really care about. But I haven't changed my body for him. I'm in fighting shape for myself and my work.

"How about Nobu?" I ask. "I can order fish."

"Good idea. Remember that crab dish you had that you loved so much you ate half of mine?" He's sweet that way; he enjoys watching me eat. That's much better than having a spouse who monitors your weight and makes you walk on eggshells. Yet like my father with my mother, I have to keep retraining my spouse not to overfeed me.

Something rustles in the grass beyond the short metal fence as we walk by.

"It's eerie out here now, among the rodents and the homeless," Jake says, inching closer to me. "I think we should go home."

"Don't worry, I'll protect you. Come on. You have to speed up. I usually do six miles in sixty minutes. You don't burn up enough calories going two miles an hour. You're too snail-paced," I say, grabbing his arm to push him forward.

"I am not. Slow down and smell the weeds—and the junkies. You're walking too fast," he says as he always does, pulling me back toward him.

"Liz, give her another Diet Coke," Bonnie orders her assistant as we sit in the back of the limo on our way uptown to Rockefeller Plaza at 5:45 the next morning. Liz hands me the can while Bonnie drinks her Starbucks double latte.

"Thanks." I hand her an empty can and stick my straw in

the new soda. I've been switching to water and tea, but this very special occasion calls for an Erasmo-approved one-hour caffeine relapse.

"What about the green shirt I told you to wear?" Bonnie shakes her head, inspecting my size-six black miniskirt, black V-neck shirt, short blazer, and five-inch high heels.

· "I look better in black. You don't like the suit?"

"What's with the pin?" she wants to know.

"It's an antique. It was a present from Jake. He picked it out himself," I brag.

"How cute. Get rid of it. The glare is all the audience will see. For Rachel Day's last book, she went on TV wearing a bug pin and they got three thousand calls from viewers saying it was ugly." Bonnie undoes my brooch and puts it in her pocket. "Okay, here's another question for you. What does your family in Illinois think of your book?"

"They hate it," I say, still half asleep despite being on my second caffeinated soda.

"No! They don't hate it! Nobody hates your book on national TV!" Bonnie yells. "They love your book! Everyone · loves your book! Now try again. So what does your husband think of your work?"

"He's threatening to write a rebuttal called *How to Tame the Shrew Beside You.*"

"No threats! No rebuttals! No shrews who need taming!" Bonnie screams. "Are you nuts? There'll be millions of people watching!"

"Well, how do you want me to answer?"

"Smile and say, 'He loves *Food Crazy*, though he'd prefer I write cookbooks.'"

"I can't say that! I wouldn't marry a man who'd prefer cookbooks."

She shoots me daggers, then in a singsongy voice continues quizzing me. "In your book you talk about the difference between emotional and physical hunger."

"Yes, my shrink said food is the hardest addiction to conquer because you can't quit eating."

"Wrong! No shrinks!" Bonnie shrieks. "Whatever you do, don't say shrink!"

"I'm sorry. My therapist," I correct. "Or should I say addiction doctor or psychoanalyst?"

"No therapists, doctors, shrinks, or psycho anything!" she insists.

"But the whole book is about going to an addiction specialist to lose weight. That's what I recommend, that food addicts go see a good shrink."

"That's not what you recommend! You're the specialist here! Middle Americans do not want to hear a neurotic New Yorker telling them to pay thousands of dollars for therapy!"

"What about Dr. Phil? He's from Texas," I argue. "Dr. Robin is from Philadelphia. Middle Americans like them."

"That's because Oprah said to like them," Bonnie snaps. "Look, you nixed the Girl Gurus and wanted your own solo TV gig, so I got it for you. Now are you going to sell Dr. Phil's books or Dr. Robin's books or your own books?"

"I'm just saying some non–New Yorkers like therapy."

"I'm from North Carolina and I see a shrink," Liz throws in.

"Are you in North Carolina now?" Bonnie asks Liz, gritting her teeth. "No, you're working in Manhattan publishing for twenty-two thousand dollars a year."

"That's why she needs a shrink," I add.

"Listen." Bonnie lowers her voice to a near whisper. "Your audience does not want to see a shrink. They want to pay twenty-one ninety-five for your book to get fixed instead. They want you to be the health expert. So say, 'In *Food Crazy* I realized food is the hardest addiction to conquer because you have to eat three times a day.'"

"When they buy the book they'll see it's about therapy." I finish the second Diet Coke, starting to wake up though the sun hasn't yet risen over the city streets. "Don't you think that's false advertising?"

"There's only one kind of advertising. Just smile and say a nice sound bite so they like you. After they shell out for your book, you can shove therapy down their throat. Don't you want to play in Peoria?"

"Yes. I want to play in Peoria. Really, I do," I say. I really do.

"So Julia, what's your method for losing weight?" She returns to her interviewer voice.

"In *Food Crazy*, I explain how you have to learn the difference between physical and emotional hunger," I answer.

"Oh, here, I brought something for you," says Liz, pulling out a cupcake with chocolate icing from her Starbucks bag and handing it to me.

I look at it, stunned. "Are you kidding me? You brought me a cupcake?"

"'Cause your cover shows the guy eating a cupcake." She sounds proud of herself.

"That's not a guy, it's Sigmund Freud," I say. "And it's ironic. Did you even read the book?" I take the cupcake from her hand, roll down the window, and throw it outside, into the traffic.

"I can't believe you did that," Bonnie says. "Is that your diet method? Somebody brings you a present and you act like a psycho and throw it out the window?"

"Yes! That's how I got to back to 128 pounds! By being a psycho! You're supposed to put as many obstacles between yourself and your addiction as possible."

"I read your book. You say sprinkle pepper on desserts you don't want at restaurants, which I find disgusting," Bonnie says. "There's nothing about throwing cupcakes out car windows."

"It's not called *Food Normal*. It's called *Food Crazy*!" I defend myself.

"I can't believe you threw a three-dollar cupcake out the window," Liz laughs.

"What are you, twenty-two years old and weigh 110?" I ask.

"One hundred and seventeen," she corrects.

"What if you hit a pedestrian?" Bonnie asks, laughing now too. "I can see the *New York Post* headline, COP KILLED BY FLYING CUPCAKE."

"I'm sorry. It's too early for me to have willpower or manners," I tell Liz.

"Oh, God, we're here. Look at the crowds!" Liz opens her window too, her mouth agape.

"This is so fucking awesome!" I can't help but squeal.

"The crowd's not for you," Bonnie says. "Shakira's debuting her new CD right after you're on."

"Wow. Really?" Liz asks. "I love her song 'My Hips Don't Lie.'"

"Good. You can give her the cupcake," I say.

"Do you think I can get her autograph?" Liz wants to know.

"You need us to get you anything else?" Bonnie asks me. "Bottle of Evian? Piece of diet cheese? A stick of gum?"

"She quit gum," Liz jumps in. "That was in her last book."

"Good, you read that one," I say, as the limousine pulls up to the curb in front of the NBC entrance. As we get out and walk toward the sign-in desk, people from the crowd point to me and wave. I wave back, pretending they know who I am, feeling elated and sated, and at least for the moment not hungry for anything else.

acknowledgments

I would like to express my deepest gratitude to:

• My fabulous book editor, Katie Gilligan, who said yes to a book on food addiction while I was fasting on Yom Kippur.

• My amazing literary agent, Ryan Fischer-Harbage, who said, "I have no doubt in the world."

• To my great publicist, Katy Hershberger, and my magnificent PR guru, Barb Burg, who said, "This should be a Shrink-aholic series."

- To Kathryn Glasgow, who read three pages at midnight at Shutters and said, "This is your new book."

- To Bob, who said, "I see no heartbreak this year."

- To my Thursday pillars (Hilary Davidson, Alice Feiring, Harold James, Kristen Kemp, Liza Monroy, Sarah Norris, Tony Powell, Rich Prior, Wendy Shanker, Kate Walter, and Royal Young), who said, "Not this again!"

- To my critical eyes (Sally Arteseros, Jami Bernard, Roberta Bernstein, Nicole Bokat, Laura Mazer, Devan Sipher), who said, "Put her on *Oprah* or give her a dead sister; it's fiction."

- To my book event angels (Donna Rauch, Daryl Mattson, Jessica Stockton, Michael Shapiro, Lisa Applebaum, Karen Sosnick, Jane Wald, Gary Rubin, Lee Hilton, Sara Goff, Amy Stanton, Keith Hewitt, Susan Stoddard, Taffy Akner, Mara Piazza, Max Roberts, Jeffrey Penque, Nancy Bass, Gina Ryder, Linda Friedman, and Sharon Preiss), who said, "How about Tuesday night at seven?"

- To my favorite editors (Julie Just, Frank Flaherty, Christina Gillham, Joanna Douglas, Esther Haynes, Patti Greco, Jerry Portwood, Gail Zimmerman, Paula Derrow, Ruth Ellenson, Bruce Tracy, Claire Lambe, Margo Hammond, David Wallis, Kara Uhl Gebhart, and Zach Petite), who said yes.

- To my teaching colleagues (Jackson Taylor, Luis Jaramillo, Robert Polito, Laura Cronk, Lori Turner, Leah Iannone, Deborah Landau, and Elizabeth Maxwell, who said, "The check is in the mail," when it really was.

- To my Midwest and West Coast crews (Arlene Cohen, Judy Burdick, EJ Levy, Laura Berman, Cindy Frenkel, Scott Grant, Howard Lyons, Ronit Pinto, Karen Buscemi, Krysten Weller, Lori Monheim, Jody Podolsky, Timmy, Alison Powell, Julie Greenwald, Caren Emmer, and Amy Alkon), who have been saying, "That's okay, I'll drive," for the last twenty years.

- To my beloved mentors (Harvey Shapiro, Ian Frazier, Grace Schulman, Gerry Jonas, and the Fasts), who said, "Plumbers don't get plumber's block," "No doesn't mean no," and "Mazel tov."

- To Danny and Karin Brownstein, who—while trying to take sexy author photos on the roof—said, "You look like you need a drink and a joint."

- To Elizabeth Kaplan, who heard about my shrink quest and said, "You have to write about this."

- To Danielle Perez, who said, "You found your novel voice."

- To Amy Koppelman, who said, "It has to be present tense."

- To MH, who asked, "Have you left the cupcake underworld behind?"

- To JC, who said, "The younger brother in the dream is me."

- To CR, who said, "Shrinks always think they're the characters in your dream." (And "I do.")

- To my family, who said, "Thank God, finally—it's fiction."

About the Author

Susan Shapiro's work has appeared in *The New York Times Magazine*, *The Washington Post*, *Newsweek*, the *Los Angeles Times*, *The Boston Globe*, *The Village Voice*, *The New York Observer*, *The Forward*, *Detroit Jewish News*, *More*, *Glamour*, *Cosmopolitan*, *Salon.com*, *The Huffington Post*, and *The Daily Beast*. She's a columnist for *Writer's Digest*, coeditor of the anthology *Food for the Soul*, and author of *Five Men Who Broke My Heart*, *Lighting Up*, *Secrets of a Fix-up Fanatic*, and *Only as Good as Your Word*. She lives in Manhattan with her husband, a TV/film writer, and has taught her own "instant gratification takes too long" method of writing at NYU and the New School. You can visit her at www.susanshapiro.net.

DATE			